FATAL

FRIED RICE

VIVIEN CHIEN

St. Martin's Paperbacks

First published in the United States by St. Martin's Paperbacks, an imprint of St. Martin's Publishing Group.

FATAL FRIED RICE

Copyright © 2021 by Vivien Chien.

All rights reserved.

For information, address St. Martin's Publishing Group, 120 Broadway, New York, NY 10271.

www.stmartins.com

ISBN: 978-1-250-78259-5

33614082228601

Our books may be purchased in bulk for promotional, educational, or business use. Please contact your local bookseller or the Macmillan Corporate and Premium Sales Department at 1-800-221-7945, ext. 5442, or by email at MacmillanSpecialMarkets@macmillan.com.

St. Martin's Paperbacks edition published 2021

Printed in the United States of America

10 9 8 7 6 5 4 3 2 1

For Sasha,
the best little dog there ever was.
Thank you for 15 years of unconditional love and
companionship.
You'll always be in my heart.

ACKNOWLEDGMENTS

A world of gratitude goes to my agent, Gail Fortune; my editor, Nettie Finn; to Kayla Janas, Allison Ziegler, Mary Ann Lasher, and all of St. Martin's Paperbacks.

Hats off to the Sisters in Crime—both locally and nationally—and to the Crime Writers of Color.

Much love to my family and friends who always have my back during the good, bad, and the ugly.

And a very special thanks to my readers, who are some of the finest people an author could ever ask for.

CHAPTER
1

"If you tell anyone about this, I'm gonna have to kill you," I said, staring my best friend squarely in the eye.

"Okay, geez, Lana. I won't tell anyone. No need to be so dramatic." Megan rolled her eyes as theatrically as possible.

"No one can know what I'm doing or where I'm going. Not even Adam. If they were to find out—" I paused. "Well, I don't even want to think about what would happen."

"I said okay, Lana Lee. Now will you get going? If you don't leave right now, you're going to be late."

I checked the time on my cell phone. I hated it when she was right. "Fine, I'm leaving. If anyone comes looking for me—"

"No one is going to come looking for you. Would you relax?" Megan stood from her seat at the kitchen table and waved her hands at me, shooing me out of our apartment.

I patted my black pug, Kikkoman, on the head and made my way out the door.

As I hurried through the parking lot, I debated whether I was being dramatic. Perhaps. But if my mother found out that her youngest daughter, and manager of the family restaurant, Ho-Lee Noodle House, was taking a Chinese cooking class—with strangers—her hair would probably light on fire.

A few weeks ago, my older sister, Anna May, who can be an absolute thorn in my side, had begun giving me an extra-hard time and teasing me persistently on my lack of cooking skills in the Asian cuisine department. Did I love Chinese food? Yes. Did I want to cook it myself? Not really.

Aside from making rice, the whole thing was an ordeal that I'd rather not get mixed up in. But now that I was in charge of the family business, it was a little odd that I didn't know how to make eighty-five percent of the items on our menu. Not that there was really a need for me to do much cooking at the noodle house. Our head cook, and one of my very best friends, Peter Huang, was miraculously never sick, and didn't request many days off. In the instances where he was out for the day, our evening chef and backup, Lou, would pick up the slack. My sister and mother were then next in line for kitchen duty. So, really, was any of this necessary? It was still a question I couldn't answer.

But man, did it eat at me that my sister was being this

relentless. So here I was on a Tuesday evening, driving out to Parma, a large suburb of Cleveland, Ohio, for an adult course in ethnic cooking. I'd been nonchalantly watching the course listings at a local learning center as each quarter offered classes to the community on cooking for different cultures. The last class had been for Mexican food, but oddly enough I can wrap a burrito like nobody's business, so I figured I was okay in that department. When I saw that they were featuring Chinese food for the next eight weeks, I signed up for the class posthaste.

Northeast Ohio in September can be an interesting place. Things either get cold really fast and we're forced into an early winter, or we're blessed with random spurts of eighty-degree days that trickle all the way into December. Right now, we were experiencing a warmer than usual beginning to the fall season. And that was perfectly fine with me since I was not a huge fan of chilly weather.

I took I-480 eastbound toward Brook Park, blasting my stereo and singing along to the Arctic Monkeys. The car is the only place you'll catch me testing my vocal abilities. All things considered, I was in pretty high spirits. It had been a rough summer at Asia Village, the plaza that houses our family's restaurant, and it was nice to look forward to doing something regular and mundane. I homed in on the fact that eight weeks from now, I was going to have some impressive Asian culinary skills and would wow my sister and my mom. Of course, my boyfriend, Adam Trudeau, would be amazed too, but he didn't really seem to care if I could cook Chinese food. I think the man would be happy if we had chicken wings and curly fries every night of the week.

I merged off the freeway at the Tiedeman Road exit, and turned right heading toward Barton's Adult Learning Center right across from the local community college. Within ten minutes, I was turning into the parking lot of the two-story, glass building and feeling the excitement of my secret jump around in my belly.

When I got out of the car, I turned toward the street to look across the way at Cuyahoga Community College. It had been a long time since I'd been on this side of town. Memories of times past flooded my mind as my eyes swept over the length of the Tri-C campus. Though Megan and I had graduated from Cleveland State University, I had spent a little time at the local college. Aside from the community events they held, like music festivals and Fourth of July celebrations, I'd taken a few courses there back in my college days.

My line of sight traveled over to the southern entrance of the school, and I visualized a younger, more innocent version of myself scurrying to the doors, rushing to get to class. A laugh escaped at the thought of how naïve I had been at the time, and though I'd mostly held on to my idealistic ways, there were parts of me that had changed. I was now more aware of the darkness that hid in society, and for a brief moment I wished for those careless days of thinking that nothing horrible could touch you. At twenty-eight years old, the times of thinking that I'm invincible are long gone.

Some of that is due to the things I've experienced in

the past year: a few murders, a boatload of deceptions, and, of course, working with the public.

I shook the thoughts away and turned to head toward the main entrance of Barton's. They'd provided a map in their course book, and I pulled it out of my tote bag to find where I needed to go. The adult learning center wasn't very big and looked like a repurposed office building. The lobby led into an open common area covered in neutral tones with couches, chairs, and dark wooden tables sprinkled throughout. Artwork by local talent adorned the walls and I vaguely remembered reading in the course book that everything was for sale. I thought that was nice of the school to support local artists, and I made a mental note to check out what was available to purchase.

I found my class at the end of the hall, and watched a variety of people walk into the room, noting that so far, I was the only one of Asian descent. Even though I'm only half Taiwanese, you wouldn't know it by looking at me. A bit of insecurity slipped in at the idea of what people would think of someone like me taking a class like this. Shouldn't I already know how to cook Chinese food? Didn't I have a family member who could teach me these sorts of things? Should I tell people that I was adopted?

I shook my head at that last thought. Nonsense, Lana, no one is even going to be thinking about you because they'll be too concerned with themselves. I squared my shoulders, took a deep breath, and continued on into the room, repeating positive affirmations in my head. This was going to be the best cooking class ever.

CHAPTER
2

I walked into the classroom with my chin up, attempting to not recreate the sensations of insecurity and doubt that come along with something like your first day in high school. Legend has it that some people actually looked forward to their first day, and rumors from past generations often said those were the best years of your life. If you're asking me specifically, that still remains to be seen. I have never actually met anyone in my age bracket that can confirm this supposed truth.

The room was almost full, and I found myself staring into a gathering of faces that well represented the American melting pot minus the Asian demographic. A mixture of ethnicities and ages sprinkled the eight cooking stations lined up neatly in two rows. A larger, more elaborate cooking island stood at the front of the class.

While I assessed the room, I hadn't realized that I'd

frozen in place near the door and was staring blankly at everyone in front of me. Suddenly, I was sixteen years old all over again and wondering if I'd forgotten to do something crucial like zip my pants.

A thin, blonde woman in her mid-fifties who sat at the table closest to the door smiled brightly at me. "Hello, are you the class instructor?"

A nervous laugh bubbled out at the insinuation and it took me a few seconds to put two and two together as to why she would assume that *I* was the teacher. "Oh, no. . . . I'm here to take the class too."

She tilted her head in confusion, but said nothing else.

I smiled awkwardly and headed to the last empty cooking island all the way in the back of the room. Some things never change, I guess. While my mother had always firmly believed that I should be front and center in any class I was taking, so that my teacher would notice me, I didn't like the attention. Never in my life have I been the person who raises their hand to answer or ask questions. Funny considering that now all I seem to do in my spare time is ask people things.

I settled my purse on the stainless-steel countertop, and placed my Asia Village tote bag on the available stool next to me. A few people turned to look my way, but I pretended to be preoccupied with putting my phone on SILENT and avoided making eye contact.

A few minutes later, a middle-aged Asian woman walked into the room carrying a box of supplies in her arms and a few tote bags slung over her shoulder. She was pretty in a simple sort of way with shoulder-length black hair that was smooth and straight and lacked definition. Her eyeliner and eyebrows were tattooed on, a fad that seemed extremely popular with her generation. Aside from that, she had no actual makeup on except for a barely visible neutral gloss.

A kind smile spread over her lips as she acknowledged the room. "Hello, I'm Margo Han, and I'll be your cooking teacher for the next eight weeks." She set the box down on the counter and removed the tote bags from her shoulder.

Scattered "hellos" floated around the room as we watched her unpack the box of utensils and bags of supplies she'd brought in. When she was finished, she turned to the large, dry erase board behind her and wrote her name in red marker in the top right corner.

Capping the marker, she turned around to address the group. "The way this class will be structured is one week of demonstration rotated with one week of hands-on learning. We will learn four popular Chinese dishes to prepare in the next eight weeks. Since I'll spend the first hour of tonight's class going over the basics of utensils, equipment, and popular ingredients used to prepare Asian meals, we'll be learning how to make a simple recipe of fried rice for our first dish. It's the least time consuming of what I have prepared for you to learn. I'll start with roll call and then we'll get right into it."

The class attendees all nodded along as the teacher spoke, and I found myself relieved that we would be starting out with something easy like fried rice. I basically knew most of the steps for that as I'd watched my mother make it quite a few times in my life. I wasn't a huge fan of fried rice and preferred white over it any day, but this was a good way to get my feet wet and build some confidence.

After she finished calling names, Margo began talking about cooking utensils and popular Asian ingredients. Within five minutes my mind and thoughts started to drift over to people-watching mode. I will be the first to admit that my attention span is not the greatest. And when left to my own devices, I tend to phase off into la-la land.

The majority of people in the class were women, but there were a handful of men too. Most of the women were older than me, but there were two who seemed to be close to my age. I took some time evaluating each person and what their purposes behind taking this class might be, wondering if I was the only one doing this to show up a family member.

At the front of the class, I noticed a rather irate-looking woman sitting next to the blonde who'd questioned me earlier. Maybe it was just her face, but she appeared to be scowling at our instructor. Her body language also seemed rigid and her hands were clenching the edge of the cooking island. I couldn't imagine what her issue would be—Margo was explaining Chinese Five Spice powder, a popular blend of seasonings that was used in a lot of Asian meat dishes.

The mixture traditionally included cinnamon, fennel seeds, anise, ground cloves, and Szechuan pepper, but different variations existed, some substituting licorice root for anise, for example. But a few potential substitutions weren't anything to get worked up over.

I decided to pay attention to Margo for a few minutes, and realized she was making eye contact with everyone in the room except for the angry woman. The speculative side of me couldn't help but wonder what that was all about. Maybe this woman had taken a class instructed by Margo in the past and didn't like her methods. Or maybe she thought she knew more than the teacher. There was always at least one know-it-all in every class.

At the end of our explanatory hour, Margo gave us a fifteen-minute bathroom break and the opportunity to stretch our legs. She would set up her station while we were gone, and the actual cooking lesson would begin when we returned.

On my way back from the restroom, I ran into one of the younger women in my class. She was considerably taller than me, and I put her at a solid five foot eleven compared to my meager five foot four. If I had to guess, I'd say she was either my age or slightly younger.

Dazzling a sparkling white smile, she approached me as I neared the brick pillar she'd been leaning against outside our classroom. "Hi, you're Lana, aren't you?"

I returned her smile and stepped to the side, getting out of the way of others returning to the room. "Yes, that's me."

"I'm Bridget. I absolutely love your hair and wanted to ask where you get it done." Her hand lifted to her own chestnut brown hair, and she ran her fingers through the loose curls that framed her face. "I am so bored with mine and I really want to do something drastically different. You know . . . make a statement." Her eyes widened with excitement as if she were sharing a conspiracy theory with me. "But I'll be honest, I'm kind of afraid to have it done."

"Oh, well, thank you," I replied. My hair was currently recovering from a bout of attempts to dye my bleached peekaboo highlights with a metallic gray that didn't go over so well. Frustrated with the results, my stylist and I were now adding in a cobalt blue color to help bring out the appearance of tinted silver. "I go to a place called Asian Accents."

Her eyes lit up and she gasped. "I knew you seemed familiar. I thought I saw you in the newspaper a while back. There was that article with you and that P.I. lady . . . Lydia something?"

I blushed. My hopes of not being recognized by anyone in the class were shot down. Although I hadn't thought it would be from the newspaper. I was more worried about running into a Ho-Lee Noodle House customer. "Yeah, that was me." She was referring to when I'd teamed up with Lydia Shepard, a local private investigator, who helped me handle a tricky situation for Donna Feng, the property owner of Asia Village.

"So, wait . . . that means you're the manager of that noodle restaurant, right? The one that's over there in Fairview Park?"

"Yeah . . ." My face continued to warm; the redness of my cheeks was going to start producing heat waves any minute now. "That's where the salon is located, in that same plaza."

"Oh, okay. Then how come you're in this class?" she

asked, pointing toward the classroom door. "I'd think if anything you'd be able to teach it yourself."

"You'd think," was my reply.

Laughing, she nudged my arm. "Don't worry, I won't judge. I'm a disaster in the kitchen. Before I started taking cooking classes, I was lucky I could even boil an egg. A few months ago, I started dating this guy and he totally made fun of me because I didn't know how to make French toast. That's why I started taking all these courses . . . to hopefully impress him with my newfound culinary skills."

I laugh good-naturedly remembering the first time I'd cooked for Adam. He'd been quite surprised that I'd known how to do anything in the kitchen at all. "I can relate. How many classes have you taken so far?"

"This will be my third course at Barton's. I took one on general cooking basics, and then a Mexican food class."

"That's great, I hope it's working out for you. You must really like him to go through all this."

"Well, everyone always talks about how the way to a man's heart is through his stomach. I didn't think I'd care about that sort of thing, but yet here I am." She ended the sentence with a shrug.

Noticing that most of our classmates had returned, I jerked a thumb over at the entrance. "Wanna get back in there? Looks like she's going to start soon."

Bridget nodded in agreement. "Yeah, we better get back, so we don't miss anything important. It was really nice chatting with you. Maybe in the next class we can sit together. It would be nice to have a partner who actually has a personality. The guy that's sitting next to me has zero social skills."

I chuckled. "I'd like that."

As we headed back into the room, Bridget turned around and whispered, "Oh, and don't worry, I won't tell anyone who you are. It'll be our little secret."

CHAPTER
3

The group of us circled around Margo's cooking station to observe as she did a walk-through of tonight's featured dish: fried rice. We watched as she diced carrots, chopped onions, minced garlic, and beat a few eggs. She included tips on chilling rice overnight and cooking times so as not to burn the rice.

As she started combining the ingredients in her skillet, the fragrant aromas of garlic and soy sauce filled the room. My mouth began to water, and I think I heard the woman's stomach next to me rumble.

Once Margo was finished, she ladled out small portions into Styrofoam bowls and offered a sample to anyone who wanted to taste test the finished product. Of course, no one refused, and we all stood around with our plastic spoons, oohing and ahhing at how delicious and simple the dish really was.

Nine o'clock had snuck up on us as we idly chitchatted about all things cooking. Before it was time to go, Margo instructed us on next week's class itinerary. "Please grab a shopping list before heading out for the evening. Everything you need to purchase is on this paper." She held up a printout for the class to see. "We'll get started cooking right away. Make sure to bring to-go containers with you. We will not be providing them like we have done in the past. We'll use the first hour for the hands-on portion of the class, and then after cleanup and break time, we'll get into our next dish which will be Orange Chicken." She wished us all a good night as we made our way out of the room.

Aside from a handful of stragglers who wanted to keep their conversation going, the room had cleared out and I felt less self-conscious. I decided to stop and talk with the instructor before leaving. I had a great idea and was hoping that she'd agree to it.

She smiled at me as I approached her cooking island. "Hi there, I hope you enjoyed the class tonight."

I nodded. "Yes, thank you. I really did."

"Is there something I can help you with?"

"Yeah, actually . . ." My eyes drifted to the countertop. "So, I manage a local Chinese noodle shop. Maybe you're familiar with it . . . Ho-Lee Noodle House?"

"Yes actually, I've been there quite a few times. It's a great restaurant."

"Thanks." I glanced up to read the expression on her face. "You're probably wondering why I'm here then, huh?"

"Not really. A lot of the younger generation is ill prepared in the kitchen. I'm guessing your restaurant is family owned and you didn't plan on working there. Am I right?"

I laughed. "How'd you guess?"

"My family owns a dry-cleaning company."

We both stared at each other for a moment, then burst out giggling.

Margo took a breath and quieted her laughter. "So, what's your question?"

"I was wondering if you could give me extended cooking classes on a one-on-one basis. I thought maybe you could teach me some more in-depth techniques. I'd pay you, of course."

She tilted her head, taking a minute to consider my request. "It would have to wait until this set of courses is finished. Is that okay? I have a lot going on at the moment."

I responded with a vigorous nod. "Yes, that's absolutely fine with me. I'll take whatever I can get. I'm trying to keep this a secret from my family, so any outside help would be greatly appreciated."

Margo chuckled. "Don't worry, I completely understand. We can discuss a schedule once we get to the final weeks, how does that sound?"

"That sounds great. Thank you so much." I adjusted the tote bag on my shoulder so I could reach into my purse. I dug into the side pocket and pulled out a business card, handing it over to Margo. "Here's my number before I forget to give it to you."

She took the card and slipped it into her back pocket. "Thanks."

"Well, I'll get out of your hair. Have a good evening."

"You too, Lana. It was great meeting you."

When I turned to leave, there was a middle-aged man with sandy brown hair and a dimpled chin standing in the foot of the doorway. He might have been one of the men in my class, though I didn't recognize him. He'd been so quiet, we hadn't realized he was standing there. Margo turned to acknowledge him, and I excused myself, exchanging a smile with her new visitor as he twisted sideways, allowing me room to pass through the threshold.

There was a sense of ease that washed over me as I left the classroom. I felt like I had accomplished something and was working toward a goal I'd been putting off for longer than I could remember.

On my way out, I noticed the girl I'd talked with earlier, Bridget, sitting in one of the lounge chairs near the main doors. She was fixated on her phone, but glanced in my direction as I approached, doing a double take. "Oh, hey," she said, giving me a wave. "So, what do you think? Can we handle the daunting task of making fried rice?"

I laughed. "I think we'll come out alive." I looked around. "Are you waiting on somebody?" I felt nosy asking, but I couldn't figure why she was just hanging out. Curiosity always got the best of me.

"Oh, I'm waiting for my Uber," she told me. "My car's in the shop because my brakes are one step away from being nonexistent." She held up her phone. "He should be here soon."

"Want me to wait with you?" I asked.

"Oh no, you go on ahead. I'm sure you have to work in the morning. I'll see ya on Thursday."

I said goodbye and when I exited the building, I spotted my car immediately as it was one of the few left in the parking lot. After turning on the engine, I sent a quick text to Megan asking if she wanted me to pick up anything on my way. Also, not being able to help myself, I asked if anyone had come looking for me. A few minutes later, she replied "no" to both.

I put the car in drive and turned up the radio, heading out onto York Road.

As I was stopped at the traffic light in front of Valley Forge High School, I realized I'd forgotten the handout Margo wanted us to take home. I made a quick right into the parking lot of the high school, and turned around to head back to the learning center.

Hurriedly, I parked the car and jogged back into the school, hoping to catch Margo before she went home. I'd only left about fifteen minutes ago, so if she'd been held up talking to that guy, then there was a chance she hadn't packed up yet.

When I re-entered the school, Bridget was gone, and the rest of the building had seemed to clear out as well. I continued on down the hallway at a brisk pace.

Nearing the classroom, it took me a moment to understand that something was amiss. I noticed a scattering of peas, carrots, and rice trailing out of the doorway. Not thinking much of it at first, I proceeded into the room, and was brought to a sudden halt by the scene before me, stopped short in the threshold gripping onto the metal trim of the doorframe. My hands felt warm against the cool metal as I gripped it for stability.

Lying sprawled and facedown in a mess of fried rice mixed with thick burgundy-colored liquid was Margo Han, a huge knife protruding out the middle of her back. As I slowly edged myself out of the room, I felt the contents of my stomach start to bubble up. I clutched at my belly, trying to force normal breath to pass through my lungs. Heat rose from my neck, traveling up to my hairline, and I could feel the sweat beginning to collect on my forehead underneath my bangs. My eyes welled with tears as my mind flashed to what I knew was coming, and before I could stop myself, I let out a blood-curdling scream that must have echoed through the entire school.

CHAPTER
4

- - - - - - - - - - - - - - -

The janitor, hearing my scream, had come running over to find out what exactly was going on. I could barely speak, and pointed to the classroom where I'd found Margo in her current state. He poked his head in the door, and after he'd witnessed the scene for himself, he pulled out his phone and called 911 without saying anything else to me.

When he got off the phone with the dispatcher, he told me to sit down and try to relax while he went to meet the police and paramedics who were on their way.

Not wanting to be anywhere near the room, I chose a couch on the opposite side of the common area, and clutched my tote bag to my chest while I waited. I took a couple of deep breaths and reminded myself that I wasn't in any immediate danger, I was safe . . . I just wished I could have said the same thing for Margo Han.

The first to arrive were two officers from the Parma

police department who made my twenty-eight years seem very advanced. I couldn't help noticing that both policemen had baby faces, and I wondered if this was their first homicide call.

The taller of the two, with a shaved head and dark, full eyebrows, approached me. His hands rested on his belt, and he acknowledged me with a respectful head nod. He appeared extremely calm in contrast to what I knew my face must look like to him. I'd managed to hold back the tears that threatened to come pouring down my face, so at least I had that going for me.

The officer gave me a comforting smile, his voice low and steady as he spoke. "Ma'am, the gentleman I spoke with, Mr. Larkin, told me that you're the one who found the body. Is that correct?"

"Yes," I replied, assuming that Mr. Larkin was the janitor.

"Can you tell me exactly what happened?" he asked. He chose the couch adjacent to mine and sat down, in what I'm guessing was an attempt to meet me at eye level.

I went through the explanation of how I came back to the classroom in order to get my weekly recipe list after having already left the school. I told him about the man I'd seen as I was leaving and that I had assumed he was another classmate.

"Do you remember actually seeing him in the class?"

"No," I admitted. "I can't really say. "He was a very average-looking man. Not really someone you'd remember."

"Would you be willing to write all this down for me?" he asked.

"Of course," I nodded. "Anything I can do to help."

He excused himself and a few minutes later returned with an incident report sheet, asking me to fill it out to the best of my ability. "You'll need to come down to the station at some point, but I do want to get your testimony fresh. Just be as specific as you can."

I took the paper from him and stared at the line that read "Name." I was having a hard time remembering anything right now.

The officer seemed to sense my frustration. "Take your time. I'm going to talk with my partner. The detective should be here any minute now."

He left me to my own devices, and I took a quick scan of the common area to see where the janitor had gone. He was nowhere in sight and I assumed he was standing guard near the entrance somewhere to lead in whomever was coming next.

Trying to focus, I filled out the report to the best of my ability. I even made it a point to write down exactly where I was when I decided to turn around. I didn't know if any of that information would help, but Adam always told me the more details, the better.

My only regret was that I couldn't really remember what the man looked like that I had seen right before leaving. If they found him, would I be able to pick him out of a lineup? Probably not.

Still, I added the small details I could remember, hoping that they'd be able to figure out more with the class registration list. If it was that man, then that eliminated all the women in the class. And that cut down the suspect list considerably.

When I was finished, I signaled the officer I'd been talking with, and he came over, pointing at the paper in my hand. "You done?"

"Yes, I hope it's okay."

He took the paper from me with a gentle smile. "I'm sure it's fine. If there's anything further we need to know, we'll be in contact." He glanced down at the form. "This is your cell phone? Or a landline?"

"Cell phone," I replied. I pulled out a business card from my purse, and handed it to him. "I manage this restaurant, and am there Monday through Friday until around five o'clock. You can always call me here if necessary. I don't have a landline at home."

Taking the card from my hand, he gave it a cursory glance before clipping it to the form with the pen I'd used. "Thank you. We appreciate your cooperation."

"Do you need me to stay? Because I'd really like to get home."

"Understandable. But I'm going to need you to hang tight until the detective gets here. He shouldn't be much longer."

"Okay." I sighed and leaned back against the couch. I knew he was going to say that, but I was hoping maybe since I'd filled out the witness form, they'd just let me go. "Is it okay if I use my cell phone to call my boyfriend?"

"Of course. Feel free to make any calls you need to. But please, don't say anything that may get passed along. We'd like to notify the family first before this gets around."

I nodded. "My boyfriend's a police detective, so he knows the drill," I said with a tiny wisp of a laugh. "If I don't tell him what's going on, I'll probably get in trouble."

The officer smirked. "What city?"

"Fairview Park."

"Oh, I have a buddy that works in Fairview . . . Steve Clark."

"I actually know him. He's answered a few calls that came through for Asia Village."

His smile grew a bit wider. "What a small world. I'll have to tell him we met."

"Weissman," a gravelly voice declared.

The officer I'd been talking with, apparently Officer Weissman, glanced up and his posture straightened. "Hello, Detective Bishop."

"Is this my witness?" he asked.

"Yes, sir," Weissman replied, sounding more official than he had since he'd first arrived.

It led me to believe that this Detective Bishop commanded a certain level of respect, and maybe instilled a little fear into the men who were of lesser rank.

I twisted in my seat to face the detective, who was standing slightly to my left. "Hi, I'm Lana."

He returned my greeting with a grunt. "I'll take it from here, Officer. Make sure you collect the statement from that janitor. What the hell was his name again?"

"Larkin, sir. Robert Larkin."

"Yeah, that guy." He held out his hand expectantly.

Officer Weismann handed him my testimony and glanced at me from the corner of his eye. Before leaving, he gave me a friendly wink then went on his way to, presumably talk with the janitor.

Detective Bishop was not by any means a large man, but the way he talked, you'd think he was bigger than he was. I put him at around five foot six and a little over 150 pounds. He had a crew cut and no sideburns or remnants of facial hair. Though I guessed him to be somewhere in his mid-forties, he'd be lucky if he could muster a five-o'clock shadow. The suit he wore was navy blue with no flair of cut like the Italian suits that our property manager, Ian Sung, wore. His belt buckle, shoes, and tie were equally drab, and offered no hints of personality.

His eyes skimmed over the report as he slowly moved to the chair opposite me. He had yet to fully acknowledge my presence. Considering the circumstances, I wasn't really going to fuss about pleasantries, but it would have been nice and put me at ease if he'd at least forced some type of smile. Though I'm guessing my comfort level wasn't really his first priority at the moment.

"This is pretty specific," he said when he'd finished reading my testimony. His charcoal eyes flicked up at me.

My palms started to sweat. If I were being paranoid, I'd say there was some accusation behind that statement. But I reminded myself I wasn't under suspicion. Not yet anyway. "I really tried to be as helpful as possible. My boyfriend is a detective, so I know how hard your job can be."

He pursed his lips. "What city does this boyfriend work for?"

"Fairview Park."

He took a moment to think. "Detective Adam Trudeau, if my memory serves me correctly."

"Yes, that's him," I said.

"Well, I hate to break it to you, but name dropping isn't going to win you any points with me if that's what you were thinking." He glanced back down at the police report, scrutinizing the form as if it were a fraudulent document.

"Oh no, you misunderstand," I said, trying to keep my voice from rising in defensiveness. "I just meant that I know how difficult things can be when you're investigating a case and I wanted to make sure I did everything I could to help with that. I didn't know Margo long . . . just met her today actually, but she seemed like a really nice person, and I'd feel better knowing I did all I could to help find out who did this."

"Uh-huh," was his reply. "So, you signed up for this class, and then met her tonight for the first time?"

"Yes."

"It says here that you work at a Chinese restaurant. You don't know how to cook already?"

A nervous chuckle escaped. "Well, no. It sounds strange, I know. But I've never been interested in cooking Chinese food. I only took over my parent's restaurant this past year, so I figured I should learn."

"And there's no one there who can teach this stuff?" he asked, sounding unconvinced of my story.

"Technically yes, but it was supposed to be a surprise." Call me crazy, but I didn't think he'd want to hear about the feud with my sister right now.

"Did you know anybody else in the class?"

"No. I did talk with one girl earlier this evening, but I'd never met her before tonight either."

"And this man you claim to have seen after the class was over . . . you don't know if he was in your actual class or not?"

A breath caught in my throat. *Claim to have seen.* I didn't like the sound of that. "No, I'm not entirely sure about him. I didn't pay too much attention to who else was in the class at the time."

"I see." He let out an exaggerated breath and stood from his seat.

I wasn't entirely sure why, but I felt like I had better stand too. "Do you need me to come down to the police station tonight?"

He sized me up, not at all trying to hide the fact that he was. "Not at this time. Although, we may want to speak with you in the next couple of days, so make sure you're available."

"Yes, Detective, I'll be sure to do that. You also have my business card if you can't reach me by cell phone."

He gave me a curt nod, and turned to leave. No "Goodbye"; no "Thank you for your time"; no nothing.

Instead of letting it get to me, I decided to shrug it off for the moment. Not everyone was going to be as nice as the officers and detectives I was used to dealing with. I made my way back out of the school wondering what had happened with the janitor. I thought maybe I'd see him on my way out, but there was no sign of him anywhere.

As I stepped out into the cool evening, I took a breath of fresh air and savored it like someone who'd just been released from a long prison sentence. Now with the light breeze that wafted through, I realized that I'd been sweating considerably, and parts of my clothing were sticking to my body. Especially my jeans.

Getting into the car, I pulled out my phone, put it on speaker, and dialed Adam's phone number. I had a sinking feeling he was not going to be happy about this new predicament.

CHAPTER
5

Adam's car was already parked in the lot of my apartment complex when I arrived home. I checked for Megan's car and noticed she was home as well. I shut the engine off, grabbed my tote bag, and headed inside, taking deep breaths all along the way. I was still feeling shaken up and had driven home with the windows down on the freeway attempting to blast a sense of normalcy back into myself. It hadn't really worked.

When I opened the door, Kikko rushed at me, snorting and wiggling her curly tail as she pawed at my ankles. I bent down and gave her a scratch between her ears, happy to see that smooshy little face after the night I'd had.

Even more relief washed over me when I saw Megan and Adam sitting at the kitchen table with beers in hand. By the look of his clothing—black undershirt and ratty jeans—I could tell that he'd come over in a hurry. The fact that his reddish-brown hair was also tousled and sticking up in clumps on the sides of his head gave it away completely.

They both rose from their seats, and Adam came rushing over to give me a bear hug. My head only comes up to his chest, and I felt the definition of his muscles as he smashed me against his body.

He kissed the top of my head. "What on earth am I going to do with you, Lana Lee? You can't even take a cooking class without getting into some kind of trouble." He released me from his embrace and stared into my eyes. "Are you okay?"

I studied his face. His forest green eyes were filled with worry, and his full lips were curved down in a pout. I hated knowing that I was the cause of his upset. Tears threatened to form, so I bit my lower lip and gave him a head nod.

"Come sit down." He put an arm around my lower back and led me to the kitchen table where Megan was standing, hands on hips.

"My god, woman. Are you all right?" Her eyebrows scrunched together as she looked me over. "You're pale as a sheet."

"I feel like throwing up," I admitted. "Why did I have to go back for that stupid grocery list?"

"Well, have a seat and calm your nerves," she said, pointing at the chair across from hers. "You're probably going to need some of this." She slid an unopened bottle of Crown Royal across the table, and followed it with a shot glass. "This should calm your nerves a little bit."

I sat down at the table, and stared at the empty shot glass. My mind was on hyperdrive thinking about what I'd seen and what I imagined had happened before I'd gotten there. *How* could this happen?

Adam broke the seal on the bottle of Canadian whiskey, poured some into the shot glass, and set it near my hand. "Drink this. And then when you're ready, tell us what happened tonight."

I did as he said, and drank the contents of the glass without thinking twice. The amber liquid burned my inner cheeks and warmed my chest as it slid down my throat. I puckered my lips, and then after another deep breath began my story.

When I was finished, the three of us sat and stared at the table in silence.

Adam was the first to speak. "That Bishop guy is a total bastard." His eyes narrowed as he fixated on a coffee stain on the otherwise clean table. "I've never liked him. Not only have I heard some real crazy stories about him, but I've had a few run-ins with him myself. Has some kind of Napoleon complex."

"Yeah, I kind of got that impression myself," I replied.

Megan rested her chin in her hands. "So, what now?"

Adam turned to her, incredulous. "What do you mean by that?"

Megan lifted her head. "Well, it's obvious to me that he's going to try and pin this whole thing on Lana. We can't just sit here and let that happen. Lest you forget, we're women of action."

I groaned, but said nothing.

"Oh no," Adam said, shaking his head. "Let's just

leave this to the police. If need be, we'll get Lana a lawyer. If you tamper with a Parma police investigation and get caught, I can't help you."

"A lawyer?" I shrieked. "I don't have money for a lawyer."

He turned to me, putting his hand over mine. "Don't worry about that right now. I'll help you if it comes to that."

I stole a glance at Megan who winked in return. Without anything needing to be said, I knew she meant that we'd talk in private later.

"Okay . . ." I responded. "I just think . . ."

"Think what?" Adam's eyes widened. "You're going to somehow fix this on your own?"

"It's not that outlandish," I grumbled.

"Lana, it's not a good idea. There are literally no witnesses aside from you, and you found the body. You took a class on how to cook Chinese food and you are the manager of a Chinese restaurant. It doesn't look good for you so far."

"Yeah, but what about fingerprints?" I asked, feeling myself becoming defiant. "They won't find mine on the murder weapon."

"Well, one, if the killer was smart, there won't be any fingerprints to find on the murder weapon aside from this Margo Han's, assuming it was hers to begin with. On top of that, you guys were working with a lot of oil while cooking. It's very possible that there isn't a decent print to be found anyhow."

"Oh," was my reply. "I didn't think about oil being a factor."

"And, may I also remind you that your boyfriend is a detective."

"Yeah? So?"

"That's not really going to help you in this situation. If I know Bishop, he's going to think you have experience in covering up crimes."

I gaped. "That's even more reason I should figure this thing out. I'm like a sitting duck." I knew I should shut my mouth, but I couldn't help myself.

That thought became even more loud and clear as I noticed his jaw starting to clench. It was typically the first sign of his agitation beginning to form.

Megan seemed to notice as well and interjected. "Okay, okay, kids. Let's do this instead. Emotions are running high, and everything just happened a couple of hours ago. Why don't we all chill out? I'll order us a pizza and we can veg out for the rest of the night. Hell, maybe we can even pretend for a few hours that this whole thing didn't happen."

Adam and I glanced at each other, and nodded in agreement.

"Fine," I said. I didn't want to talk about it anymore anyway.

The next morning, I woke up a little earlier than usual to see Adam off to work. After I kissed him goodbye and he'd walked out the front door, I heard Megan come out into the living room. When I turned, she was standing in the hallway with her arms crossed over her chest, staring at me with determination on her face.

"So, we're getting all up in this case, aren't we?"

My chin dropped to my chest, and I sulked to the kitchen to prepare some coffee for the both of us. Kikko followed behind me, and seemingly sensing my unease, let out a whine of discontent. "I don't see how we can't get involved. I mean, you're absolutely right, it does look like they might try to pin this on me. Or at the very least, I'm going to be a suspect in their investigation."

"Do you think there are any security cameras that could help your case? After you guys went to bed last night, I was thinking there's a slight possibility that maybe they'll rule you out with some basic detective work."

I filled the coffeepot with water and poured it into the machine's reservoir. "I don't know, honestly. I couldn't even tell you if there were cameras in the building. The parking lot is a free-for-all, so it's not like I had to talk to an attendant who could vouch for me or anything. Then I thought about maybe traffic cameras, but I don't think there's one until you get to Pearl Road. So, there's no record there either since I didn't make it that far."

She seemed to contemplate this, nodding her head repeatedly as her eyes moved side to side. "We'll find something. Don't worry, we're going to figure this out. We always do, right?"

After I pressed BREW, I joined her at the table. "Yeah, but how many times can you come out of something like this unscathed before you run out of luck?" I asked.

"Well, if you're a cat, then nine. Nine times," she joked.

I forced a laugh. "You know what I mean."

"Chin up, buttercup. Adam may not be on board right now, but maybe he'll change his mind at some point. And even if he doesn't, who cares, you'll always have me."

I smirked. "Best friends forever."

Megan leaned back in her chair and smiled wide. "Ride or die, baby."

CHAPTER
6

Asia Village is my home away from home. I probably spend more time in the Asian shopping plaza than anywhere else. Thankfully, we have it all under one roof. If you need to pick up the latest psychological thriller by Jennifer Hillier, you can swing by the Modern Scroll, the plaza's bookstore. Or maybe you're searching for a birthday gift for your aunt Linda who happens to like fine porcelain vases. No problem, you can head to Chin's Gifts and even have it gift wrapped and everything. On your way out, you may be inclined to stop into Shanghai Donuts and grab a dozen sweet treats for you and your coworkers . . . or just yourself, depending on if you like to share.

On top of that, you can sing your heart out at our karaoke bar, the Bamboo Lounge, grab a few cosmetics items from the Ivory Doll, or even stock up on herbal supplements at Wild Sage where you will be greeted by the wise Mr. Zhang who may or may not be celebrating a centennial.

Of course, you may also be tempted to have lunch at Ho-Lee Noodle House. And that's where you'd find me. At least five days a week, I'm tucked away in the restaurant, managing the books, ordering supplies, and filling in as a waitress when needed.

We keep our staff small and we're all like family. Aside from me and my sister, Anna May—who fills in from time to time between law school obligations. My mother's best friend, Nancy Huang, is our split-shift server. Her son, Peter, is our head chef, and as previously mentioned, one of my very close friends. Lou handles our nights and weekends kitchen duty, and Vanessa Wen—the teenager who keeps me on my toes—is a night hostess and waitress. My parents, of course, come in and help at random times. You never know when either of them will pop in.

Since my grandmother from Taiwan came to stay with us, my mother has been coming in less and less, which is how I ended up taking over all the managerial duties. It definitely wasn't planned, I can tell you that.

I pulled into the plaza's parking lot, driving through the wrought-iron gate with its golden dragons greeting me as they did every morning. The sun sparkled on their metallic scales, which wrapped around brightly painted red poles.

Asia Village's façade was designed to mimic pagoda-style buildings, and the effect it created was a little town all of its own. When you walked inside the enclosed shopping center, you were greeted by a courtyard covered in cobblestone floors and a sky-light ceiling adorned with hanging paper lanterns and twinkle lights. In the center of the plaza was a large koi pond complete with footbridge and fish food machines to feed our aquatic friends. Wooden benches were sprinkled around the perimeter of the pond, and many people lounged to enjoy the scenery or chat with friends. It was an especially popular place to hang out during the city's colder months . . . which, truth be told, were about nine months out of the year nowadays.

I walked into the plaza, passing the hair salon, Asian Accents, the only place I trusted with my hair, and then passed Wild Sage herbal shop and spotted Mr. Zhang sweeping the sales floor. I smiled brightly at him as he lifted his head, and he returned the gesture with a toothy grin of his own. Next, I passed China Cinema and Song, an Asian entertainment store where you could find just about anything that had to do with Bruce Lee, Yo-Yo Ma, Teresa Tang, and Gong Li. My friend Kimmy Tran and her parents run the shop and have been friends with my family since well before Kimmy and I were born.

The shop right next to my family's restaurant is one of my personal favorites—Shanghai Donuts. Sweet smells of frosting and dough were already wafting out into the plaza as I made my way past to Ho-Lee Noodle House. My stomach growled as I thought about the doughnut holes I would be devouring once the plaza opened.

Inside the darkened dining room of our beloved restaurant, I moved through the maze of tables without worrying that I would bump my knee on a table or chair. I could walk this room blindfolded if I had to. The light switches—placed inconveniently if you asked me—were against the back wall near the kitchen.

Flicking them all on at once, the red and black décor-filled room was brought to life. The soft yellow lighting highlighted the sparingly used gold decorations that were meant to complete the traditional Chinese design that my parents chose a little over three decades ago.

My mother's current method of making me jump through hoops was to have me redesign the restaurant while somehow still keeping our original style intact. I had presented her with a few ideas that she had not taken to. In hindsight, I realized I should have followed the old adage "Act now, ask for forgiveness later." But alas, I was trying to be a good daughter, and thought if I showed her my ideas, she'd give me the go-ahead. It did not go as planned.

I made my way into the kitchen and headed to a second pair of swinging doors that led to the back room, which was used as a community break room. Off to the left was a door that looked like it led to a broom closet. That was my office.

Opening the flimsy wooden door, I turned on the light in the small room I considered home base and let out a sigh. Sometimes my life felt like the movie *Groundhog Day*—Bill Murray and me just living that same day on repeat.

I set my purse down on the wooden desk that was once my mother's, and riffled through a few notes I had left for myself. Wednesdays can be kind of slow for me at the restaurant, and I needed to find a way to keep myself entertained and occupied so I didn't think about the events of the previous evening too much. I didn't know how much time I had before things started to escalate with the police department and their investigation, and I needed a little break to gather my thoughts and sort things out. I had essentially been with Adam and Megan the entire time since I'd left the learning center, and I needed some alone time to truly process what was going on inside my head.

I checked the time on my cell phone, and saw that I had about fifteen minutes before Peter would show up for his shift. Heading back out into the dining room, I decided to go about my duties as usual. Maybe doing commonplace things would bring some normalcy back into my life.

I stopped by each table and booth to make sure the place settings were all perfect. Cloth napkins, silverware, and chopsticks were all present, along with bottles of soy sauce, salt and pepper shakers, sugar canisters, and alternative sweetener packets.

At the hostess station, I skimmed through the menus to make sure they were all wiped down—which they were—and that the cash register had been reset to its till of fifty dollars in coins and small bills—which it had.

I hopped onto the stool and stared out into the plaza, noting the darkened shop of Yi's Tea and Bakery that stood directly across from our restaurant on the other side of the koi pond. The shop had been closed for a few weeks, and the rest of us Asia Villagers were unclear on if and when it would reopen.

I tried to think about anything else. But, of course, my mind couldn't stay away from Margo Han's murder. I wondered if she knew her assailant. Clearly, they'd stabbed her in the back. Literally. They'd been up close and personal. From the brief moments I'd been in the room with her dead body, I hadn't picked up on the sense that there'd been much of a struggle. Aside from the scattered ingredients that had spilled to the floor—which could have been a result of Margo unintentionally hitting the bowl of leftovers with her arm as she fell forward—the rest of the room hadn't been disturbed. But they couldn't have snuck up on her. There was only one way to get in and out of the room, and you'd see the person coming. So, what exactly had happened in there? I couldn't make sense of it.

If the man I'd seen as I was leaving the class was in fact a student, what reason would he have to kill her? Did he know her previously? Was he *even* a student? Could he have been another instructor for a different class? I couldn't remember him.

I mentally rewound to when I entered the classroom and the chain of events that followed. I'd stopped and assessed the room, but I'd been so nervous walking in, I hadn't focused on many details. All I could remember was the blonde woman in the front row who'd asked me if I was the instructor. And then me proceeding to the back of the room as quickly as possible. The next thing I could remember distinctly was the woman with the sour expression on her face who'd been sitting near the front. And, of course, chatting with Bridget during our bathroom break.

I drummed my fingers on the hostess stand in front of me, zoning out to the rhythm I was inadvertently creating. *Think, Lana, think.*

A sharp rap on the glass door jolted me from my thoughts. When I looked up, Peter was waving and sticking his tongue out at me.

I got up to let him in. My alone time was over.

"Were you in dream land or what, man?" he asked as he entered the restaurant. He adjusted his baseball cap, which always sat low over his eyes, his shaggy black hair sticking awkwardly out of the sides. If I was in a more playful mood, I might tease him about needing a haircut.

"Yeah, just got a lot on my mind this morning. No biggie," I replied. Peter wasn't a huge fan of my propensity to investigate, so I didn't want to start our morning with an argument.

"Is it girl related?" he asked, turning to face me. "Because you know I can't deal with the girl stuff conversations. But if it's anything else, then I'm your guy."

"Yeah, it's girl problems," I lied. "Nothing to worry about. I'm sure I'll be fine later."

He gave me a thumbs-up. "Well then I'm off to my cooking cave. Gotta get ready for the Matrons."

The Mahjong Matrons were our most loyal customers and they arrived at nine o'clock sharp every day. They were never late, and they never altered their order. See? *Groundhog Day.*

I glanced up at the clock on the wall—only ten minutes before we open. Peter was later than usual this morning.

I returned to my stool as he walked away. A mix of feelings ranging from wanting to get this day over with to not wanting it to begin were having a full-on battle in my head. I began to mentally prepare myself for the necessity of "turning it on." The customer-service voice and smile would have to come out, and Detective Lee would have to take a back seat for the time being.

Then again, maybe the Mahjong Matrons could enlighten me with some information. They were, after all, the eyes and ears of this community.

CHAPTER 7

Helen, Wendy, Pearl, and Opal, our beloved Mahjong Matrons, filed into the restaurant at nine o'clock sharp. The four widows didn't bother to pause at the hostess station for a seating assignment. They had their own table they occupied every morning, always sitting in the same spots. When I'd first started working full time at the restaurant, I'd bring them menus as a formality. They really didn't need them as they ordered the same thing without fail, day in and day out. After a while I gave up on bringing the menus and just headed straight for the kitchen to place their order with Peter and prep their tea.

When I returned to the dining room and approached their table, the elderly women turned to greet me with pleasant smiles and twinkles in their eyes.

"Good morning, Lana," Helen sang in a cheerful voice.

"Good morning, ladies," I returned, giving them all a smile as I set the teakettle down in the center of the table.

Helen, who often acted as mother hen, reached for the kettle, and as the women flipped over their teacups, she filled each one to the brim. "Have you heard the latest news?" she asked, setting the kettle back down.

"The latest news?" I thought it best for right now to pretend like I hadn't heard. Anyone who knew me was well aware of the fact that I did not read the newspaper or watch the news. I was usually the last person to know about current events unless they went viral on some social media platform. It wasn't that I didn't care about what was going on in the world, but my sensitive nature had grown tired from trying to keep up with what always seemed to be bad news.

Pearl, Opal's older sister, leaned forward and whispered, "Yes, the news about Margo Han. She was killed last night. Stabbed in the back!" She lifted her hand, balled it into a fist and made a stabbing motion.

I paused for a minute realizing my potential error. If the case continued, there may be a point where it would come out that I was the one to find her body. Then the Matrons would know I lied to them and probably be furious with me. "Oh, *that* news." I replied. "Yes, I did happen to hear about that. Such a shame. Did you ladies know her?"

Wendy, whose sensibility often kept the group from going overboard, was the next to speak. "We only knew her a little bit. She was a nice woman, but did not seem to be close to anyone. She was not married, and did not have any children."

"How did you know her then?" I asked the group.

Opal was the next to reply. The petite woman was so dainty in even her speech, that sometimes it could be hard to hear her if you weren't listening closely. Barely above a whisper, she said, "She would come to the hair salon sometimes on Saturday mornings. She asked a lot of questions about mahjong and we tried to have her come play with us, but she always said no."

I tucked that information away in my brain. Interesting that she had visited the salon, yet I had never seen her. Which reminded me that she had mentioned she'd been to Ho-Lee Noodle House on a few occasions. But I couldn't place her.

"So, what do you ladies think about what happened to her?" I asked.

The four women glanced at one another, then Helen answered for the group. "We think she probably made somebody mad at the school. From what we know, all she did was work."

The bell in the kitchen rang, which signified that Peter had completed the Matrons' order. I excused myself to retrieve their food.

I returned to the table and set down their daily breakfast choices: Chinese omelets with chives, century eggs, pickled cucumbers, and a large bowl of rice porridge.

Right before I turned to return to the hostess station, Wendy glanced up at me and said, "Usually the ones

who look innocent have the most to hide. I bet someone like Margo Han was keeping a secret or two."

When the lunch rush had died down and Nancy had
things under control, I decided to take my break and
head over to the salon to find out if anyone there had
some information on Margo Han. If she didn't have a
husband or kids, I wondered who her next of kin would
be. I vaguely remembered her saying that her family
owned a dry-cleaning business. Were her parents still
living? Maybe she had siblings who ran the business?
Or maybe a secret boyfriend no one was aware of. Usually women liked to chat about those sorts of things
while getting their hair done, so I was hoping there'd be
some knowledge to gain.

I opened the door to the salon and was immediately
met with acrylic-nail fumes and Chinese pop music.

Yuna, the salon's receptionist, was jamming out to
a song playing over the salon's speakers, singing into a
round hairbrush she'd probably plucked from the shelf
of hair supplies they sold. Her normally pin-straight,
long hair was now wavy and mermaid green with a few
braided strands wrapped around her head. Metallic tur-
quoise clamshells dangled from her ears and complemented her aquatically themed hair perfectly.

The young twenty-something showed no signs of
embarrassment as she realized that I'd walked in and
caught her in mid-refrain. "Oh, hi, Lana. Did you come
to join the party?" She held her makeshift microphone
out toward me.

I held out a hand in protest. "Oh no, trust me, you don't want me to sing. Not unless you want the whole place to clear out."

She giggled in return. "Really? Come on, you can't be that bad. We're all going to the Bamboo Lounge tonight after work. Jasmine wants to start having monthly outings as a team. I've been warming up my vocal cords since this weekend! You should totally come along and hang out with us."

I had to admire her enthusiasm for life. Yuna was always in a cheerful mood and ready to take on whatever challenge you threw at her. "Well, if Jasmine is going to sing, maybe I should stop by," I joked.

Jasmine Ming was the owner of Asian Accents, my personal hair stylist, and the only person I trusted near my head with a pair of scissors. A few years back, I'd had a disaster of a haircut at another salon. It was so bad I'd contemplated wearing a paper bag over my head. After my mother scolded me for not supporting the plaza to begin with, I decided to give Asian Accents a try. I've never looked back or thought about going to another salon since.

"Is Jasmine here?" I asked, peeking around the wall of product that separated the cutting stations from the reception area. "I need to ask her something."

"No, she actually stepped out for lunch. She should be back in an hour if you want to try her then. I can tell her you stopped by."

"Actually, maybe you can help me," I suggested, stepping up to the reception desk. "Does the name Margo Han sound familiar to you at all?"

She tapped her chin with her index finger. "Han . . . Margo Han . . . hmmm."

"If it helps, she's middle-aged, about yay-high." I held my hand up a little below my own head. "Thin . . . kind of plain . . . is a cooking instructor."

"A cooking instructor?" Yuna repeated, her face lighting up. "I think I do know a Margo who comes in who's a cooking instructor. She's kind of quiet and doesn't get much done. Usually just a trim or something. Definitely no frills like you and me."

"That's probably her then," I said with a nod. Even though I'd only met her once, she struck me as a plain sort of person. "Do you know anything about her?"

"Like what?" Yuna asked, tilting her head.

"Something more on the personal side. Like if she has a boyfriend, a brother . . . what she did in her spare time."

Yuna's eyes widened. "Like why? Did something happen to her? Are you doing one of your investigation thingies?" She started to bounce with excitement.

I glanced around to see if anyone was in earshot. Thankfully no one was close enough to hear our conversation. "Um, kinda. I don't know what I'm doing yet, so please don't say anything. It could really complicate things."

"Don't worry," she put her hand up to her lips and acted as if she were zipping them up. "My lips are sealed. *But* you have to tell me what happened."

Checking over my shoulder again, I leaned in and whispered, "Margo was murdered last night after one of her cooking classes. Right now, the police have no real suspects and the whole thing just bugs me. I thought if I could find out something about her, it might lead to a helpful clue that could help the police track down who did this."

Yuna gasped, covering her mouth. "Seriously?"

"Yeah . . ." I left out the part about me being there because even though Yuna promised to keep this conversation between us, she was almost as bad as the Mahjong Matrons. I knew the first person she would tell would be Jasmine, and I was okay with that. I'd just rather tell Jasmine the details myself.

"Wow . . . that sucks. She always seemed like a nice lady. I didn't really know much about her though. She did mention she had a sister one time. But she never said anything about a boyfriend or whatever."

"Do you remember the last time she was in?"

Yuna shook her head. "No, but I can look." She turned to the computer on her countertop and started typing away on the keyboard, her eyes narrowing as she skimmed the screen for details. "Okay, it says here that her last appointment was about three weeks ago. She was due in next week for a trim." She sighed. "I guess I can cancel *that* appointment."

"Who cuts her hair?" I asked. "Does she always go to the same stylist? Or did she just take whatever available appointment she could get?"

"Hmmm . . . let me see." Yuna clacked away on the keyboard again and then tapped her fingers on the counter as she waited for the information to load.

"Well, it looks like she gets her hair done by Nicole. There was only one time she had her hair done by Jasmine, and that was over a year ago."

"Great." My eyes scanned the salon. "Is Nicole here today?"

"No, but she'll be in tomorrow. She comes in at two o'clock."

"Okay, thanks. I'll be back in tomorrow then," I said.

"Do you want me to tell Jasmine you stopped in?"

"That's okay. I'll try to catch her when I stop by tomorrow."

We said our goodbyes and I headed back to Ho-Lee Noodle House. I was hoping that Nicole could tell me a little more about Margo's personal life, and maybe point me in the direction of her sister. It wasn't much to go on, but maybe if I could track down Margo's sister I'd be able to learn more about Margo herself.

CHAPTER
8

The afternoon went slowly and gave me the opportunity to get caught up on all my managerial duties. With everything taken care of, I was able to spend the rest of my day in my office running potential scenarios. I considered that Margo might have had an affair and that's why she didn't have a known boyfriend. Or maybe she had an angry student lurking about who wanted revenge. I also thought about the fact she may have made an enemy out of another faculty member.

One thing I knew for certain is that I needed to go back to Barton's and do some snooping around. Earlier in the day, I had received an e-mail from the school letting me know that a tragic event had taken place and that the class would currently be cancelled. We had options of receiving a refund or applying the money spent to the next class they would offer. At this point, I didn't know what I wanted to do. I had really wanted to take this class in particular, but it seemed fate was working against me.

I had no plans that evening, so what better time to check out the learning center and see what I could find out. I sent a text to Megan letting her know what my ideas were and asked if she wanted to tag along.

As luck would have it, she didn't have to work that evening. I told her I'd pick her up when I was finished at the restaurant.

Around five thirty, I pulled into the parking lot of our apartment building and texted her: *I'm here.*

A few minutes later, she poked her head out the door, waved, and jogged to the car.

She hopped into the passenger seat. "Kikko was going bonkers as I was heading out, so I left her with a bone. I think she knows something is up."

I chuckled. "Most likely. She was doing laps around the apartment this morning." I put the car in reverse and pulled out of the parking lot, heading for the main road. "I'm feeling kind of jittery myself."

"Who can blame you?" she replied, her attention directed at the scenery outside the window. "Have you found out anything useful at the plaza?"

"Not really," I admitted. "It's a lot of general information. I do have a potential lead at Asian Accents tomorrow with the woman who used to do Margo's hair."

"Good call on that. Most stylists are honorary therapists. Margo must have told her something at some point in time."

"Let's hope." I paused as I entered on to the freeway ramp. "It seems as though she kept her personal life pretty close to the chest. But I may have just talked to the wrong people." While we drove, I filled her in on the conversations I'd had earlier that morning.

When we arrived at the school, we took a moment in the parking lot to come up with a game plan.

I turned the engine off and stared at the glass building. "I figure what I'll do is pretend that I have no idea that an e-mail was sent about the class cancellation and see what I can find out that way."

"What should *I* do?" she asked.

"I'd like for you to go to the actual classroom. I'm not sure if it's sealed off or not. But take a look and tell me what you think about the layout. I want another opinion on what the scenario could have been that night."

She gave me a thumbs-up. "You got it."

We headed into the school, and after I directed Megan on where to find the classroom, we separated and promised to meet near the main doors.

I knew from the few classes I'd taken here in the past that the administration office was open until seven o'clock to help any students who took night courses, but the staff was cut in half after the majority of classes were done for the day.

I was so focused on my next steps that I hardly noticed the cheery blonde waving at me as if I were a family member she hadn't seen in ages. It took a moment to place her as the woman who'd been in my cooking class, front and center, and who'd asked me if I was the instructor.

"Hey there." She stopped abruptly in front of me, and

put her hands on her hips. "Fancy running into you here. Lena, wasn't it? I'm Jan."

I returned her chipper attitude with a cordial smile. "Hi. It's Lana, actually."

"Right, Lana. That's it. I apologize, I'm terrible with names."

"Oh don't worry about it," I replied. "How are you?"

She blew a raspberry and threw her hands up. "Oh, just trying to find something else to sign up for. None of the classes I'd like to take are at the right times, and I really like my away time from home. Moms need time for themselves too, you know."

A bell dinged in my head. "Do you take classes here often?"

"Oh sure." She nodded. "I take at least one a quarter—two, if I can swing it. Especially when the kids get back in school."

"Did you happen to know our teacher, Margo Han? Prior to this cooking class, I mean."

Jan tsked and shook her head. "Shame what happened, isn't it? I can't imagine what her poor family must be going through. I'd taken some of her other cooking classes in the past, yes. I think that woman could cook just about anything under the sun."

"Did she have any children that you know of?" I asked

"She definitely didn't have children. And no husband, I can tell you that too." She leaned in and raised an eyebrow at me. "And it seemed as though she wanted to keep it that way."

"Why do you say that?"

"Well, at the beginning of the Mexican food course, she got a bouquet of flowers sent to her during class. They were a beautiful ordeal. Lots of roses . . . all different colors, and in the most beautiful crystal vase. But then she did the oddest thing." Jan held out her hands, palms up and shrugged her shoulders. "She threw them in the garbage at the end of the class. Mostly everyone had cleared out, just a few of us hanging around. I'm never in a rush myself, so I'm usually the last to leave."

"Really?"

"Yeah, can you believe it?" She shook her head in disappointment. "What a waste of money. You know they had to have cost a pretty penny. Delivered flowers ain't cheap."

"Did you know who they were from, by chance?"

"No, I didn't want to put her on the spot. She was clearly upset at whomever they came from . . ." She paused. "And then there was that other thing with one of the students."

"Thing?" I asked. "What kind of thing?"

Jan glanced over her shoulder as if worried someone would sneak up on our conversation. "There was this attractive man in that same Mexican class. Didn't seem to have much between his ears, but he was nice enough. Well, I overheard him ask her out to dinner after class one night, and she flat out said no and wasn't very nice about it either. Didn't even give the poor sap an explanation. She could have at least lied to him and said she was involved with someone or something. The kid was so embarrassed he never came back to the class."

"Do you happen to know his name?"

She gave me an apologetic shrug. "It started with an *R*, Randy or Rick . . . maybe Ron?"

It was flimsy at best, and I contemplated the likelihood of someone getting turned down for a date as a cause for murder.

Jan glanced at her watch and sighed. "Well, Lana, it was nice talking with you, but I'd better get going. The kids are going to be expecting dinner soon. You take care now. Maybe we'll bump into each other again sometime."

I said goodbye and watched her head toward the exit. For whatever reason, it seemed as if Margo was shying away from relationships, and had a potential admirer to boot. I made a few mental notes before turning my attention back to the administration office.

When I walked into the narrow room, I found two people behind the main counter, one of them appeared to be super young and potentially an intern. She had a hopeful smile, and cheery hazel eyes that were both welcoming and kind. In a way, she reminded me of Yuna from Asian Accents.

The older woman did not appear as welcoming or kind. The scowl on her face seemed to be a permanent fixture, and the beady eyes that scrutinized me spoke of annoyance with a dash of impatience.

No one was in the office but me, so I had my pick of the two. Despite my better judgment, I chose to go with the older woman because she probably would have more intimate knowledge about the faculty and their interpersonal relationships.

Unfortunately, the older woman did not look at all pleased that I was heading in her direction. She acknowledged me with a curt smile, lifting her chin as if to say, *"What?"*

Despite the discouraging feeling I had in the pit of my stomach, I forced my customer-service smile into place, showing teeth and all, and stepped up to the counter. "Hi, my name is Lana Lee, and I was taking a cooking class here . . . the one with—"

The woman held up a hand. "Yes, the ethnic cooking class with Margo Han. You should have received an e-mail with further instruction on your options."

I let out a fake, nervous laugh. "Oh, duh, I didn't even think to check my e-mail. Probably could have saved myself a trip up here."

The woman pursed her lips. "Uh-huh."

"Such a tragedy, what happened and all that," I said in a conversational tone. "I can't even imagine how the rest of the staff feels."

The woman stared blankly at me. "I can help issue you a refund if that's what you would prefer."

I will be the first to admit that my facial expressions often betray me. *Poker face* is something I continuously strive to achieve, but don't always succeed with. At this current moment in time, I was trying my damnedest not to reveal the fact that I was severely disappointed in her response. I thought for sure my mention of the staff might warrant her to say something along the lines of

"Yes, she had so many friends." Or *"I'm not surprised this happened to her. She just didn't get along with people."* Something. But, perhaps, that was asking for too much.

I must have been focusing on maintaining the positive expression on my face so intently that I'd completely forgotten to answer her, because she jutted out her chin and said, "Ma'am?"

Ma'am. Who was she calling ma'am? I loathed the word.

"Okay, let's do a refund," I said, through clenched teeth. "It's probably safer that way."

She clucked her tongue. "The facility is safe—I can assure you of that. We've heightened security and plan to install additional cameras in the lobby, common area, and hallways."

The defensiveness in her tone showed me what route I needed to take in order to get her talking. "Well, that's good," I replied, not sounding the least bit convinced. "But I'd still feel safer not attending. No one has been caught yet, and who knows if it was another instructor or something crazy like that."

If smoke could have come out of her ears at that point, it totally would have happened. "I can assure you, *young lady*, that another teacher being guilty of this . . . is absolutely *not* the case. We carefully screen all of our faculty members before they're hired. And you'll do well to remember that. Now if you'll just give me a moment, I'll begin your refund. Do you have your identification card with you?"

While "young lady" sounded much better than the

dreaded "ma'am" that I despised so much, coming from her it still hit my ears as condescending and rude. I dug around in my purse for my wallet, pulled out the appropriate card, and handed it over.

She snatched it off the counter and began aggressively typing on her keyboard.

The intern and I exchanged a look. Her expression was a mixture of apologetic and shocked. Maybe I'd picked the wrong person after all.

It took about five minutes for Grumpy Pants to complete my refund. She'd slid a processing form across the counter and slapped a pen on top of it. "Please fill this out, *Ms.* Lee."

I did as she said without responding, and then smacked the pen back down when I was finished. My streak of sass was starting to bleed through and "customer-service Lana" was slowly fading away.

The printer behind her started to spit out papers, and she swiveled around in her office chair to reach for them.

She slapped the first sheet down on the counter. "This is your check—you have ninety days to deposit it." She slapped down the next piece of paper with the same intensity. "This is your acknowledgment form stating that you've received your check and we are no longer accountable to refund you anything further. Please sign and date this."

With a scowl, I reached for the pen she'd left on the counter for me and scribbled my name in a frenzied hand. As I set the pen down, I smiled sweetly at her, hoping that the sarcasm would not be lost.

"Thank you, Ms. Lee. You're all set. Have a nice evening." The lack of smile and deadpan look in her eyes told me she didn't mean it in the least.

"I hope you have a better one," I replied, and whipped around to exit the office.

As I entered the common area, I let out a groan of frustration. Not only was that completely useless, but I'd aggravated myself beyond belief. My only comfort was the check I had in hand.

I headed in the direction of the doors where I was supposed to meet Megan, hoping that she would have something useful to tell me that might make this trip feel like it was productive. But when I got near the main entrance, Megan was nowhere to be seen.

I pulled out my phone and began to text her. Out of the corner of my eye I noticed movement, and thinking it was Megan, momentarily stopped typing and glanced up. But it wasn't Megan, it was the intern who'd been working in the administration office. She appeared to be out of breath and also looking for me.

She was a petite girl who made me feel like a giant in comparison. Rail thin and somewhat athletic, she reminded me of someone fit to be a gymnast.

When we made eye contact, her eyes lit up and she waved. "Hey. There you are. You walk really fast, you know that?"

I dropped my phone back into my purse. "Sorry, I'm supposed to meet up with someone."

"I only have a minute because I told Bernice that I was going to the bathroom," she said. "Sorry you had to deal with her. She's like that with everyone, so don't take it personally."

"I think she's in the wrong line of business then."

The girl laughed. "You're not the only one to have said that."

"What can I help you with?"

"I just wanted to tell you that she's full of crap," the girl said, glancing over her shoulder in paranoia.

"About what exactly?"

"That the faculty is innocent." She shrugged. "I mean, yeah sure, they are all evaluated and looked into before being hired, but there is such a thing as first-time offenders. The police were here earlier today questioning staff, and the impression I got was that some of them are being investigated. But I haven't found out who exactly." She looked down at her feet. "No one is talking to me about anything because I'm just an intern. And they assume I'm gonna spread it all over the school since I really have no loyalties to any of these people. I did happen to see them talking to the one janitor guy, Robert, on my way to the bathroom. I tried to eavesdrop on my way back to the admin office, but by the time I came out of the ladies' room, they were gone."

"Do you know if he's around today?"

She shook her head. "No, he's out for the rest of the week taking some personal time."

My mind started to race. So, there *were* questionable faculty members.

I pulled a business card out of my purse. "If you find out anything more specific, would you mind giving me a call? I know that seems kinda weird, but if you don't mind?"

She took the card from me and skimmed over the information. "Sure. Can I ask why you want to know?"

I didn't want to tell her that I might be on the police radar for potential suspects, so I just replied with, "Margo was planning on helping me with something, and even though she never got to, I feel like I owe her a favor."

The girl nodded with understanding. "Sure, I get that." She held up the card before slipping it into her back pocket. "I'll give you a call if any sort of info comes my way."

We said goodbye, and she jogged off in the direction she came from, passing Megan in the process.

Megan jerked a thumb over her shoulder as the girl disappeared down the corridor. "What the heck was all that about?"

CHAPTER
9

"Let's not talk in here," I said, my eyes darting around the lobby. The last thing we needed was for someone to hear our bizarre conversation. "Outside is probably safer."

As we made our way through the parking lot, I told her about the run-in with my classmate, my experience at the administration office, and the intern coming to find me afterward.

Megan shook her head in disgust. "Wow, some people are so miserable."

"For real. But hopefully this girl can find out something for me." I smacked my forehead. "Duh, I forgot to get her name. Anyways, tell me what happened on your end."

We got into the car and Megan sighed. "Well, the room itself was closed off, door shut with crime-scene tape, typical stuff. But I still scanned the area to see what I thought, and you're right: there's only one way in and out, and not many places for someone to disappear quickly. How there was no one in the vicinity to hear her scream is beyond me. Didn't the person get blood on their hands? Did they walk through the school like that? Run to the nearest restroom? Like what did they do?" Megan's tone was a little agitated and her speech hurried as she went through the various options.

"There's a restroom not far from the classroom, so that's a possibility. Someone could have easily hidden in there, cleaned themselves off, and waited until the coast was clear to leave."

"But what about noises that would have come from the room?" Megan reminded me. "How did she not scream? Or was there a fight beforehand that someone might have heard? Wouldn't someone hear raised voices and then report that?"

"Assuming they would wanna come forward and involve themselves. We both know people can get tight-lipped when these kinds of things happen."

"That's true."

"Also, when I went back to the classroom that night, there was no one around but me. The place had cleared out pretty fast, but the janitor must have been somewhere nearby because he did hear me scream. He was there in what seemed like seconds. And with her being stabbed in the back, she may have been caught off guard and couldn't scream. She was only stabbed once too, so clearly they made it count," I replied.

"Who do you think the flowers were from?"

"No idea. Ex-boyfriend trying to win her back? A secret admirer?"

"Well, whoever it was liked her enough to send flowers. What about this janitor? Do you think it could have been him?" she asked.

"It's crossed my mind," I told her. "He's definitely on my list of people to consider. But he seemed genuinely surprised when he found her. I don't know if he's just a really good actor or was in fact equally as shocked as I was."

"We need to look into him for sure," Megan said with resolve. "Do you think we should go back inside?"

I shook my head and started the car. "No, that intern told me he's out for the rest of the week on a personal leave. We'll have to come back a different day. Plus, that lady put me in a bad mood."

"You're probably hungry. When's the last time you ate?"

"Early this afternoon," I replied, pulling out of the parking spot.

"Let's stuff our faces and get ourselves organized with this case. It seems like we're going to have to play the waiting game a little bit with this one."

"Stuffing our faces," I repeated. "Now that sounds like a plan.

On the way home, we picked up a pepperoni pizza and some teriyaki wings for our brainstorming session. Kikko, of course, greeted us at the door with anxious sniffs, dancing on her hind legs in anticipation of getting some pepperoni from at least one of us.

I dug underneath my mattress—the official hiding

place of my detective journal—grabbed the tattered spiral notebook, and brought it to the kitchen table where Megan and I hunkered down with greasy food and speculations.

The hard part of this whole thing was that Margo didn't have much affiliation with anyone I knew, and I didn't know anything about her on my own. Normally, should a situation like this arise, I could always count on the people who worked or shopped at Asia Village to help me do some digging.

My only hope at this point was that Margo's hair stylist, Nicole, would be able to shed the tiniest of lights on the deceased woman's private life.

I'd just finished jotting down the limited information we knew about Margo when Megan let out an exaggerated groan. Her eyes were focused on the page I'd been writing, and my guess was that her frustration was due to the fact that most of the page was untouched. All we really knew for sure was that her family owned a dry-cleaning company, and that she had a sister. We concluded her sister must run the family business, but even that we couldn't be sure about just yet.

"How are we going to pull this one off?" Megan asked. She removed the elastic band from her hair and readjusted her ponytail.

I slapped the pen down on the notebook and gawked at her. "Wait a minute, you're always the one with the *can do* attitude. You can't just go and change tactics on me."

She crossed her arms over her chest in mock protest. "If I'm always the one encouraging you, why don't *you* have a turn? Put those positivity podcasts and self-improvement books to the test."

I stuck my tongue out and she responded with a snicker.

In recent months, I had taken to the positivity movement that seemed to be spreading like wildfire. Not only had I purchased a variety of books on mindset from the Modern Scroll, but I was dutifully listening to motivational and uplifting podcasts on a daily basis, and Megan couldn't resist regularly teasing me about it.

"Okay, fine," I said, matching her crossed arms. "I accept your challenge. I can be positive about this, no problem."

"Oh yeah?" She raised an eyebrow at me. "Look at that empty page and then tell me that again."

I sighed. "But this is how all of our cases start. We think we're doomed and then something opens a door that leads us to another door, and then another . . ."

"Well, I hope you're right. I don't say this often, but I don't see this being so easy."

With a laugh, I replied, "It's never easy."

"You know what I mean."

"Don't worry, I have a good feeling about this lead with Nicole. At one time or another, Margo had to say something of use to her, and we're gonna use that to break into this case."

Looking unconvinced, she leaned forward and reached for another slice of pizza. "Like I said, I hope you're right."

"Don't worry," I replied, smiling wide. "How often am I actually wrong?"

* * *

The next morning, I found myself feeling quite determined. As I put on my makeup, I wondered if that was Megan's purpose all along. She knew I'd been feeling combative lately, which is exactly why I took the cooking class to begin with. Maybe this was her way of getting me on top of my game.

Whatever the case may be, it had worked. I got myself dressed and ready for the day, my mind moving from one idea to the next. Of course, most of these ideas were just me making assumptions, since I knew next to nothing about this woman.

Asia Village was quiet when I arrived, and I took a couple deep breaths on the way to the restaurant to calm myself. I felt jittery even though I'd barely had any coffee that morning.

I went through my usual morning routine of prepping the restaurant, greeting Peter when he arrived, and getting the Mahjong Matrons situated when they walked through the restaurant doors.

Nicole wouldn't be starting her shift until two o'clock, so I had to go almost the entire day before finding out if she even knew anything important to begin with. I could very possibly be waiting on a big fat nothing.

And naturally, because I was waiting for something to happen, the day dragged on with little to no excitement to keep me occupied. At that point, I would have even taken a customer complaint to get things moving. Talk about feeling desperate.

Nancy arrived at eleven, and I disappeared into my

office until the lunch rush so I could prep the bank deposit to take with me later that day. Per usual, I would use the bank deposit drop-off as a way to leave the restaurant without being questioned by anyone.

I made a couple quick notes to myself about things I wanted to order for the restaurant at the beginning of the following week before heading back out to the dining room. To my utter dismay, there was nothing "rush-like" about lunchtime. Only a few businessmen came in and their orders were pretty light. This day was crawling.

Finally, it was ten minutes until two, and as I scurried back into the office to get my things, I debated whether it would be annoying to show up right as Nicole did. I already knew that the stylists didn't get their first appointment until about a half hour into their shift unless there were overflow issues. Jasmine always preferred her workers to get situated when they arrived, so they were less likely to feel rushed and mess up somebody's hair. And since it was business hours on a weekday, it wasn't likely there would be any overflow to contend with.

I practically jogged out of the restaurant, yelling to Peter and Nancy that I would be back soon. They each gave me a curious look as I passed, but neither made any comment about my clearly anxious behavior.

I took another deep breath as I exited the restaurant and warned myself to calm down, so I didn't seem like a complete wacko as I walked into the salon.

But on my way, as I was passing China Cinema and Song, Kimmy Tran stepped out from her store and stood right in front of me. "Lana Lee!" she bellowed.

Even though I'd noticed her out of the corner of my eye, she'd startled me anyhow. I jumped a little, sucking in a gasp.

Kimmy laughed, her chubby cheeks rising with amusement. "You are too easy to scare!"

I groaned. "Kimmy, you're going to give me a heart attack one of these days."

She shook a finger at me. "You need to calm down, Lee. How much coffee have you had today?"

Pursing my lips at her, I refused to answer.

She put her hands on her hips and jutted out her chin. "Uh-huh. That's what I thought."

"Okay, well I'll see you later then," I said, attempting to express just how agitated I was with her.

"Wait a minute. What are you up to?"

"Nothing," I replied. "Why would you think I was up to something?"

"You have that look on your face. I know that face . . . I've seen it plenty. Now spill."

"I don't know what you're talking about," I said. I started to inch away in the direction of the salon.

"I don't know why you bother hiding these things from me. It's becoming insulting. You know I'm going to find out anyhow."

"Well, when you find out, you let me know." I waved and turned away before she could say anything else. She was right though. It was only a matter of time before someone ratted me out for snooping around. I just hoped it was later rather than sooner.

CHAPTER 10

I stepped into the salon and felt heat rise up my neck. The pressure was on because I felt like I had something to prove. Me and my big mouth had gone on quite a bit the night before with Megan about how I knew this meeting with Nicole was going to be just what we needed to get the ball rolling. Needless to say, I was reluctant to hear her say the words "I told you so." She loved to say it too much.

Nicole is not hard to pick out of a crowd. There aren't many Asians running around Cleveland with bleach blonde hair. I don't know how the girl did it, but she made it work. And I always say, if you can rock it, flaunt it.

I waved to Yuna, who was chatting with a customer who was cashing out. She gave me a wink and nudged her head in the direction of Nicole's workstation.

The fashion-forward stylist was slouched in her

cutting chair, flipping casually through a hair magazine when I walked up. She tilted her head upward
and smiled, and then did a double take when she realized it was me who had come to see her.

"Well, if isn't Miss Lana Lee," she said with a wide
grin. "It's been a while since I've seen you."

"I know, we always seem to miss each other," I replied, feeling the muscles in my body relax. Nicole and
I had known each other a long time. We didn't talk
much, but there was a comfort level there that I'd forgotten existed. Maybe this wouldn't be so bad after all.

"What brings you by? I know it can't be to let me cut
your hair," she joked. "Because Jasmine would have
both our heads on a platter."

"True story," I said with a laugh. "No, I actually came
to ask about one of your clients, if you have a few minutes to spare." I glanced over my shoulder to make sure
no one was around.

She closed her magazine and straightened in the
chair. "Oh yeah? Are you, you know . . . ?" She gave me
an exaggerated wink.

"Possibly." I felt the palms of my hands begin to
sweat. My previous stints in detective work were no secret around the plaza, but I always tried my best to keep
a low profile whenever possible.

"Cool. I kind of have an idea on who you might be
here about."

"Oh yeah?"

"It's not every day that one of your clients is murdered."

"Okay, well good, I can skip the backstory then. What

can you tell me about her?" I don't know why, but it felt like both of us were avoiding saying her name out loud.

"Not much really. She was pretty standard procedure as far as haircuts go. She'd get her hair trimmed every four weeks, even if it didn't look like it needed it. And everything she talked about was pretty much surface stuff. She never got into the nitty-gritty with me."

"Did she talk about her family at all?"

Nicole took a moment to think. "Not in-depth, but I do know that she had an older sister. I think she ran the family business or something. I wanna say it's called Lucky Lotus Cleaners."

Point for me. At least my assumption about the sibling running the family business was correct. "How about a love interest? From what the Matrons told me she wasn't involved with anyone. But I did hear from someone else that she received flowers a couple months back."

"Oh, she had a boyfriend for sure." Nicole said with a smirk. "Well, at least someone she wanted to be with. . . . What the extent of the relationship was, I can't really say."

I thought about her throwing the flowers in the garbage. If it was someone she wanted to be with, that didn't seem like an appropriate response. "But did she *say* she had a boyfriend? Or are you just guessing?"

"She never called him by a title. She always called him her *friend*," Nicole replied, holding up her hands and using her fingers to make air quotes. "However, that's absolutely what he was whether she wanted to admit it or not."

"How can you be sure about that? Maybe they were platonic?" I wanted clear confirmation that it came out of Margo's mouth versus speculation.

"Well, no one can really be sure of anything, can they? But you know as well as I do that a woman just knows about this sort of thing. And I could definitely feel it. The little she talked about him, you could tell she was super invested in him. But she struck me as a timid woman who wasn't going to speak up for the things she wanted in life. Just the tone in her voice— she'd get soft if he happened to come up in a story she was telling me."

"She never mentioned a name?" I asked.

"Nope, always *her friend*. She'd tell me they went to a movie or went out for dinner. She liked to cook for him too. She'd mention a lot of times how she'd prep meals for him to take home. I guess he was not a genius in the kitchen."

"Did you get the impression that he was Asian?" I didn't know if that mattered, but I felt like it would at least help me eliminate some of the people who'd end up on my list of suspects.

"I don't think so. From time to time she said how her family didn't approve of mixed relationships. They were pretty old-fashioned from what she said. The two topics were never mentioned at the same time. But it left me with the impression that maybe that's why she was keeping things in her personal life quiet. Honestly, it's hard to say which scenario I believe. One of them didn't want to seal the deal, that's all I know for sure."

I started making mental notes of angles I wanted to explore. If her family was close-minded, then it could have been a factor in her intimate relationships. Also, a possibility that she'd rejected someone and inadvertently offended them.

Nicole observed me while I collected my thoughts. "What do *you* think happened?"

I sighed. "At this point, I have no idea really. I didn't know her in the slightest. Tuesday night was the first night I'd ever met her."

"How did you guys meet anyways? She doesn't come around here too often."

Blushing, I said, "I was taking her cooking class. Please don't tell anyone."

Nicole's hand flew up to her mouth to stifle a laugh. When she composed herself, she gave me that look people give you when they think you're being ridiculous—it often comes with a tilt of the head and pursed lips. "Lana, just let Peter teach you. He's not going to make fun of you or something. Is that what you're worried about?"

"It's not that, I guess. I don't know, I really wanted to surprise all of them. Especially Anna May."

Nicole chuckled. "I can understand that. Your sister is a little . . . well, no offense, she's kind of a know-it-all."

I laughed. "Believe me, I know that fact firsthand."

"So now what? I'm guessing the class is cancelled?"

My shoulders dropped. "Now I put learning to cook on the back burner . . . again."

"Cheer up, Lana," Nicole said, flashing a bright smile.

"One of these days you'll learn to sauté with the best of them."

Before leaving Nicole to begin her shift, I asked her to let me know if she thought of anything else that might be significant. She promised she would, and I left feeling mildly productive.

Hoping that no one from Ho-Lee Noodle House noticed me leave the salon, I scurried out the main doors and headed for my car. I'd been at the salon for about twenty minutes, and if I was lucky, going to the bank wouldn't take too long.

On the way there I thought about what Nicole had said concerning Margo having a boyfriend and that maybe it had been a secret relationship. My own sister, Anna May, was entertaining a "private" relationship at the moment. As liberal as I tend to be about most things, matters of the heart was not one of them.

Normally I attributed those types of relationships to some type of deceit. That maybe she'd been a mistress, or maybe the guy was dating multiple women on the side. But hiding an interracial relationship would not have dawned on me.

My parents, as old-fashioned as they were, had always been open-minded in that department. Neither one had discouraged me from dating—or not dating—a specific type of person. And though I knew those feelings of prejudice still resided in society today, they were usually not at the forefront of mind. I suppose that was the idealist in me.

There weren't many cars in the bank parking lot, so I hurried inside to handle my business and was back in my car less than ten minutes later.

For a September afternoon it was unseasonably warm, and I rolled down the windows to let some air in the car. The drive back to Asia Village was more relaxing than the one to the bank, and I realized just then how much tension I had been holding onto.

Unfortunately for me, when I returned to the restaurant, I had a visitor waiting for me that would reinstate that tension and multiply it tenfold.

Detective Bishop had come a callin'.

CHAPTER
11

Upon my walking into the restaurant, Nancy, who'd been sitting on the hostess stool, sprang up with alarm on her face, eyes widening and sliding in the direction of my surprise visitor. Detective Bishop was sitting at a two-seater table near the entrance, facing the door. He had what appeared to be an untouched cup of tea in front of him. His arms were folded across his chest and he was leaning back in his chair with an air that spoke of wasted time.

As if the detective being there wasn't bad enough, my mother and grandmother were also there, seated at their usual booth near the kitchen. My mother was glaring intently at Detective Bishop from over her bowl of noodles.

Trying to remain calm, I smiled good-naturedly at Nancy. If I acted like this wasn't a big deal, then maybe my mother wouldn't flip out and cause a scene.

Before Nancy could say anything to me, the detective rose from his seat, adjusted his tie, and approached the lobby area where I'd slowed down my pace considerably.

I didn't have to pretend to be surprised to see him because I was. "Detective Bishop, nice to see you again." Which was a lie, of course.

"Miss Lee," he said in response. "I hope I'm not catching you at a bad time. There are some things I'd like to discuss with you if you have a moment to spare."

My palms started to sweat. "Sure. We can go back to my office if you'd like to talk in there."

Without realizing it, my mother had walked up behind Detective Bishop, and she made a production of clearing her throat. Undaunted by my mother's presence, the detective turned around to acknowledge her. "Hello again, Mrs. Lee."

My mother planted her hands on her hips. She was about two inches shorter than me, but she always seemed larger than life, at least to me. I wasn't sure she had the same effect on our new friend. "Now my daughter is here. You tell me why you are here to see her." Her tone was so authoritative there was no mistaking that she wasn't asking, she was telling.

Detective Bishop's stance didn't budge an ounce. "Mrs. Lee, right now I need to speak with your daughter in private." He talked slower and louder than he had when addressing me, and it was obvious that it was in a condescending way, as if my mother couldn't understand what he was saying.

Points for her because she picked up on it right away. "I'm Taiwanese, I'm not stupid."

His jaw clenched, and he took a step back. "No one is suggesting that you're stupid, Mrs. Lee. I simply wasn't clear if you understood English all that well."

She scowled in return. "I understand more than you think."

He turned to me, clearly perplexed. "Miss Lee? May we speak in private? I have places I need to be."

I sighed heavily. "Mom, we can talk after he leaves." Turning to Detective Bishop, I said, "Right this way, Detective."

My mother clucked her tongue as we walked by her. "My other daughter is a lawyer; you better be careful."

I heard Detective Bishop mumble something under his breath that sounded like "Yeah okay," but I couldn't be sure. I kept my back straight and my head held high as I led him to my office. I wasn't going to bother with pleasantries and ask if he wanted water or anything to make him more comfortable. I was pretty sure that he would never extend the same courtesy to me.

When we got to my office, he assessed it, taking the seat closest to the door. His demeanor told me he was unimpressed with the space, and frankly, I couldn't blame him.

I sat in my chair, folded my hands in front of me and waited for him to speak. I had no idea what to expect.

He reached into his suit jacket and pulled out a tape

recorder. "I hope you don't mind me taping our discussion. I like to make sure that everything is above board and I have a clear record of all communications."

"No, that's perfectly fine," I said, keeping my voice flat. I knew right now it was important that I didn't show much emotion.

He turned the recorder on and recited a script I'm sure he'd said a hundred times, explaining who he was talking to, where he was at, and what the purpose of his visit was. He then stated that I was aware of the recording and asked me to say my name and that I accepted the conditions of our conversation.

I complied.

"Now, Miss Lee, you told me that you left Barton's Adult Learning Center and returned to retrieve some type of shopping list for the class requirements. Is that correct?"

"Yes, sir."

"And when you returned, the victim, Margo Han, had already been stabbed, correct?"

"Yes, sir."

"Did you walk into the room? Or try to call out to her, seeing if she needed any help?"

I didn't know why he was asking me these things again. I had already made my statement and, as he'd said, written an overabundance of detail. My only guess was that he was trying to see if I was being consistent with my story. "No, I did not walk into the room. I could see everything from the doorway. I did not call out to her, but I did scream."

"And that's when Mr. Robert Larkin, janitorial employee for Barton's Adult Learning Center, came onto the scene?"

"Yes, he must have heard me screaming and came to see what was happening."

"And did he enter the room and offer assistance to Margo Han?"

"No, he stayed outside of the room, and when he realized what had happened, he called nine-one-one."

"Do either of you possess any medical knowledge or training?"

My eyebrows furrowed. "Well, I can't speak for Mr. Larkin, but I definitely do not have any medical training."

"Yet you were able to assess that she was in fact dead from the doorway?"

"I think it was pretty obvious from the state she was in that she was . . . deceased."

"I see." He sounded skeptical.

"I think that it was. It's not the first dead body that I've seen." The moment it came out of my mouth, I knew I shouldn't have said it.

"So, you've been in this particular type of situation before?" he asked.

Now I understood the purpose of his visit. It was to get on record that this wasn't my first rodeo.

"Yes, unfortunately, I have."

"I see."

"I'm sure you know about the murder of Thomas Feng, our former property owner here at Asia Village."

"Yes, Miss Lee, I am aware."

"And I'm sure you also know that someone else was

found guilty of that murder," I replied firmly. Echoing my mother's previous sentiment, I'm not stupid. I knew perfectly well when my integrity was in jeopardy.

"Yes, Miss Lee. And for the record, you were the person to apprehend the guilty party, correct?"

"I was."

"And interestingly enough, you were also involved in the Yeoh, Pan, Chow, and Kam investigations as well, correct?"

My face was heating up fast. "Yes, I was."

"So, it's fair to say that you're familiar with a crime scene and how things operate?"

"I suppose I am."

"And you also mentioned that your boyfriend is Detective Adam Trudeau of the Fairview Park Police Department. Is that also true?"

I glared at him. "Yes."

"Then is it also fair to say that dating an officer of the law may further any personal knowledge when it comes to the act of committing a crime?"

I was losing my patience. My blood was boiling, and I wanted to punch this guy straight in the mouth. But before I could say something that could possibly get me arrested, the door to my office flung open, and my sister stormed in wearing a scowl that would rival my mother's facial expressions any day.

Behind her was the infamous secret boyfriend—and high-powered attorney, Henry Andrews. He was no doubt dressed to impress in a charcoal Armani suit, crisp dress shirt, and baby blue tie that matched his eyes perfectly. His sandy blond hair appeared freshly cut and was kept short and professional, along with a clean-shaven face that allowed him to display a rather remarkably defined jaw line. I had to give my sister points for taste in men, that was evident.

Detective Bishop uncrossed his legs and shifted in his seat to face the door, clearly annoyed at our interruption. "Excuse me, I'm conducting some questioning here."

"And you'll excuse *me*, Detective Bishop, is it?" Henry said it with the elegance of a peacock fanning its feathers. "I'm Henry Andrews, Miss Lee's attorney. I was just informed that you were conducting a private interview with my client without my presence."

Detective Bishop hit STOP on the recorder and rubbed his temple. "There hasn't been a charge against Miss Lee, I'm just asking her a couple of standard questions."

"And what are the nature of these questions?" Henry asked. He crossed his arms holding onto his left wrist with his right hand, showcasing the expensive Cartier watch he wore. "Sounded to me as if you were trying to make my client incriminate herself."

Bishop narrowed his eyes. "Were you eavesdropping on our conversation, Mr. Andrews?"

Henry scoffed, his crooked smile producing deep-set dimples that just made him look all the more charming. "Hardly, Detective. I think it's perfectly obvious that these walls are paper thin. I merely heard the tail end of your conversation with Miss Lee, and I'll be frank with you, I didn't like it."

"I can assure you, *Mr. Andrews*, there isn't anything

to not like. I'm just gathering some information to help with a murder investigation that I'm working on."

Henry grinned with amusement, as if to let the detective know that he'd accepted the challenge. He extended his hand, waving the detective on. "Please then, by all means, continue. I'm sure that you understand I'll need to be present for this so that Miss Lee does not unintentionally incriminate herself."

"You know," Detective Bishop began with a sneer, "usually people only need a lawyer in the event that they're guilty."

Henry wagged a finger at him. "Not always the case, Detective. I'm sure you've heard of several recorded instances where innocent people are found guilty by unwittingly incriminating themselves *or* have been coerced into saying something they didn't mean." He let that hang in the air for a moment before he added, "Of course, I'm not accusing *you* of such behavior. But as I've learned over the duration of my criminal law career, one can never be too safe."

"Fine," Bishop replied curtly. He turned the tape recorder on and made note that two more people were present in the room as legal representation and then asked Henry and my sister to state their names for the record.

Once that was complete, he turned back to me and said, "Miss Lee, do you have any involvement with, or have you ever met, Robert Larkin prior to the day of Margo Han's murder?"

I shook my head. "No sir, I have never met Robert Larkin before that day."

"Thank you," he replied. "That will be all for today."

He turned the recorder back off and stood up. I notice he tried to puff up his chest and make himself larger as he stood next to Henry, who was roughly six foot two.

Henry gave the detective another sly smile. "Now see, was that so bad?"

Bishop didn't respond, but turned to me instead. "Miss Lee, I'm sure we'll be in touch in the near future. Please make sure to have your *lawyer* on standby." He gave a final glare to my sister and Henry before saying, "I'll see myself out."

When he left the office, I took a deep breath and flopped backward in my chair. I had developed a headache and it was more than warm in my tiny office with four people having occupied the space.

After a minute had passed, Anna May stuck her head out my office door, peeked around the corner, and then returned, folding her arms over her chest. She looked down at me, and in a no-nonsense voice, she said, "Lana Lee, you have *a lot* of explaining to do, so I suggest you get started."

CHAPTER
12

It wasn't long before my mother and grandmother joined us to find out what was going on. Now with five people in that cramped space, I couldn't take it anymore and asked to move into the employee lounge area directly outside of my office.

My grandmother, who had been in the United States for less than six months, still had no idea what was going on half the time. She was slowly picking up words commonly used by my mother, like "bingo," "shopping," "dinner," and "casino."

My dad was trying to help her learn, but from what I gathered, he wasn't having the best of luck.

With a red face, I began explaining the story to my family and Henry. I think him being there made it a little worse, because I knew almost next to nothing about the man. I'm sure my reasoning behind taking the cooking class to begin with sounded petty to him, because as I said it out loud, it sure sounded like that to me. Plus, I still wasn't sure what I thought about him secretly dating my sister. Though Anna May had informed our small family about the true nature of her relationship with Henry—unbeknownst to him—I knew it wasn't "out there." She had sworn all of us to secrecy. Anna May had not told any of her friends, and from the limited information she'd given me after I'd begged to know, none of Henry's colleagues were aware of it either. Their outward appearance was an innocent friendship, perhaps a slightly older established attorney helping a young woman interested in law. And something about that gave me a yucky feeling.

Her internship had recently ended, but someone like Henry had enough pull to keep her hanging around the law firm to help on a case that had begun during the middle of the summer. Anna May's involvement in the actual trial was minimal, but it was enough distraction to keep her away from helping me at the restaurant as much as she normally did. This annoyed me thoroughly because I was feeling burnt-out to the max. Of course, my parents—mostly my mother—were happy about it because it kept her front and center with who they hoped would be their future son-in-law.

When I finished the whole story, my sister let out a loud, infuriated groan. "I can't believe you, Lana. Is it so important to show me up that you would stoop to this level? Now look what you've gotten yourself into. And, of course, you'd have to be the one to find the body."

"Hey!" I said, raising my voice. "If you hadn't started

picking on me so much in the past couple of weeks, I wouldn't have even taken the stupid class to begin with. You can't let up on me *ever*. Here we are, me in my late twenties and you in your early thirties and you still have to tease me about my entire life."

"Cry me a river, Lana. It's what big sisters do. Get over it." She pointed at the swinging door that led out to the kitchen. "Also, may I remind you that *Peter* is right out there! He would have gladly helped you out-cook me any day. You guys are supposed to be the best of friends, aren't you?"

My mother tsked at both of us. "Why can't you two girls be nice to each other, you are sisters. We are all family, and you should not be this way."

My nostrils flared, and right before I could go into a tirade, my grandmother asked my mother what was going on.

We all paused while my mother translated for her in Hokkien, the Taiwanese dialect my family spoke. I understood most of what they were saying, though I couldn't speak the language myself. My sister knew exactly what they were saying too. So, when my grandmother stuck up for me and reminded my mother of her own difficult relationship with my aunt Grace, Anna May pouted.

Henry, who had been observing but hadn't commented, held up his hands. "Okay, ladies, let's all take a breather. I think we're getting a little sidetracked with the emotions behind this. If we're going to help Lana, we have to talk this through with logical minds and leave the rest of the backstory out of it."

As cordial as I could possibly be at the moment, I turned to him and said, "I appreciate your kindness and for saving me from Detective Bishop, but I don't have the money to pay for an attorney right now, especially someone of your status."

He seemed to take pride in that statement, and suddenly his shoulders appeared a little broader. "Think nothing of it, consider it a gift for a friend."

I snuck a glance at my sister, who I knew was melting with adoration on the inside, but outwardly she appeared unfazed by his generosity. Ten bucks said that she would have planted a big ole kiss on his smacker if none of us had been around.

"I appreciate that, Henry," I replied. "How did you guys end up here anyways?"

"Mom called me," Anna May explained. "She told me that a detective was here, and she thought something was fishy about it. She figured you might be in trouble and asked us to come by. Lucky for you, we were available."

I ignored my sister's comment, and asked Henry, "So, now what do we do?"

"Well for now, keep a low profile," Henry answered. "I have a few friends in the Parma police department who might let me pick their brains. Let me find out what they're thinking in regard to this situation. It seems that whoever this Robert Larkin is, he's a person of interest for them. I thought it was curious the detective wanted to know if the two of you had any associations."

"I did too," I admitted. "Before you guys showed up, he asked me if either one of us had any medical training. And I was thinking to myself, how the hell would I know if Robert Larkin had any type of medical background whatsoever?"

Henry nodded. "I heard him ask you that. We actually *were* eavesdropping outside the door. I wanted to see how far he would take his questioning before we came barging in."

"Well, I'm glad you stepped in when you did. I almost lost it on him toward the end."

"My best guess is that he was trying to get you to slip up somehow," he suggested. "And you really don't know this Robert Larkin character, right?"

"No, I really don't. Tuesday night was the first time I'd ever seen the man in my life."

"Okay, good." He pulled a hand out of his pocket and produced a business card. "This is my card, and it has my cell phone number on it. Use it if the detective shows his face again. Don't hesitate to call."

I took the card and thanked him again.

"Don't thank me yet, Lana. Detective Bishop isn't someone to take lightly. I assume the next time he shows up, the questions are going to be even more difficult. But like I said, just keep a low profile, and we'll get this whole thing squared away. After all, you are innocent."

After Henry and Anna May left, I endured a twenty-minute lecture from my mother about adjusting my viewpoints on the relationship with my sister. She also suggested that I have Peter teach me how to cook instead of entertaining any type of direction from an outsider.

Though I wasn't surprised she felt that way, I was a little thrown off that she hadn't offered to teach me herself. Perhaps it was my impatience and short attention span as a teen that discouraged her from attempting to teach me anything now.

The whole ordeal from aggressive detective to un-invited parental guidance had taken up the remainder of the afternoon, and it was nearly five o'clock when everyone was done berating me. I couldn't have been more relieved at the realization that I would be going home soon.

I shuffled out into the kitchen to see what Peter was up to and if he had any extra spring rolls laying around. Being interrogated always made me hungry.

When he saw me coming, he shook his head in disappointment. "Mama Lee told me about your little secret."

"I figured she would," I replied, leaning against the stainless-steel counter next to the grill where Peter was browning some teriyaki strips. "Are you mad at me?"

He responded with a noncommittal shrug. "Eh, you know me, I get over things quick. I just don't know why you wouldn't ask me in the first place. This whole thing could have been avoided."

I sighed. "I know, but I didn't want you to laugh at me."

"Dude, I wouldn't have laughed at you." He paused. "Okay, maybe a little," he added with a smirk. "But still, after that short laugh, *then* I would have shown you how to run this kitchen like a champ."

"Well . . . I don't know what you want me to say.

Hindsight and all that. I'm sorry if it offended you at all. That really wasn't my intention."

"Don't sweat it. Do you still want to learn?" he asked.

"Kinda, but not right now, I guess. I don't know. It would feel sort of frivolous right now with everything going on."

"We can do it whenever. You think on it and let me know."

"Okay, thanks. But can I ask you to do me a different favor in the meantime?"

"What?"

"Can you make me something to eat?"

That evening when I got home, I felt the weight of the day wearing on the muscles in my neck. I wanted to take a nice, long bath—something I never did—until my toes and fingers started to prune.

I noticed Megan's car in the parking lot, which was a pleasant surprise because on most days she had already started her shift at the bar by the time I got off of work. Now that she was the lead manager, it was easier for her to customize her schedule a little more than she'd been able to previously.

I found her and Kikko sprawled out on the couch, relaxing. Shutting the door, I said, "Okay, where is Megan Riley and what have you done with her?"

Upon hearing my voice, Kikko's head popped up and she yawned, just waking from a nap. Her pink tongue curled out and she sighed as her mouth closed, as if in protest of being disturbed from sleep. Hoisting herself

up, she flopped off the couch and scuttled over to give
my shoes a good sniff.

Megan stretched her arms over her head. "What do
you mean by that?"

"You're not doing anything. There are no projects
on the table, you're not knitting anything or designing
some kind of jewelry. That's not like you." I hung my
keys on the hook near the door, and bent down to pet
Kikko before she started yipping.

"I can relax," Megan replied defensively. "I do it all
the time."

"No, no you don't." I moved toward the couch, and
batted at her knees. "I don't think I've seen you relax
since 2005."

Megan adjusted herself, giving me room to sit next
to her. "Oh, stop being so dramatic, Lana. I already have
a headache."

"You feeling okay?"

"I guess." She leaned her head in her hand. "I think
I'm just agitated with this whole situation."

"Well, wait until I tell you what happened to me
today."

"Oh brother, what now?"

Before I fully unloaded the entire story of the whirl-
wind that was my day, I went to the fridge and pulled
out two bottles of beer to help take the edge off. When
I was settled back down, I went through all the details
of what happened, trying not to leave anything out. The
more I talked, the more rushed my speech became and
I had to keep backtracking to add in details that I'd forgotten to mention.

Megan drummed her fingernails on the side of her beer bottle. "This is ridiculous. If this Detective Bishop gets in our way, he could ruin our chances of figuring anything out. Couldn't this have happened in Fairview Park instead so it would be Adam we're dealing with?"

"Well, ideally this wouldn't have happened at all," I said.

"Yeah, obviously. But you know what I mean."

"I agree, this guy might make things complicated for us. But hopefully there won't be much in the way of run-ins with him."

"Are you going to do what your sister's boyfriend said and keep a low profile?" she asked.

"We tend to try and do that anyways," I reminded her. "It's not like we broadcast our movements for everyone to know about."

"True." She nodded. "So, what's next on our agenda?"

"Clearly I need to talk with Robert Larkin."

"And we also need to get to Margo's sister. See if there's anything she can help us figure out. Maybe she'll know if Margo had any enemies . . . or who the flower guy might be."

"Why don't you let me approach her alone?" I asked. "You can come with me to talk with Robert Larkin?"

"How come? Are you worried she won't talk while I'm there because I'm not Asian?"

Megan was referring to the possibility that Margo's family wasn't into her mixed-race associations.

"No, nothing like that. I'm more concerned she'll view it as a two-against-one type of thing. I want to make sure she feels comfortable with me and that she can speak candidly."

"Good point." She sipped her beer. "Well what should we get started on?"

"Right now?"

"Yeah."

"Well, right now, I am taking the longest bath known to man. After that, I say we pig out and update the notebook. Maybe do some digging online and see what we're getting ourselves into as far as Robert Larkin goes. If we can find anything, that is."

"Okay, sounds good to me. Anything to keep me in leggings for the rest of the night. What do you want to eat?"

"Dealer's choice," I said, getting up from the couch. I could hear the bathtub calling my name.

"Mexican food!" Megan reached for her cell phone on the coffee table. "I could really go for an enchilada."

CHAPTER
13

After my bath and the large amount of Mexican food I consumed with Megan, I found my eyes starting to close involuntarily. Though Megan had cracked open her laptop and started working her magic to find something interesting about Margo, within fifteen minutes we both ran out of steam. Deciding to skip our investigative session, we promised each other to hunker down and focus more during the weekend.

When I woke up on Friday morning, it was hard to believe that so much time had passed and I felt as if I'd gotten nowhere. As I prepped for work, I tried my best to motivate myself into thinking that all of this would be no problem. I'd done it before, and I could do it again. I just needed to be patient with myself and take everything one day at a time. Each piece of new information would bring me one step closer to my objective.

Before I hopped in the car, I checked my phone for

a text message from Adam. He was working on a new case, and I had barely been able to see him much in the past two weeks. It was tricky dating a detective at times. I admired the dedication he had for the work he did, but sometimes I felt like I would always be on the back burner. I tried not to have selfish thoughts like those because I knew that what he did for a living was really important, but sometimes I just missed him.

With no text messages to review, I left the parking lot of my apartment complex and headed east.

I didn't see today being the best day for Megan and me to try to track down Robert Larkin. Since the only place I knew to find him was at the school, we'd have to wait until at least Monday. For today, I'd try my luck with a quick visit to Lucky Lotus Cleaners and perhaps get the chance to meet with Margo's sister, Joyce.

I felt a little weird about approaching her, considering her sister had just been murdered and she didn't know me whatsoever. Aside from it being intrusive, it was also a little on the odd side to someone who wasn't familiar with me. What would she think about some random stranger getting mixed up in their family affairs? And I couldn't help but wonder if it would make me look like I was guilty.

As I pulled into the plaza's parking lot, I realized I didn't have the luxury of worrying about it. If I wanted answers, and wanted them on my own terms, then I'd just have to do whatever it took.

I went through the motions of any typical morning at the restaurant. When Peter arrived, I noticed that I wasn't feeling very social. We mumbled a few attempts at "hello" and "how are you" before he headed into the kitchen.

This wasn't totally unprecedented because neither one of us were morning people, but I had to admit that I was not feeling entirely myself this particular morning.

The Mahjong Matrons arrived at nine o'clock, and when I returned with their tea, the four women looked at me with expectation.

"Lana," Helen began, "I cannot believe you didn't tell us about what happened with Margo Han."

Wendy tsked and shook her head in disappointment. "We have been through a lot together. Is it that you don't trust us?"

Pearl and Opal did not chime in, but both ladies appeared to be saddened.

I directed my confusion at all four of them. "What do you mean?"

Helen wagged her finger at me. "Lana, do not take us for fools. We know that you were taking Margo's class and found her body."

My face reddened. "Oh, that." I hugged the round tray I'd just emptied. "It's not that I don't trust the four of you. But I really didn't want anyone to know that I was taking a cooking class. It's kind of embarrassing."

Opal, who'd been gazing out the window into the plaza, turned to face me. "Lana, this is nothing to be ashamed of. We understand why you would do this. Sometimes family can be difficult."

Pearl gaped at her younger sister. "I hope you are not talking about me."

Opal blushed. "Of course not, dear sister. How could I ever think such a thing?"

Helen looked up at me and rolled her eyes. "Listen to us. Do not worry about these small things or feel bashful. The Mahjong Matrons will help you find information about who killed poor Margo Han."

The four women nodded in unison, determination set on their faces.

"How did all of you find out anyway?" I asked.

Wendy laughed. "Do not worry about this, young lady. The Mahjong Matrons always find out."

After the Matrons left for the day, I tended to a couple of odds and ends around the restaurant. When I was finished tinkering around with soy sauce containers and place settings, I headed to the front to lounge on the hostess stool. Whenever I had free time, I'd hop on Pinterest and check out ideas for remodeling the dining area. I still had no idea what I could do that both my mother and I would agree on.

I didn't get too far into my search before the bells above the door tinkled. I closed out the app and shoved my phone under the counter, giving the new customer my full attention. But when I looked up, I realized that I was staring into a familiar face, though I couldn't place the young woman standing in front of me right away.

She smiled brightly, showing a perfect row of teeth, and I experienced a moment of déjà vu. It was Bridget, the girl from my class who had befriended me on our break.

"Hi, Lana," she said, her eyes scanning the dining room behind me. "Wow, this place is a lot more beautiful than I remember. It's been a long time since I've been here."

I couldn't wipe the stupor off my face. She wasn't someone I had expected to see walk into Ho-Lee Noodle House. But perhaps I could use it to my advantage.

Noticing my surprise, she let out a nervous laugh. "Sorry to show up like this. I came by to check out that salon you were telling me about."

I'd completely forgotten all about our Asian Accents conversation, and after she mentioned it, I nodded in recognition. "Oh that's right, the salon. Decided to brave the unknown, huh?"

She chuckled. "Yeah, I thought I'd go in for a consultation and see what the stylist had to say. Then I figured since I was already here, I'd might as well kill two birds with one stone and stop in to see you. I've been wanting to talk to someone about what happened to Margo Han. Crazy, right?"

With a frown, I said, "Yeah, completely crazy." I didn't know what else to say about it other than it was a tragedy, so I left it at that.

Bridget, however, didn't seem to pick up on my discomfort. She continued: "I could hardly believe it when I first saw it on the news. I mean, just think, we were there *right* before it happened."

"I know," I replied. "What are the chances of that?"

Thankfully details of how the body was found were not released by the police. A general statement was given saying that a student and school employee found the body and called 911. As long as Robert Larkin kept his mouth shut, no one would be the wiser.

"And the chances that'd you be in that specific class. Am I right?" She shook her head in bewilderment.

My breath caught in my throat. "What do you mean by that?"

She hesitated. "Oh, all I meant by that was you like to investigate things and have experience with this sort of stuff. I mean, this has really got to have your wheels turnin'. For me, well, this is a first-time deal. I don't even know what to make of it."

It felt like I visibly gulped just like they do in cartoons. "I can see why you'd think that, but I haven't really thought about it."

She tilted her head. "Really? You aren't the teeniest bit curious about what happened to Ms. Han?"

I tried to keep my facial expressions in check, and the tone of my voice. Even though Bridget was a friendly person, and her general curiosity was normal, I didn't want to divulge my secrets to a stranger. Who knows who she might tell? But I did need to try and see if she knew anything useful. I cautioned myself to tread lightly. "No, really I'm not."

She did not appear convinced by my answer.

"Honestly," I said, attempting to sound very matter of fact and not at all defensive. "The only reason I got involved in those other cases is because they affected people I knew directly. They were more personal situations. I didn't know Margo Han outside of that class or even that day."

"Hm." Bridget pursed her lips. "Well, I can't say the same for myself. I'm dying to know what happened to her. How strange that someone would just kill a person like that in a classroom. And with potential witnesses around, no less!"

The conversation was making me a tad anxious because, of course, I also wanted to know what happened to Margo. "You know, Bridget . . . didn't you mention that you took the Mexican food class that she taught last quarter?"

She nodded. "I did, and I am proud to say that I can make a fajita with the best of 'em. Why do you ask?"

"Oh, I was only wondering if you knew Margo on a more personal level, and that's why you're curious about what happened to her. I mean, like I said, that's what happens with me. If you're somehow invested, it's hard to help yourself."

"No, I can't say that I did," Bridget replied slowly, shaking her head. "Do you find it odd that I'm being inquisitive about what happened?"

I couldn't tell if she had taken offense by my question or was in the process of questioning herself. "I just wondered is all."

"I'm sure this is probably old hat for you, Lana. But this is . . . well, this is something you see on TV for people like me, you know?"

I took her reply as a signifier that she might be offended. "I'm sorry if you took that the wrong way—"

She waved at me with a dismissive hand. "Oh no, nothing like that. I just didn't know her is what I'm saying."

"I heard that she had a secret admirer. Were you there the night she received flowers from someone?"

She laughed. "See? You *are* interested in this! I knew it!"

"Oh no no," I said, shaking my head. "I was only thinking about what a shame it was for that person to have lost her. She must have meant something to whomever that person was."

Bridget smirked. "Whoever gave them to her must have done her wrong because I saw her throw them out after the class was over. You know," she said, leaning forward, "what if the person who gave her the flowers is the killer? Wouldn't *that* be something?"

I didn't want to admit to her that I was worried about the same thing. She appeared to be a little hyped up about this situation, and I didn't want to make it worse. If we got too into this conversation, I might slip and say something that I shouldn't.

She seemed to notice the tension I felt, and shifted to a more casual body language. Her shoulders slouched a little bit and she repositioned herself against the podium in a more conversational manner, as if we were just two buddies discussing the weather. "So, anyways, enough of that awfulness. What are you planning on doing about your cooking dilemma? Are you going to sign up for a new class?"

"Um, not right now," I admitted. "The head chef here offered to give me a few lessons when I feel up for it. So, I'll probably just do that."

"Oh." Her eyes widened. "I guess the cat is out of the bag about you taking the class then?"

"Yeah, you could say something like that."

"Well, if he's giving out free lessons, I'd be happy to sign up." The enthusiasm in her statement was followed by a blush in her cheeks. "Oh, I'm sorry. That's incredibly forward of me. We don't even know each other."

I gave her an encouraging smile. It was obvious that her nerves were rattled. She was probably embarrassed about her morbid curiosity and was trying to overcompensate. "I'll ask him about it and see what he says."

"Great. I mean, I would also pay for him to teach me, of course," Bridget replied. She began digging around in her purse, found a loose piece of paper, which turned out to be a receipt, tore it in half, and grabbed a pen off my counter. "Here's my cell phone number. Even if he decides he doesn't want to give out lessons to a perfect stranger, we should keep in touch anyways." She handed the paper over with a grin.

"Yeah, we should," I said, taking it from her. Reaching for the business card holder on the counter, I grabbed a card and flipped it over, writing my cell phone number on the back. "Here's my cell, and of course, the restaurant is a good place to reach me if you need to. I'm here more often than I'm not."

She skimmed it over and nodded. "Cool. We'll talk soon. Maybe we can grab a drink or something?"

"Sure, that sounds like fun."

"Well, I better get going. I've got some errands I have to run." She held up the business card and smiled before putting it in her back pocket. "See you around, Lana."

After she walked out the door, I grabbed my cell phone from under the counter and was ready to hop back on Pinterest, but before I could even get started, Megan called.

CHAPTER
14

When Megan asked how my day had been so far, I told her about my unexpected visit with Bridget. And I was surprised to find that my best friend did not approve of the situation. She solidified her distaste for Bridget's random appearance at the restaurant with a hearty "Something smells fishy to me."

"It's totally possible that she's just one of these people who's fascinated by murder," I said. "I think it only comes off weird because of who I am and the situations I've been involved in."

"Yeah, but doesn't she have her own friends to speculate with?" she asked.

"I'm sure she does, but it's different when someone is closer to the situation. Her telling a friend who had no involvement in the class at all doesn't have the same impact. They're too far removed."

"I have no involvement with the class," Megan stated plainly.

I cringed. "That's not what I meant, and you know that."

Megan didn't reply, and I thought the phone had cut out.

"I just meant for someone who's never been through this before, they'd want to talk to someone who knew the deceased party."

"I'm putting her on our suspect list," Megan said, dismissing my roundabout apology. "It's weird and I don't like it, but it's also convenient."

"How so?"

"You may have to get close to this girl, Lana. This could be your way in to finding things out."

"I don't see how. She knew Margo Han about as much as I did." I took a moment to think about whether that statement was actually true. Bridget had said to me that she'd taken a few cooking courses at the learning center. Maybe she did know Margo more than I thought.

"Do you think she's capable of killing your teacher?" Megan asked.

"I mean, I guess. Bridget is pretty tall . . . and somewhat muscular, I suppose. Margo was a small woman and could probably be easily overpowered. But I don't see a logical motive to her doing something like that."

"Doesn't matter. Right now, I'm just concerned with possibilities. We can weed people out later." I could hear Megan scribbling on a pad of paper. "Do you know this girl's last name?"

"No. It's never come up. I know Margo said it out loud at the beginning of the class when she was taking roll, but I wasn't paying attention."

"If we can't get any leads from Margo's sister or find out anything from Robert Larkin on Monday, you might have to chat up your new friend Bridget to see if there's anything worth looking into."

I grunted in agreement. I wasn't taking much stock in this conversation, but I didn't want to argue with Megan about something so trivial.

"Don't forget, Lana, everyone is a suspect until we prove otherwise."

We hung up after I promised to check in with her once I'd completed my adventure out to Lucky Lotus Cleaners. I was planning another bank deposit cover story for when Nancy came in for the day.

An hour later, she strolled in the door. Her gentle smile always put me at ease.

Friday at lunchtime is usually pretty busy. With people getting hyped up for the weekend, more office workers seemed to come in with anticipation of their workweek ending. Almost as if it were a precursor to their upcoming freedom from desk life.

Nancy and I worked the dining room in a rhythm we had nailed down to perfection. We never found ourselves running into or stumbling over each other when things got hectic. Sometimes working in the food industry felt like an art form.

Things finally started to slow down around one o'clock, and my stomach was protesting loudly at the lack of food in my system. Before heading into my office to get the money out of the safe, I asked Peter to grill some teriyaki sticks for me to take on the road.

I let Peter and Nancy know that I had to run an additional errand while I was out at the bank, and since that wasn't very unusual, neither questioned what it was that I was going to do. Not having any connections to Margo was also helpful, as I didn't think either one of them would suspect I would get involved in this case. Really, it was a great cover. My only hope was that it stayed that way until I figured out who the killer really was.

Lucky Lotus Cleaners was on the east side of Cleveland, where most of the Asian businesses reside in the city. When the original owner of Asia Village, Thomas Feng, built the Asian shopping mall on the west side, his move was intentional. Though many had discouraged him at the time to stray from the already established locations that had been set up by previous generations of immigrants, Thomas felt it was important to expand the radius. He wanted to offer the same Asian products to people who might be unwilling to travel, though it wasn't all that far. Most Clevelanders, especially the older community, tend to stay on their side of town.

Within twenty minutes I was pulling my car into the small and extremely cracked parking lot of the Han family business. The sign outside was old and faded with a barely visible pink lotus blossom flourishing next to green block letters that read: Lucky Lotus Cleaners.

I turned off the engine and stared at the dilapidated building, wondering what the heck I was going to say to Margo's sister. I shifted in the driver's seat to look in the back at the two dress shirts I'd brought along with me as a cover story. This morning, I'd grabbed them right before leaving the house, thinking it would be a good idea that I didn't show up empty-handed. The only problem was I didn't know how I was going segue into the topic of her recently deceased sister. Truth was, I had been feeling so scattered and anxious that I wasn't thinking as clearly as I should have been. And now, my mind was drawing a blank on any possible conversation starters, making me feel as if this whole thing was a big mistake.

Prepared or not, I knew I couldn't drag this out any longer. I was losing time. Without giving myself the opportunity to back out, I opened the car door and forced my foot to plant itself firmly on the ground. I was going in no matter what. Opening the back door of my car, I reached for the shirts and held onto them as if they were life support.

I was trying to find the positives of this, and one thing on my side was that there were no other cars in the parking lot. I didn't know what that meant as far as how their business was doing, but I also didn't know how busy a dry-cleaning company was supposed to be. In all my lifetime, I had never once utilized a dry cleaner.

Approaching the entrance, I could see a middle-aged Asian woman with cropped hair tending to something at the counter I couldn't see. Her head was bent down so I wasn't able to see her face, but hopefully this would be Margo's sister and not some random employee.

When I opened the door, the woman lifted her head and smiled cordially. "Hello. How can I help you?" She glanced down at the shirts I had in my hand.

Feeling a little awkward, I walked up to the counter, and placed the shirts down in front of me. "Was I supposed to put them on hangers? I've never done this before."

The name tag on her shirt read JOYCE. She laughed pleasantly. "I have hangers here that I can use. Will this be all?"

"Yes, just these two shirts."

She smoothed out the shirts and grabbed two hangers from the metal rod that hung behind her. It was filled with blouses, pants, and dresses covered in plastic. "I can have these ready for you by tomorrow," she told me. She slipped a hanger through the collar of the first top.

"Oh great, that's faster than I thought."

"We haven't been too busy lately. I had to close a few days this week, and I will be closing again next week. You came in at the perfect time."

My stomach fluttered; this was my chance. "Oh really, how come? Are you going on vacation?"

The smile from her face disappeared and she frowned, shaking her head. "I wish that were what I was doing. But there has been a death in the family."

"Oh no, I'm sorry to hear that," I said.

"Thank you. It has been a great shock to our family." Joyce moved the first shirt off to the side and put the other hanger through the next collar. "Life can be so short for some people."

I didn't know what to say in return. I felt insensitive

even being there and trying to pump this woman for information when she was clearly hurting. What had I been thinking?

Most likely, she took my silence as discomfort, which to be fair was accurate. But probably not the discomfort she assumed I was feeling. She sighed. "I'm sorry, I did not mean to be too personal with you."

"No, not at all," I said, trying to assure her the best I could. "It's terrible to lose a family member. I'm surprised you're even open at all."

She moved the second blouse on top of the first and looked up at me, tears welling in her eyes. "I had to keep myself busy. So, I opened for a few days while we wait for the funeral. Otherwise, I would just sit at home and cry. And I know that will not help bring my sister back."

"I can understand wanting to keep busy. I'm the same way."

"Next week I will be closed for maybe two weeks. Maybe more. I'm not sure. So please be sure to pick up your things tomorrow, otherwise it will have to wait until I reopen."

"No problem, I'll be back tomorrow."

She handed me two green tickets. "You can pick them up any time after noon. I'll be open until five and you can pay when you pick up your things."

I took the tickets from her and smiled. "Thank you, I'll see you tomorrow."

She nodded, picked up my shirts and disappeared behind the metal rack. I stood there for a minute staring at the tickets before turning to leave. I had no idea what I was going to do, but I had less than twenty-four hours to figure it out.

I remained preoccupied for the rest of the workday. It had slowed down considerably, and I attributed that to the nice weather we were having that afternoon. If you didn't know any better, you'd think it was spring.

When I got home that evening, Megan was already gone for the night. We hardly got to spend any time together on the weekends unless I went up to the bar for a visit. Which usually I did. But you couldn't really consider it "hanging out" when you were interrupted every five minutes.

It had been hours since I'd even checked my cell phone and I'd completely forgotten to update Megan after leaving the cleaners.

After I walked Kikko around the apartment complex, allowing her to sniff every bush and tree stump at her leisure, I reviewed the text messages I'd missed from earlier that day. There was one from Anna May checking in and asking if I was behaving myself. I responded with the eye-roll emoji and left it at that.

The next one was, of course, from Megan wanting to know why she hadn't heard from me. I waited to respond on that one.

And the last one was from Adam, who had sent me five messages wanting to know if I was free in the evening, why I hadn't answered, and whether he needed to send the cavalry. At this point, I was surprised the police department wasn't already knocking on my door.

I quickly texted back to tell him I was free, and included three kissy-face emojis. Within a minute, he responded and told me he'd be by in an hour to pick me up. I confirmed and then rushed to the bathroom for a quick shower and to get myself dressed.

Maybe a night out would be exactly what I needed to clear my head. It had been a long week, and I could definitely use a night of relaxing . . . and a few cocktails to help that along.

CHAPTER
15

There was no question that Adam and I would be going to the Zodiac that evening. It had become something of a typical Friday night tradition. I'd still never responded to Megan because I'd been so busy getting ready for Adam to pick me up. So, when we walked in, she was mildly surprised to see us there.

"Oh man, you guys should have told me you were coming in tonight," she said, greeting us at our seats. "I would have told you not to bother."

Adam hopped onto the stool next to mine. "Why's that? Sick of our faces already?"

She snorted. "No, silly, we're doing a speed-dating event here tonight. In about an hour it's going to get ridiculously packed. Didn't think you guys would wanna deal with something like that after a long day of working."

Adam turned around and assessed the bar. "Really?

That kind of thing is still popular with all these dating apps there are now?"

"You'd be surprised," Megan said. "It's brought a lot of business to the bar. At first, we just did it as a one-time deal, but people loved it so much and we actually had a lot of customers ask us to hold more events. Since then, we've been working with the dating service to hold biweekly get-togethers. I'd say over sixty percent of the people who participate go home with someone that night."

"It might be fun to watch," I replied. "I've never seen one before."

Adam returned my comment with a side-eye. "Uh-huh. Fun to watch."

"What?" I batted his arm playfully. "It's not like I want to participate or something."

Megan giggled. "Okay kids, I'll grab your drinks."

"I just don't want you to get any crazy ideas." He grinned and put an arm around my shoulders, pulling me close and kissing my cheek. "I haven't been around much these past two weeks and if I leave you unattended too long, you tend to go stir crazy."

I gave him a theatrical eye roll. "Ohmigod, I am not that bad. And, trust me when I say that you have nothing to worry about. You're stuck with me, Trudeau."

Megan returned with a whiskey and Coke for me, and a Great Lakes beer for Adam. She promised she'd be back in a few after she finished helping adjust the tables around the room for the upcoming event.

Adam's eyes drifted to the row of televisions above the bar. Three of the six TVs were on sport channels, two were on news programs, and the sixth one might have been an infomercial program or just a painfully long commercial about hearing aids. "So, what have you been up to this week?" He sipped his beer, never breaking focus on the TV tuned to News Channel 5. It made me wonder if he was waiting for something specific to air.

I hadn't told him about what happened with Detective Bishop earlier in the week. In some ways, I was slightly surprised he hadn't found out through the grapevine somehow. I knew that I had to tell him. Not just because we had promised each other to be one hundred percent forthcoming in situations like these, but because he really would find out anyway. Better that he heard it straight from the horse's mouth.

My pause caused him to turn his attention away from the TV. "Lana? Did you hear me?"

I took a deep breath and began telling the story about Detective Bishop's impromptu interrogation at Ho-Lee Noodle House and that it had come to an abrupt halt when Anna May and Henry had barged in to save the day.

His jaw muscles tensed, and he started to shake his head in disapproval. "That guy's got some nerve comin' at you like that. If I wasn't worried about making things worse for you, I'd have a word or two with him off the clock."

I rested a hand on his leg, giving him a light squeeze for reassurance. "Henry said that he'd take care of it if Bishop shows up again. I have his card and he told me to call him no matter what time of day. He's currently trying to find out from his own sources if there's any-thing I need to worry about. So, he's definitely on top of it."

Adam nodded. "Well, that's good, keep your head down, and let this Henry guy take care of it. He's got a good reputation with this sort of thing. No need to put yourself in the middle of this if you don't have to."

"Uh-huh," I said, chewing on the straw in my drink.

"That didn't sound very comforting," Adam joked.

"Well, I am nervous about this. I mean, Henry did agree the detective's questions were kind of specific. Seems like he thinks he's going somewhere with this."

Adam shrugged. "Maybe, maybe not. He's fishing around in the dark right now. I'm sure he's doing the same thing with other students from the class. It's not like you were the only person there that night."

I hadn't given too much thought about the other stu-dents from my class and whether or not the police had questioned them yet because none of them had been around. It made me wonder if Detective Bishop had in-terviewed Bridget already and if not, would he? If and when that time came, would my name somehow come up and what would she say about me?

"Where'd you go?" Adam asked, rubbing my arm. "You off in la-la land again?"

"What about family?" I asked abruptly. My mind had moved on to the potential interviews Detective Bishop would conduct.

"I don't get what you mean?"

"Like interviewing the family—how does that work during such a critical time? It's really invasive considering what they're going through." I was referring to my own experience with Margo's sister, Joyce, of course, and how difficult it had been for me to even begin asking her anything.

In previous instances, I had some kind of connection to the person who had been murdered. Talking with people seemed less intrusive and rude because the situations meant something to me at a personal level that wasn't just self-serving. But in this scenario, it felt purely selfish. I needed to solve this murder to get myself out of hot water. And was asking Adam his viewpoint on it even going to help me suss that out? People expected police to ask questions, not someone like me.

Adam tilted his head. "It can get rough sometimes, but you try to do it with tact, and that's all you can really do. You have a job to perform, and if you let yourself get too emotionally involved, you may hurt your chances of reaching the objective. And then there are times where you suspect the family, so you don't feel quite as bad about questioning them."

"But you do sometimes feel bad when you ask the family questions?" I asked.

Megan returned, hearing the question that I was posing to Adam. "Oh good, I came back at the right time. What did Margo's sister have to say when you went to see her today?"

I froze. My focus was on Megan who I was now giving the death stare to.

She looked between Adam and me, confused for a few seconds before she must have come to the realization that I had been asking a generic question.

She let out a nervous chuckle. "Oops, so I'm guessing you didn't get to that part yet, huh?"

The awkward silence had been followed by a stream of lecturing from Adam about how this was proof I could not be left to my own devices for too long. I tried to interrupt a few times to explain that I was fueled by Detective Bishop's questions with the assumption that my character and credibility were under fire. How could any person just sit by and take that from someone when the accusation was so horrible?

Adam wasn't buying it. "I'm sure this has been rolling around in your head since the moment it happened. I already had to convince you that very night to not give this another thought. I should have known that you and Megan would continue scheming the next day."

"I'll admit that might be around fifty percent accurate."

He smirked. "How did you come up with that percentage?"

"I was thinking about it . . . but casually."

"Yeah right. You went to get your money back at the school. Was that the *only* reason you went that day?"

I blushed. "I had to go anyways. It wasn't going to hurt anything to ask a few measly questions."

"See? I knew it. Lana . . ." Adam scrubbed his chin with the back of his hand. "If you don't think I know you by now, you're living in a dream world."

"Exactly."

He turned to me, seemingly confused by my answer.

I continued. "If you know me so well, then you know I can't sit idly by and let things play out on their own. Especially when the finger might be pointed directly at me. I told you Detective Bishop even brought up the fact that you're a cop. Don't tell me he isn't trying to make some kind of leap with all of this."

Adam didn't respond at first. He sat staring at the TV, but it was clear he was thinking about something other than the seven-day forecast that was displayed on the screen.

Megan returned for the first time since she'd dropped the bombshell about my visit to the dry cleaners. After she'd realized what was happening, she'd fluttered away to avoid being yelled at by yours truly.

In her hands she had two plates, one filled with BBQ chicken wings and the other filled with bacon and cheese-smothered fries. She didn't say anything, but gave me an apologetic look before walking away. I suspected tonight's order would be on the house.

Adam stared at the wings, but did not fill the empty plate that sat in front of him like he normally did. It wasn't often that Adam wouldn't immediately jump on whatever food was put in front of his face. "Did you touch anything in that room?"

"The classroom, you mean?"

"Yeah."

"Earlier in the night, yeah. I was up there at her cooking station with the rest of the class. And then again when I was talking with her before I left the first time."

"Did you touch any of the cutlery or utensils whatsoever?"

"No, we didn't participate in any of the cooking aspects. All we did was eat the finished product. Everything she gave us was plastic and Styrofoam, and it was all thrown out after. Easy cleanup."

He paused his questioning to think some more.

I eyed the smothered fries in front of me and worried about them being left untouched for too long. If the cheese hardened before I got a chance to eat some, Megan wasn't going to be the only person I would be mad at in the bar.

Adam drummed his fingers on the bar top. "At least you have that going for you, I guess. If they can't actually find any forensic evidence against you, that will make it much harder for them to pin it on you."

"I got the impression that he was trying to insinuate I would think of that because we're dating, and I know things about police work that others may not know."

Adam scowled. "Doesn't matter, that only counts as speculation."

I let out a heavy sigh. "Look, let's not worry about it tonight. Now you're all up to date on my shenanigans, and you always like to let things marinate in your brain to make better sense of them. So, tonight can be the night to marinate. We can worry about this tomorrow."

Behind us I heard a commotion as the door opened and what I can only describe as a "gaggle of girls" walked in. The cluster of early twenty-somethings were all scantily clad in mini-skirts, high heels, and crop tops that seemed better suited for July than September.

I watched them gather at the registration table to pay

and collect name tags before heading to the group of tables that had been set up for the evening.

Turning back around, I noticed that Adam had not joined me in people watching, but was instead staring at the bar, obviously deep in thought. I feared that I had lost him to "detective mode," and sometimes when that happened it was hard to get him back.

Gently, I nudged the empty plate in front of him to get his attention. He glanced up at me, his eyes softening as he studied my face.

I gave him a wry smile, jerking my head in the direction of the tables that were filling up fast. "Eat your wings, it's about to get interesting in here."

CHAPTER
16

Adam spent the night, and when we woke up the next morning, it was the first time in a while that we didn't have to rush off to meet some type of obligation. We lay in bed for an extra hour, relaxing and listening to the wind rattle the trees outside my window before I absolutely had to get out of bed for coffee.

I wasn't the only one anxious to get the day started. Kikko was also becoming restless waiting for one of us to let her out for morning tinkle time. Adam offered to take her while I prepared the coffee and toasted some bagels.

Upon returning, Kikko scuttled into the kitchen, no doubt smelling the toasted bread. She let out a few whines as I carried the plates to our seats at the table.

Adam drank his coffee black, and the minute the mug was put in front of him he took a long sip. "Too many beers last night," he commented as he set the mug down. "Probably could have done without those last two."

I added some cream and sugar to my cup. "Well, who can blame you losing count with all that chaos going on last night?"

He laughed, picking up a slice of his bagel. "And those two girls fighting over that guy with the leather pants on? I mean, come on . . . let's get real here."

I giggled. "I'm getting you a pair of those pants for Christmas."

"You'll be sorry when I wear them to Sunday dim sum with your family," he teased.

"You wouldn't dare." I kicked him playfully under the table. "My mother would have your head on a platter."

"But, Mrs. Lee, your daughter bought these for me. I didn't want to hurt her feelings."

"You stop." I laughed.

The door to Megan's room creaked open, and a messy bun of blonde hair poked out. "Hey, can you guys keep it down out there? Some of us didn't get to bed until four a.m."

"Sorry," I said, stifling a giggle. "We're just messing around."

Megan shut the door, and I heard a muffled, "There better be a bagel out there for me when I get back up."

Adam smirked at the now empty hallway before turning his attention back to me. In a lower voice, he asked. "So, what are your plans for today?"

I finished chewing my bagel. "Well despite your extreme protests, I have to go back to Lucky Lotus today.

My dry cleaning has to be picked up before she closes today at five."

He grunted into his coffee.

"What do you have going on? I'm surprised you're not working."

"The chief gave me the day off. We're kind of at a stalemate while we wait for some results to come back from the lab."

"How is your case coming in general?" I asked. I knew I wouldn't get much information about what he was working on, but I still liked to show that I cared about what was going on in his life.

"It's coming along slow. The circumstances are sketchy, so I can't say I'm entirely surprised by that."

"Do you get discouraged when things don't move faster?"

"Sometimes, but you have to remind yourself to be patient. If things move along too quickly that can be a sign a piece of evidence was missed somewhere along the way."

If there was one thing that I needed work on outside of my poker face, it was being patient. Often, I found myself moving along faster than I should with things because I wanted results and I wanted them yesterday.

"Do you want to come with me to the dry cleaner?" I asked. Originally, I hadn't thought it would be a good idea to have someone with me. The last thing I wanted Joyce to feel was ganged up on while I questioned her, but it might be handy having a professional along for the ride.

He leaned back in his chair. "I better not, dollface. If she happened to bring up at any point that another department's detective was snooping around on an active case, it could cause problems. Especially considering that you're my girlfriend and Bishop's already trying to make that connection without any help from us."

"Good point," I replied. I hadn't thought about how it might come back to bite us on the butt at a later date. "Wanna meet up later then? Maybe we could go to a movie or something. You know, do normal-people things."

Adam laughed as he finished off his bagel. "Sure, let's meet up later and do normal-people things. It's been a while."

I got myself dressed and ready to head over to Lucky Lotus after Adam went back to his place to handle a few chores he'd neglected through the week. Megan was still asleep, and I didn't want to wake her up again, so I left a sticky note on her door telling her where I was going.

Traffic wasn't too heavy for a Saturday, but I was relieved I didn't have to contend with on-street parking because there still wasn't a space in sight. I found the parking lot to Lucky Lotus fairly unoccupied. There were only two other cars there.

I dawdled in the car a little bit to give the customers some time to pay up and leave. When a man walked out with an armful of suits, I opened my car door and headed in.

I should have waited a little longer, because when I got inside a woman who had come to pick up her clothes was fumbling around in her purse. She turned to look at me as I walked in and gave an apologetic smile. "You can go ahead. I can't seem to find my pick-up ticket."

"Oh, that's okay," I said. "I'm not in a rush."

"No really, it's all right. I'm not in a rush either and I don't want to hold anyone up because the inside of my purse looks like a tornado. You go on, young lady."

What do you do when someone counters your kindness with more kindness? I couldn't refuse her, especially in this situation. It would seem weird. I thought about also pretending to have lost my ticket, but that appeared a little too contrived.

Joyce recognized me from the day before and smiled, ushering me to step up to the counter. "Hello again."

I was stuck. I moved ahead of the woman in front of me and returned Joyce's smile. "Hi, how are you today?" I handed her the ticket I'd had in my back pocket.

"I'm managing," she replied. She held up the ticket to inspect the numbers. "Just give me a minute."

She flipped through the bagged clothing items on the rack behind her and pulled out my two shirts, showing them to me for confirmation.

I nodded and she began the process of ringing me up.

After I'd paid, I noticed the other woman still hadn't found her ticket. What the heck was this lady's problem?

Feeling discouraged, and with no real reason to hang around, I said goodbye to Joyce and headed out the door. Just as I stepped out onto the sidewalk, I heard the woman behind me say, "Aha! Here it is."

I mumbled a curse under my breath and continued on to my car. What was I going to do now? This was my last chance before Joyce took off of work for a week, maybe two, and how would I get to her then? It's not like I could just show up at the funeral. How tacky would *that* be?

I unlocked my car, tossed the freshly pressed shirts into the back seat, and flopped down onto the driver's seat. Maybe no one else would come and I'd just have to wait for this lady to leave. It wouldn't take that long for the woman to pay up and be on her way, right?

Ten whole minutes passed, and the lady still hadn't come out. My foot began to tap as I waited—very impatiently—for something to happen. Plus, I had to pee, and I couldn't sit here for much longer. I watched the apron of the driveway, slightly nervous that someone would pull in at any moment and I'd have to wait even longer.

Finally, a minute later, the woman walked out in no particular hurry. I lunged myself out of the car and headed back into the building. The woman gave me a curious glance as I passed her, but didn't say anything though her mouth began to open.

When I got back inside, Joyce was nowhere to be seen.

"Hello?" I called out.

A few seconds later, Joyce popped her head out from the back room. "Oh, I'm sorry, I didn't realize anyone had come back in. I didn't hear the door chimes."

"Sorry to bother you," I said.

"No bother at all. Did you leave anything behind? I gave your credit card back, right?"

"Oh yes, that's not the problem."

She came into full view and approached the counter. "What can I help you with?"

"This may sound like a strange question, but do you happen to be related to Margo Han?"

Joyce lost a little color in her face. "Why are you asking? Are you a reporter? I've already told the newspaper I won't be a part of any articles on this murder investigation."

"Oh no!" I said, holding up my hands. "No, no, I'm not a reporter at all."

"Then how would you know that Margo is my sister?"

"It's a total coincidence," I lied. "I was in her cooking class and found out she was murdered this week. Then yesterday when you mentioned that your sister had passed away and it was a shock to your family, I thought wouldn't it be weird if we knew the same person?"

She eyed me with suspicion. "You were in her class?"

"Yes, she even offered to help me with private classes. I manage my family's restaurant and I get teased a lot because I can't cook Chinese food to save my life." I was hoping this little bit of information would show her that I was friendly and no one to be concerned about.

Joyce still didn't seem totally convinced by this odd occurrence, but her shoulders visibly relaxed. "It's a tragedy about what happened to her. She was an amazing woman. You would have been lucky to have learned to cook from her."

"She seemed like a really nice person. I can't imagine her having any enemies. Can you think of anyone who would want to harm her?" I tried my best to keep my voice light and conversational, like I was just asking for my own curiosity.

Luckily, she didn't appear offended by my question. "No one that I can think of. The police asked me the same thing—if there was anyone I knew of who was causing problems in her life before this happened. I would have told them immediately, but there really wasn't. At least not anything she mentioned to me."

"Well, then there probably wasn't. I mean, I know I tell my sister everything." I lied again.

She tilted her head back and forth. "We really weren't all that close when it came to things like that. If she was having problems at work or something, she might not have said anything right away."

"What about guy problems?" I asked. "My sister and I always gab about boys."

Her eyebrows crunched together, and I held my breath wondering if she was starting to think my questions were a little strange. But instead she said, "I don't know if she'd talk to me about that either. I know she had been seeing someone casually a while back, but she hadn't brought him up recently."

I decided to push on, wondering if this might be the man who'd sent the flowers Margo had thrown away. "Did you ever get to meet the guy?"

"No, she never brought him around. I thought I'd meet him at some point, but it never happened. I don't even think I know his name, to be honest with you."

That feeling of disappointment was bubbling back up.

This woman knew just about as much as I did. Which was a big fat nothing.

The door chimed behind us as a man walked in. Just as well, I wasn't going to learn anything significant here anyways. I was about to turn around and say goodbye to Joyce, but then I realized the man who walked in was Detective Bishop.

Busted.

CHAPTER

17

"Miss Lee," Detective Bishop stated with satisfaction. "Interesting to see you here today."

I stepped off to the side so I didn't have my back to Joyce. I could feel her staring at me, probably waiting for some type of answer as to why the detective knew me by name.

"Hello, Detective. I was just picking up some dry cleaning," I said plainly.

He looked at my hands, which were empty of proof, and then raised an eyebrow at Joyce for confirmation.

She gave a solemn nod, but did not speak.

"What a coincidence that you use this dry cleaner. On your report, you listed that you live in North Olmsted. Isn't this a little out of your way? I'd think it would be an inconvenience for you to drive out here just to drop off and pick up a few items of clothing."

"I was in the neighborhood yesterday and dropped

off some shirts I had in my car that needed to be dry-cleaned."

"What brought you out this way?" he asked.

"Tink Hall," I replied, coolly, rattling off the name of a nearby Asian grocery. "I come out this way a lot actually."

"I see," he replied, taking a step toward me. "And it just so happens that you use the dry cleaner of your cooking teacher's family? Now that's a small world."

Before I could try and defend myself, Joyce interjected. "The Asian community is fairly small, Detective Bishop. It's really not that unusual."

His eyes narrowed. "You might think differently about that, Ms. Han, if you knew that Lana here was the one who found your sister's body."

Both Joyce and I gasped. For different reasons, obviously. I was appalled at the way he talked about Margo's body being found in such a cavalier manner to a family member. An immediate family member, no less.

Joyce gawked at me as if I'd sprouted two heads. I wanted to explain, but I knew that I couldn't do that in front of Bishop. If he knew that I was snooping around, he'd probably try to arrest me right on the spot.

I didn't know where to go with this. It was the second time today that I felt trapped in my circumstances and I didn't like it. That's when I realized I had a card to play. "Do you plan on asking me any further questions? Because my lawyer requested that he be present for any interrogations. I can give him a call right now if that's the case."

The detective's cheeks reddened. "No, that won't be necessary. I don't have anything further to ask you at this time."

"Fine, then if you don't mind, I was actually on my way out." I turned to Joyce and tried to apologize with my eyes. "I hope everything goes all right next week. I'm so sorry for your loss."

Joyce gave me a nod, but did not thank me or say anything further. I couldn't tell if that was because the detective was in the room with us or because she was that disgusted with my presence. I couldn't imagine what was going on in her mind right now. If it were me, I would be thinking all sorts of crazy things.

I spun on my heel, trying to pull up an air of indignation, but as I've mentioned, my poker face isn't very good. Curtly, I said, "Detective." And then headed out the door.

Halfway through the parking lot, I got that nervous jitter in the pit of my stomach that was telling me to run. But I knew that Bishop was watching me from inside. I was right, too, because right before I got into my car, he stuck his head out the door and yelled. "Miss Lee! Don't forget, I've got an eye on you."

To anyone listening, it would have sounded like a friendly reminder, but I knew enough about him to hear it for what it was: a threat.

When I got home, my first thought was to plant myself on the couch and throw blankets over my head. But Megan was finally up, and she was occupying the sofa with

Kikko at her side. She had her laptop out and seemed to be enthralled by whatever was on the screen.

"Took you long enough," she said, not looking up. "I have to go into work in a few hours, you know. If we're gonna work on this case at all, it needs to be now, missy."

"Ugh." I hung my keys on the hook, and rubbed my temple.

She glanced in my direction. "What's your problem? Did you pick up your dry cleaning?"

"Crap, I left it in the car." I shook my head. "Whatever, it can stay there." I trudged to the couch, feeling a temper tantrum coming on. "Today did not go well."

"What happened? You and Trudeau were all laughs this morning." She set the laptop on the coffee table, and I could see she was viewing our county's clerk of courts website.

"Not only did I run into Detective Bishop while I was chatting up Joyce Han, but she didn't even know anything of use to begin with. The whole thing was a wasted trip, and I've probably increased my guilt in his book."

Megan's jaw dropped. "Oh no, what did he say?"

I went through the events that took place at Lucky Lotus. Megan couldn't help but cringe as I shared the details of Bishop informing Joyce about my involvement in the night of her sister's murder.

"She has got to be going crazy with questions," Megan said when I'd finished. "Do you think she asked Bishop for more details about that after you left?"

"I'm sure that he offered them up willingly and probably also told her that I was a potential suspect in their investigation."

"Hopefully she'll realize that you wouldn't be stupid enough to question a family member if you were guilty."

"Let's hope," I said. "But I still feel bad because she knows that I was lying to her, and that's enough to make anybody mad, regardless of the reason behind it."

"So, what are you going to do?"

I leaned back against the couch, and rested my head, staring upward as if some answer would come to me from the textured popcorn pattern that was our ceiling. "I guess all I can do is leave it alone for now. Maybe if I give it some time, she'll come back around."

"Probably a good idea. If you try too hard to convince her of anything, she may think that's a sign of your guilt."

I turned to face her. "So, what were you doing before I got home?"

"Oh!" She clapped her hands together. "Right. I was looking at Cuyahoga County's Clerk of Courts website to see if I could find anything about Robert Larkin. There are two in the system, and I wanted to ask you how old you thought he was. We have options of thirty-four years old or forty-six years old."

"I would say that he's most likely forty-six." I tried picturing the janitor in my mind again, remembering a few laugh lines around his eyes, and wrinkles around his mouth. The ones around his mouth were pretty deep set and had reminded me of parentheses. "If he's only thirty-four, he's had a rough start."

Megan laughed, and then bent forward to pick up her laptop. She ran her finger across the mouse pad to access the screen. She tapped a few times, and then turned the laptop around for me to see. "Well, our man, 'Bobby,' seems to have a record. I don't know if it means anything because most of them seem to be drunk and disorderlies, but he's definitely no angel, that's for sure."

I looked over the screen, noting the dates of his offenses and the outcomes. Everything seemed to stop about a year ago when he'd spent a little time in jail for assaulting an officer. I rested my head back again, searching the ceiling for any signs of hope. "At this point, we need to take whatever leads we can get."

The rest of the early afternoon was pretty uneventful aside from a few searches Megan and I fumbled around with online. We tried looking into Robert Larkin a bit more, and then dug a little into Margo's sister just in case. As I suspected, we found nothing interesting about her. Even though I'd only met her twice for short periods of time, she appeared to be someone living a normal life who didn't get into much trouble.

I jotted down a few things in my trusty notebook, hoping that writing down what scarce new information we had on paper would help. It didn't.

When Megan left for work, I paced the apartment until Adam called me. We made plans for him to pick me up around six o'clock for a movie at Crocker Park.

I forced myself to get ready, putting on a dressy tunic

top with leggings paired with dark gray ankle boots I'd splurged on a few weeks ago from Aldo. I took extra time applying my makeup, and coordinating jewelry. They say to look how you want to feel, and right now I wanted to feel put together.

Adam arrived shortly before six—I was alerted by my alternate doorbell, Kikko. I rushed from my bedroom as she started to yip and whine, batting her paw at the crack in the door.

As soon as I opened the door, Adam scooped me up and twirled me around, planting a sloppy kiss on my cheek. "Hey there, dollface."

I giggled. "What's got you in such a good mood?"

He set me down and kissed my forehead. "We're going to do normal-people things, remember? It's exciting." He took a step back and assessed my outfit. "Whoa, you're all decked out. Where exactly do you think we're going?"

"I thought it might help me feel better," I said, turning away to find my purse and keys. "I had a run-in with Detective Bishop today."

"Uh-oh."

I told him the same story I'd told Megan earlier that day. He grunted a few times, but made no comment. I could tell he was thinking things through and assessing whether or not this would be a big deal later on down the line.

After I found my purse and keys, we said goodbye to Kikko and headed out the door.

Crocker Park is about a fifteen-minute drive from my apartment, but the movie we wanted to see didn't start until seven, so we had plenty of time. When we pulled into the outdoor shopping complex, my cell phone rang. Figuring it was Megan, I picked up without checking the readout.

"Hey girl," I said into the phone.

"Um, hello?"

I pulled the phone away from my ear and realized that it was a number I didn't recognize. "Hello, sorry, I thought you were my friend. Who's this?"

"This is Lana Lee, right?"

"Yes . . ." I said with caution. "Who's calling?"

Adam glanced over at me, furrowing his brow.

"Hi, this is Sabrina Crawford."

"Okay . . ." I said, drawing a total blank. "I'm sorry, the name isn't ringing a bell."

"Oh, duh, my bad. I'm the intern from Barton's Adult Learning Center. We spoke on Wednesday . . . in the lobby."

I smacked myself in the forehead. "Right, sorry, I completely forgot to get your name that day."

"That's all right. I was in such a hurry to get back, I wasn't even thinking about names. Anyways, I found out some info and was wondering if you had time to meet."

"Meet?"

Adam nudged me with his elbow from the driver's seat. He mouthed, *"Who is it?"*

I waved a hand at him and turned my attention back to the phone. "When were you thinking? I'm not really available right now." I was slightly put off that she wanted to meet in person. Couldn't she just say what she had to right now?

"Maybe tomorrow afternoon then?" she suggested.

"I think I can swing that . . ." I said, feeling anxious. "Can I ask why you don't want to tell me over the phone?"

"Well, I could, but I wanted to show you some stuff too. I stayed at work later than everyone last night so I could do some digging. There's definitely something off going on at the school. I found some things in my personal locker that were meant for Ms. Han. Our lockers are right next to each other and I think whoever left them must have messed up."

"What kinds of things?"

"There was a note and some pictures. I think Ms. Han knew something about someone having an affair. From what I gathered, she was probably going to tell the wife. That's why I wanted you to see the note. To see if that's the conclusion you come to as well."

Alarm bells went off in my head. I wanted to meet with her right now. I glanced over at Adam, and remembering his excitement before leaving my apartment, I told myself to chill out and asked Sabrina, "Can you meet me tomorrow at three?"

"Sure, I can do that."

We discussed the logistics of where we lived and where to meet, deciding on the I-480 exit at Tiedemann Road. There was an Irish pub with a nice patio right off the freeway that we were both familiar with and we confirmed it was a suitable place to get together.

We said goodbye and wished each other a good evening.

"Well, what the heck was all that about?" Adam asked. He had parked the car in a multi-floored garage while I'd finished up my call. "I'm over here on pins and needles."

"Come on, let's go. I'll tell you on the way to the theater."

CHAPTER
18

I hardly paid any attention to the movie. Since Halloween was just a little over a month away, Adam had wanted to see something scary. I half-heartedly watched as a woman with a tear-streaked face ran through a darkened house—always in the wrong direction—up the stairs.

On the way into the theater, Adam had warned me, "Don't touch anything that girl shows you. She needs to turn whatever she has into the police right away."

"I know, I know," had been my reply.

This was potentially what I needed to clear my name. If Margo was about to rat someone out for having an affair, then that obviously had nothing to do with me, and Detective Bishop could leave me alone.

For Adam's sake, I tried to appear as if I weren't preoccupied. But considering the man was a detective and trained to read body language, I'm sure he knew that I wasn't a hundred percent mentally present.

The movie ended fairly late, so our options for dinner were limited. We decided to head up to the Zodiac instead of being those jerks who show up at a restaurant ten minutes before the place closes. Being in the restaurant industry, I was all too familiar with those people and despised their thoughtlessness thoroughly.

The Zodiac was pretty busy when we walked in, and all the stools were taken at the bar. We waved down Megan and she handed us some drinks before we went over to one of the bar-top two-seater tables.

"You know, Lana . . . honey," Adam said after he'd taken a sip of his beer. "You give me a lot of crap when I'm lost in a case and we're out on a date . . . yet . . ." He let the rest of his thought hang in the air. He didn't have to finish the sentence because he knew that I would know exactly what he was talking about.

"Ugh, I know. I'm sorry." My chin dropped and I shook my head, disappointed in myself for letting him down on what was supposed to be our normal-people date. "I'm being a total jerk tonight. It's just that I can't stop thinking about the note and photos that Sabrina found in her locker. I wish she had called me yesterday instead. I could have met with her already and maybe this whole thing would be behind us by now."

"Okay, I'll admit something to you," he said, shifting on his stool to lean forward. "I've kind of been half thinking about this the whole time too."

I pointed an accusatory finger at him. "Aha! See? I'm not the only one."

He chuckled. "Calm yourself, woman. If I didn't already know you were thinking about it, I would have been able to put it out of my head."

"Uh-huh."

"Do you want to hear what I have to say or not?" he asked, raising a playful eyebrow at me.

"Okay, okay, sorry. Continue."

"I think it's odd that this intern wanted to help you to begin with. What business is it of hers? And why did it take her so long to find the note and photos? It's already been five days, and that stuff would have had to be there before the murder if the person who left them wanted Margo to see them. Obviously, they're of no use if Margo is already dead. And that is, of course, assuming that someone was trying to threaten her to begin with."

I thought that over while I sipped my drink. He did have a point. Why had it taken Sabrina so long to find this evidence? Although, if she was guilty, why would she even bother to inform me of this news? Wouldn't she want to distance herself from me as much as possible?

"And then . . ." Adam tapped his index finger on the table. "Then she waits until a Saturday evening to tell you this information? Why didn't she tell you last night after she originally found it? Or better yet, why mess around with telling you at all? Why not go straight to the cops? If these photos are legit, then what do they have to do with you?"

"All valid questions," I replied. "But, I don't think she would reach out to me if she was actually the guilty party. How stupid would that be?"

He tipped his beer bottle in my direction. "Keep your friends close, and your enemies closer. It wouldn't be the first time I've seen it in action during an investigation."

"Well, I guess I'm going to find out either way tomorrow. Now that I've agreed to meet with her, I can't take it back. Plus, it's going to drive me crazy if I don't get to see what she has."

"I agree. But, I'm thinking that maybe I should follow you there . . . wait in the parking lot in case this is some kind of setup. You know, just to be on the safe side."

"Really?" I asked. "You're aiding and abetting me?"

He smirked. "Yeah, but don't get used to it."

Sunday morning, Adam and I woke up at a decent time so we could lounge with some coffee before heading to dim sum with my family. Adam was coming with me today since he didn't have any work he needed to tend to. After almost two weeks of barely seeing each other, it was nice having him to myself for a whole weekend. Once tomorrow came, who knew what our schedules would be like?

Around eleven o'clock we got in the car and headed to the east side of Cleveland to Asia Village's competitor, Asia Plaza. My family and I met there every Sunday to have dim sum at one of Cleveland's most popular Chinese restaurants, Li Wah's.

The plaza's parking lot was packed, but Adam was fortunate enough to find a spot where someone was getting ready to pull out. We skimmed the parking lot for my sister's car and saw it near the entrance. I was usually the last to arrive, and I preferred it that way. Any time that my sister isn't around, my parents tend to grill me more about my personal life—even with Adam around—and I didn't like all the attention to be on me.

Considering that my mother was now aware of the cooking class debacle, I'm sure she'd already told my dad. Knowing that he'd have an opinion about it, and warnings about meddling in the aftermath of the murder, I was a bit surprised that I hadn't heard from him all week. It gave me the impression that he was saving his lecture for a face-to-face visit.

Adam and I entered the bustling restaurant, smiling and waving at the staff as we passed by. Everyone here knew the Lee family, and not just because we came here nearly every week, but because my mother makes her presence known. For as small as she is, she does not have any problems being heard over a crowd.

As we neared the group of dining tables, my mother shot up from her seat and waved her hands in the air. "Lana! We are here!" She pointed at the table and waved again before sitting back down in her seat.

A few people turned to look at us, and my cheeks warmed as we wove through the tables to get to my family. To my surprise, Henry was seated next to my sister. I wanted to say something about him being there, but I decided to just let it go for the moment.

"Can't you guys ever get a table near the front?" I asked. "Hi, Dad," I said, acknowledging him as I sat down next to my grandmother.

"Hi. Goober." My dad grinned at me, and then regarded Adam—who was seated in between Henry and me—with a head nod.

Henry and Adam exchanged pleasantries, and I greeted my temporary lawyer with a delicate head nod and smile. As I studied his face, I wondered if he could tell that I knew their little secret or not. Adam, of course, was clued in—because let's face it, I couldn't keep this juicy gossip from him—but his ability to hide things like that far surpassed my own, so I knew the undisclosed-relationship status was safe with him.

If I didn't know any better, I would have thought the seating was strategically orchestrated to put the two men together. Anna May had mentioned to me in the past she thought it best that our significant others get along should they be around for the long haul. It made me wonder just how deep her feelings were for this man. Although, it was more than likely that my sister just didn't want Henry to be too close to my mother. It would have been easier for her to give him the third degree that way.

Anna May is put together very well at all times. Her nails are always done; her glossy ebony hair is forever perfect, and her makeup, though neutral and barely visible, is eternally on point. She's a classic sort of gal and without a doubt, my older sister had grown into a beautiful woman over the years. However, you'd sooner see me set on fire before I'd admit such a thing to her face. But I digress.

However, today Anna May was decked out to the nines, and I'm sure it had everything to do with her new beau being present. Her hair was styled in large, loose curls that hung just below her shoulders. The makeup she'd chosen was a little more colorful than usual. Smoky mauves accented her almond-shaped eyes, and both her eyeliner and mascara were the darkest shades of black you could find. On a normal day, you'd be lucky to see my sister wear any at all. Her lips were accentuated with a deep burgundy gloss that complemented the tone of her skin perfectly. I had to confess, I was a tad jealous because I could never find a deep shade that didn't make me look like a goth chick trying to relive her glory days.

It took everything in my power not to comment on my sister's new look. I knew that it would only stir up trouble, and frankly, I wasn't in the mood for it.

My mother picked up the teakettle and leaned over my grandmother, pouring tea for me and Adam. "This is so nice to have everyone together today." She finished pouring and set the kettle down, taking her seat. "It is very nice for Henry to come. He is such a busy man."

Henry flashed a charming smile. "I'm honored that you asked me to come. It's not every day I get to enjoy lunch with such an amazing group of people."

My mother actually blushed. "We wanted to say thank you for helping Lana get out of trouble. This is very kind of you."

Adam squeezed my leg under the table.

I had to stifle a grin. Talk about laying it on thick. He must really like my sister.

My dad rested an elbow on the table and leaned forward. "I second that. We really do appreciate what you did for my little Goober. She's always getting into trouble one way or another. If you hadn't come to save the day, she may be sportin' black and white stripes and we'd be visiting her from behind shatterproof glass."

"Dad!" Now it was my turn to blush.

Adam wrapped an arm around my chair and tickled the back of my neck with his thumb. "Now, Mr. Lee, you know that's not true. Inmates usually wear orange now."

The three men shared a chuckle at my expense.

"Oh look, the dim sum cart," I said, raising my voice above their laughter and signaling the server to stop by. "Mom, why don't you get some food on the table to keep these men's mouths busy?"

My mother greeted the server and they chatted for a few minutes in Mandarin before she started selecting some dishes for the table. I watched as the server pulled out plates of pan-fried dumplings, shrimp noodle rolls, turnip cakes, black pepper short ribs, a large bowl of white rice, watercress, and BBQ pork.

"Mom . . . aren't you forgetting something?" I asked, eyeing the cart.

"Oh yes," my mother said, clasping her hands together. "And some chicken feet."

I groaned.

My mom laughed. "Spring rolls, please."

It's not that we *couldn't* order for ourselves, but we just didn't. My mother was always in charge of what went on the table for dim sum. Only on rare occasions had my sister or I taken over that duty. It was never left to my father to decide, because if we let him, he'd order seven plates of short ribs and call it a day.

We all busied ourselves with filling our plates. I noticed that Anna May chose her selections sparingly and I wanted to tease her about it. But I was doing so well at staying quiet, I wanted to see how long I could go with keeping my mouth shut.

I never hid my appetite from anyone. I like to eat, and I don't apologize for it. If Adam hadn't been okay with that, I would have sent him packing on my way to the doughnut shop. But thankfully, my guy wasn't that sort of man.

It was quiet for a few minutes while everyone dug into their plates, enjoying what was probably their first meal of the day.

A-ma held up a short rib and beamed, her two silver front teeth shimmering as she smiled. "So good!"

I laughed. "Very good."

"So, Lana," Henry said, wiping the corners of his mouth. "Have you had any more problems with Detective Bishop?"

For a moment, I thought about lunging over the table at him for even bringing it back up. Maybe I should have picked on Anna May after all. At least then the topic would be on something besides Detective Bishop and me.

I was just about to lie to him and say no when Adam piped in. "You might as well tell him."

Before answering, I gave Adam the stink eye and then turned to Henry. "As a matter of fact, I did have a short run-in with him yesterday. But it's no big deal." I made a production of investigating my spring roll.

My mother gawked at me. "You did not work yesterday—did he come to your house? Why did you not tell me this?"

"No, I ran into him while I was out." Offering up as little information as I could seemed like the best route to take. There was no point in announcing to the table that I had been at Lucky Lotus Cleaners the day before.

I hadn't realized it, but my sister had been scrutinizing me the whole time. "Lana . . . what did you do?"

"Nothing, I didn't do anything. Why is everyone always accusing me of doing something? As if I'm totally incapable of controlling myself."

Adam started to open his mouth.

I held up a finger in his face. "If you say anything at all, you will lose your ability to finish what's on your plate."

He chuckled and held up his hands in defense.

Anna May pointed her chopsticks at me in accusation. "This isn't a joke. Henry has been nice enough to offer you his help *for free*, and you're making more trouble for yourself. This is serious business, Lana."

I felt the frustration rise in my chest—smoke would start pouring out of my ears at any moment. And before I could help myself, I blurted out, "Yeah? Well so is that lipstick. 1997 called—"

"Now, girls," my dad interjected before I could finish my sentence. "Let's play nice in front of company."

If I wasn't twenty-eight years old, I might have used the argument that she started it, but it didn't seem right at this stage in my life. Instead, I stabbed my noodle roll and settled for glaring at my sister instead.

The rest of dim sum went by without any more outbursts, and my parents took over the conversation talking about a cruise they planned to take my grandmother on in the coming months.

After the bill was settled, we walked out into the parking lot and said our goodbyes. When Adam and I were alone in the car, I turned to him and smacked his arm. "Thanks a lot for having my back in there."

He stuck the key in the ignition and laughed. "Dollface, I was just trying to lighten the mood and make you laugh a little bit. Don't be so mad at me."

"Whatever," I said, folding my arms over my chest.

"Ah babe, come on."

"Fine," I replied. "Do you want to spend the night tonight?"

His face softened. "See, I knew you couldn't stay mad at me."

"Don't get too excited, you're sleeping on the couch."

CHAPTER

19

Adam and I lounged around my apartment playing with Kikko until it was time to meet up with Sabrina. As anxious as I was, I thought the time would pass slowly as it often does when you're waiting for something. But surprisingly enough, it did not.

We left in separate cars around two-thirty and he told me that he would be situated in the parking lot of an adjoining TGI Fridays. Adam instructed me to go into the bathroom and call him right away if anything seemed strange or out of place.

As I drove, I thought about my upcoming meeting. It's funny how two people can look at the same situation and see something totally different. It really does all come down to perspective. Though I could understand his point of view, it wouldn't have dawned on me that something appeared strange about Sabrina contacting or approaching me after I left the administration office. But for him, it raised a red flag right away.

When I arrived at Hooley House, the parking lot was much fuller than I would have expected for a Sunday. I attributed it to some sports game that I wasn't aware of.

I parked the car and nonchalantly skimmed the Friday's parking lot to see if I could spot Adam, but no such luck. I knew he was there somewhere . . . watching me casually look for him and probably mentally channeling me to act natural.

When I walked in, I was greeted by a hostess and I let her know that I was waiting for someone. She told me another woman had just walked in a few minutes prior saying that she would be meeting someone and directed me to a two-seater off to the right side of the bar area.

Sabrina was facing the walkway and saw me approach, waving me over in case I'd missed spotting her. "Hi, Lana, thanks for meeting with me."

"Sure, no problem," I said, hopping onto the stool. "I appreciate you letting me know about what you've found."

"Did you want to order anything?" she asked, fidgeting in her seat. "The bartender should be coming back in a few minutes with my drink."

"I'm okay for right now," I said. "I'm not much of a day drinker unless it involves mimosas."

"Gotcha. Well, let's just get into it then." She reached for her purse and dug around, pulling out a white letter-sized envelope. "This is what was left in my locker." She handed the envelope over for me to inspect.

"Um, maybe I shouldn't touch that," I said. "Finger-prints and all."

She tilted her head at me. "Really? You think they'll check for fingerprints?"

"Definitely."

I thought I saw a flash of panic in her eyes, but I couldn't say for sure.

"Okay, well I'll just take them out for you then." She opened the envelope and set down three photos and a wrinkled piece of notebook paper.

Two of the photos showed three people outside of Barton's Adult Learning Center at what looked to be late at night. The quality of the picture was very grainy, so it was impossible to make out many details. On the side of the building were what appeared to be a man and a woman huddled together getting to know each other in a very personal manner. Thankfully they were both clothed or I would have started blushing right there. The third person in the photo was another woman who was walking away from the building. Her head was turned toward the couple. She was closer to the camera, and I knew without having to make the stretch that it was Margo Han.

And that was partially due to the fact that the last photo was a close-up of Margo sitting in her car. She'd parked underneath a lamppost, and it illuminated just enough to make the objects in the picture more visible.

The note read I KNOW YOU KNOW. WHAT ARE YOU GOING TO DO ABOUT IT?

I studied the pictures more carefully, contemplating what they were trying to tell me. Clearly the people in the photo didn't take the picture . . . so who were the unknown parties, and why would Margo care to do something about it?

Sabrina seemed to sense that I was lost and said, "I didn't get it at first either, but look at the time stamps."

The photos that included the couple were taken five minutes before the shot of Margo sitting in her car.

A slender, blonde woman with a pixie haircut—who I assumed to be the bartender—approached our table carrying a drink. Sabrina grabbed at the photos and note before anything could be seen.

"Here's your drink, miss. Sorry it took so long," the bartender said as she set down a pint of wheat-colored beer. She turned to me and smiled, "Would you like anything?"

"Just a water would be fine, thanks," I replied.

Once she'd walked away again, Sabrina set the photos back on the table, taking a sip of her beer. "Ugh, I needed this today. Normally I don't drink during the day either."

"So . . ." My eyes focused on the photos, trying to come up with some scenario. "Someone took these pictures, and saw that Margo knew . . . and has proof that she sat in her car for at least five minutes. Thinking over what she's just seen, we assume? Obviously, it didn't take her that long to get to her car." I considered the man in the photo might even be the one who'd sent the flowers that got tossed in the garbage. Maybe even to make up for what was happening in the photo? That little speculation would stay with me though. Divulging too much to Sabrina might not be the best idea just in case Adam *was* right and she was guilty of something.

"Right," Sabrina said, tapping the photos. "But the questions I want answers to are, what did this person think Margo was going to do? And why would Margo care?"

"Do you recognize the people in the photo?" I squinted, trying to make out some kind of detail, but it was impossible. The only reason you could even tell that one of them was a woman was by the length of her hair.

Sabrina shook her head. "I don't have a clue, but it's obviously someone at the school."

"And look at Margo's face in this close-up of her in the car. She looks kind of devastated."

Sabrina nodded in agreement. "I thought about that too. And that she's probably sitting there deciding what to do. I don't think she was a creep or anything, like, just watching these people or something."

"How long have you been helping out at the learning center?" I asked.

Sabrina shrugged. "Not very long, just a couple of months. I need the internship credit to graduate."

"Did you know Margo well?"

"Not really. She wasn't very talkative, but she was such a nice woman. We'd run into each other at the lockers and ask about how the day had gone. She'd ask me about my schooling sometimes, but that's about it."

"Do you happen to know if she was involved with anyone?"

Sabrina paused, her eyes shifting left and right. "I

don't think so, but I did notice a difference in how she dressed herself."

"What do you mean?"

"Well, it seemed as though when I first started that she was more dressed up, at least compared to what she looked like by the time you met her. I'd say about two months ago is when I noticed a change in appearance. At first, I thought she wasn't feeling well, but she wasn't acting any different."

The bartender returned with my water, and Sabrina reached for the photos and note once again, this time putting them back into the envelope and tucking them back into her purse.

While I sipped my water, I took a few moments to contemplate what all of this meant. I had a sinking suspicion that she was secretly involved with someone. Now I started to wonder if that someone was the man in the photo. But who the heck was it?

"So, what now?" Sabrina asked, breaking the silence.

I shrugged. "I'm not really sure, to be honest with you." I didn't want to tell her too much about what I was thinking, in the event that Adam was right and there was something off about this girl. But from what I could tell right now by talking to her, I didn't suspect her of anything. Now if Adam had been in the room with me, I don't know what he would have made of all this. I wished he could have come in with me so he could see the photos for himself.

"But you think I should definitely turn these photos into the police?"

"Absolutely," I said. "This might be a huge clue for them. Can I ask you something though?"

"Sure."

"Why didn't you find the photos right away? I mean, Margo was murdered on Tuesday."

Sabrina seemed to be slightly offended that I would ask. "Our work lockers have a shelf at the top, and I don't use mine at all. I just hang up my purse and jacket if I have one. It must have been the way I opened the locker Friday morning that moved it and I saw the edge of the envelope hanging over the side."

"Did you tell anyone else about it?"

She shook her head. "No, I wouldn't dare. I mean, let's face it. This was left by someone who works there. I don't really want to get mixed up in whatever these photos are about. That's why I asked if you think I definitely need to turn this stuff in to the cops. Because what if it gets out that it was me who turned it in? Right now, the person who dropped these off doesn't realize that Margo didn't get the photos to begin with."

"That's true," I said, wondering if I should encourage her to turn them in after all. If she did and something happened to her, I'd feel responsible. I needed to ask Adam before saying anything else. "Maybe hold onto them for a little while so I can think about it. Unless you want to just go with your gut?"

She tilted her head to the side and puffed up her cheeks, then exhaled slowly. "I wish I wouldn't have found these damn pictures to begin with. I only have a few weeks left to intern there and then I could have been far removed from this whole situation. All I care about is graduating."

"Believe me, I can understand not wanting to get dragged into this kind of stuff. I feel like that's my life story at the moment."

We talked for a few more minutes and I told her I'd be in touch. I needed to get going. Adam couldn't just hang out in the parking lot of Friday's all day long while I chitchatted.

Sabrina had decided to stay so she could finish her beer. Before I left, I turned back around. "Just one more thing . . ."

She set her beer back down and gave me her full attention.

"When we talked on the phone, you said you stayed late to look into some things. What is it that you were trying to find?"

"Oh that. I was trying to compare the penmanship from the note to some of the staff's handwriting in a log-book we have in the admin office. I thought maybe if I could match up the writing, we could figure out who left the note."

"Did you find anything?" I asked.

"Nothing even remotely close."

CHAPTER
20

- - - - - - - - - - - - - -

Adam followed me back to my apartment, and I couldn't wait to get inside and talk through my sit-down with Sabrina. I really wanted to know what he thought once I told him about the photos and the note.

Megan was nowhere to be found, and I assumed she was working a shift at the Zodiac. I'd have to repeat myself again later that night.

Adam stayed silent through the entire story, not interrupting me once. He appeared to be letting everything soak in, casually petting Kikko who sat diligently at his side.

"Well? What do you think?" I asked, after I'd finished the story with a flourishing hand gesture. Vanna White had nothing on me.

Adam leaned forward, resting his elbows on his knees and steepling his fingers in front of his face. "I don't like it, I think it's too convenient," he responded. "If I was working this case, that Sabrina girl would be at the top of my list."

"Really? I will agree you made some valid arguments when we talked after the movie, but after talking with her today, she seems pretty innocent to me. I think she just got stuck in a bad situation."

Adam raised an eyebrow. "Babe, come on. She runs after you when you leave the office and agrees to help you if she can find anything useful. Normal people—and don't take this the wrong way—but they wouldn't offer to help you. You're a stranger. . . . How do they know *you're* not involved somehow?"

"Okay, true."

"Then, as luck would have it, she stumbles upon the most convenient evidence that could provide a solid motive?"

"It could happen," I mumbled.

He snorted. "You watch too many of these murder mystery shows."

"Well, what about truth is stranger than fiction? You hear that all the time."

"I doubt it. That's all I'm saying. I mean, yes, anything is possible. But is it likely in this situation? Probably not."

"Ye of little faith," I said, holding up my chin. "I think she's telling the truth. Partially because I don't know that she's cunning enough to orchestrate all this. She doesn't strike me as the elaborate mastermind type."

"The cleverest minds usually don't show their hand, Lana. They generally want you to be fooled."

"Care to make a friendly wager?" I asked with a sly smile.

Leaning further forward, he wiggled his eyebrows at me. "What did you have in mind?"

I rolled my eyes. "You wish. I was thinking more along the lines of . . . whoever's right gets to pick all the date nights and movies for the next month."

He flopped back, disappointed. "Oh." He patted Kikko on the head and shrugged. "Fine . . . I'll take it. I hope you're ready to do the most ridiculous stuff I can think of because clearly I'm right." He offered his hand.

I grabbed his hand and gave it a firm shake. "We'll see, Detective. We'll see."

Monday morning had finally arrived. Normally I wouldn't be caught saying something so absurd, but I was, in fact, excited for it to be Monday. It meant that I could make my planned trip to Barton's and hopefully speak with the janitor, Robert Larkin.

Now that I had a little bit more info about Margo, I felt more prepared to ask questions with a sense of direction. My only concern now was if I could trust Mr. Larkin, or if he was someone I should be wary of too.

Armed with a full face of makeup and determination, I set out to begin my day at Ho-Lee Noodle House. I'd have to make it through an entire shift before I could get to the part of my day I was really anxious for. I only hoped that time would move quickly.

The Matrons arrived at their usual time, and I went through the motions of getting them situated with tea and placing their order with Peter. When I returned with their food, Wendy stopped me before I left again.

"Lana, how are things going with finding Margo's killer?"

"Nothing much has happened yet," I said. I was apprehensive to tell them about the photos and note left in Sabrina's locker. "What about the four of you? Have you learned anything that might help me along?"

Helen shook her head, her lips curved down in disappointment. "So far nothing that would be useful to you. We have tried asking many questions about her with other mahjong teams, but it doesn't seem many people knew her well. She was a very quiet person and liked to ask questions about other people."

So far everything that I'd learned about this woman had led to that same point. She loved to ask others about themselves, but never divulged anything about herself. Was that the sign of a person who kept lots of secrets? It was sure starting to feel like it to me. Which made me wonder about the person who left her the note. If they really knew her, would they ever think she'd be quick to tell on anyone about what she'd seen that night in the parking lot?

Pearl broke me from my thoughts. "We will keep trying, Lana. We all have hair appointments tomorrow." She gave me an encouraging smile.

"I tried that already. Her hair stylist, Nicole, didn't know anything helpful either."

Opal held up a finger. "Ah yes, but that does not mean

another customer did not know a secret or two. Let us see what we can find with the older ladies. People often like to talk to older ladies . . . we are everybody's grandma."

I smiled at that. She did have a point. Maybe Margo wanted some grandmotherly advice at some juncture and opened up to someone in the senior population. Especially in Asian communities, there was a respect for the older generation and all the wisdom they held. I know that on several occasions in the past, I had often looked to Mr. Zhang at the Wild Sage herbal shop to impart some wise words to me whenever I was feeling truly lost.

"Do not lose hope, Lana," Helen said. "One way or another we will find answers."

After the Mahjong Matrons left, I became extremely bored. Mondays weren't typically a busy day for us, and I'd already straightened up the dining room and checked it three more times before finally giving up and returning to the hostess station. There was still about a half hour left before Nancy showed up. I thought about bumming around in the kitchen, but Peter had been in a mood since he came in that morning, and I figured it was best to leave him alone. When he'd arrived that morning, he'd mentioned to me that he hadn't slept well and didn't feel much like talking to anyone.

I opted for tinkering on my phone and indulging in some hidden-object games to help pass the time. I must have lost track of the world around me because I heard the bells jingle above the door, and when I looked up, Nancy was staring at me with an amused grin on her face.

"Now the boss is guilty of playtime at work."

I could feel my face turning pink and quickly set my phone down. I was always giving our teenage employee, Vanessa Wen, a hard time about messing around with her phone or whatever object she brought to work on any given day to distract herself. And in turn, Nancy liked to tease me any time I was caught red-handed. "I am so bored today," I admitted. "We haven't had any customers all morning . . . just the Matrons."

She glanced around the empty dining room. "Pretty soon the holidays will be coming and we will be really busy. Enjoy this quiet time."

I let out a sigh. I knew she was right. Once holiday shoppers started coming, there'd be no time for me to waste during the day searching through cluttered photos in my favorite hidden object games for random pieces of pie and mismatched shoes. And our shopping rush didn't end with the traditional holidays that everyone thinks about. We also had Chinese New Year to contend with, and that was always a busy time around here.

Once Nancy got situated, I told her that I'd be in the office prepping the bank deposit and taking care of some loose ends. I said hello to Peter on the way back to my office, and he grunted in return.

Shutting the door, I stared at the stack of paperwork on my desk and groaned. I still had to file invoices and pay bills before the growing stack got out of hand. I felt tired just thinking about it.

I forced myself into the chair and decided to start with the cash deposit since that definitely needed to get to the bank by the end of the day. It took me about twenty minutes to get everything finalized, which wasn't bad considering I drifted into a daze at least twice.

Just as I was lifting the first invoice off the top of my stack, there was a soft tap at my office door. I already knew it was Nancy because she was the only person with that delicate of a knock.

"Come in," I shouted.

Nancy barely opened the door and poked her in head. "There is a woman here to see you."

A woman? *Now what*, I thought. Had Bridget decided to stop by for another unannounced visit? "Did she give you a name?"

Nancy shook her head. "No, she just said it was very urgent she speak with you. I told her to wait at the front booth."

I sighed. "Okay, I'll be right out."

Nancy nodded and shut the door.

I huffed, and placed the invoice back on the top of my stack. It had only been a few days since I'd last seen Bridget. I didn't think she'd be back this soon. But maybe she'd scheduled a hair appointment for today that had brought her back to Asia Village.

However, when I got out into the dining room, I was more than surprised to find out that it wasn't my former classmate waiting for me. It was Joyce Han, Margo's sister.

My stomach dropped, my mouth dried, and my heart pounded. The way we'd left things at the dry cleaners, I didn't think I would be hearing from her, much less seeing her any time soon.

I attempted to gather myself as I approached the table. Thankfully Nancy had already brought tea service, and I found Joyce sipping on some tea and staring out into the plaza watching the sparse shoppers make their way to the various shops.

I cleared my throat so as not to startle her. "Hello, Ms. Han."

She turned slowly to face me and when she did, I could see the exhaustion and sadness in her eyes. It had only been about four days since I'd seen her last, but she looked as though she aged a year since then. "Hello, Miss Lee."

"Please, call me Lana," I said, taking a seat on the opposite side of the booth. I placed my hands in my lap. "I wasn't expecting to see you."

She inhaled deeply. "I wasn't expecting this of myself either. But I needed to talk to you in private. I figured if you were at all smart you would not try and reach out to me again. So, I knew it was up to me to find you."

I leaned forward, and gave her a sympathetic frown. "I'm sorry if what happened at the dry cleaner upset you. That was not my intention at all."

"Then what was your intention?" She pushed her teacup to the side. "That's why I came today. I want to know what you're up to."

Choosing my words carefully, I explained to her

what happened and how I'd come about finding Margo's body after the class was over. I included the information about seeing the dimple-chinned man right as I left the first time, and that the janitor had come to my rescue. I left out my involvement with the administration office, and that I had met with Sabrina Hartford. I hadn't yet decided if I wanted her to know about the photographs and the cryptic note.

She didn't say anything right away, and I gathered that she was trying to make sense of everything I'd told her. After a few minutes of awkward silence, she said in a hushed tone, "I believe you."

Relief washed over me, and I exhaled a deep breath, leaning backward in the booth. "I'm so glad to hear you say that," I said. "I really just want to help find out what happened to your sister. She seemed like a genuinely kind person, and I think the police are looking at this all wrong."

"I agree with that," she said, reaching for her teacup. "Detective Bishop stayed to speak with me for a while after you left. It does not seem as though he is thinking about this clearly. When he left, I found myself becoming concerned that justice would not be found for my sister."

"I can understand that," I replied.

She held my eyes with hers, staring at me with what appeared to be contempt. But I couldn't tell if it was directed at me or at the situation we found ourselves in. "I know, Miss Lee, I have done some of my own detective work and looked into who you are. I am aware of your past and your experience with these situations."

I found my mouth beginning to dry again and wished that I could have some tea too. Under the circumstances, I felt like it would be rude to help myself. "I can assure you that—"

She held up a hand. "Please, you do not have to explain."

I closed my mouth and let her continue.

"I came here to tell you that I understand what you are trying to do. I will not stop you from looking into what happened. You seem to be good at this. But, please, do not get in the way of anything the police may find. I don't know if they will find anything, but you have to be careful. And you must not tell anyone that you spoke with me."

"Of course," I said. "I won't breathe a word to anyone about this."

She seemed to relax after I agreed to keep quiet.

"Can I ask you something though?"

She nodded for me to continue.

"What concerned you about the visit with Detective Bishop?"

Picking up the kettle to refill her teacup, she said, "He seemed very interested in you, and the janitor who was there that evening. He didn't seem to think anyone else could be guilty."

"I thought they were looking into the students and staff?"

She didn't ask me how I knew this information; instead she scoffed at my question. "He says that, but I can tell that he is already convinced it is you and this man. I don't even know this man. Margo never talked about him or anyone at the school besides a couple of women she had made friends with. I find this very dangerous to think so close-minded of any situation without having more proof." She lifted the teacup to her lips, but before taking a sip, she asked, "Wouldn't you agree?"

"Of course. He couldn't be more wrong," I said. "I can promise you I had nothing to do with this."

"As I've said, I believe you," she replied. "What convinced me most was your business card."

"My business card?"

"Yes, it was found in my sister's back pocket. That's when I knew something must be off." She paused. "If you were guilty of murdering her, why would you have been stupid enough to give your business card to her that same evening?"

I'd forgotten all about that, and now that Joyce had brought it up, I was glad that I'd done it. Too bad that Detective Bishop didn't see it that way.

We chatted for a few more minutes, and she gave me the first names of the women she thought might have been friends with Margo. I walked her to the door of the restaurant, and before she left she turned to me and said, "Be careful, Miss Lee. This Detective Bishop could be a lot of trouble for you."

CHAPTER
21

- - - - - - - - - - - - - - -

It was getting close to five o'clock. The rest of the afternoon had flown by after my visit with Joyce, the lunch rush—I use the word "rush" loosely—and my managerial duties. I'd managed to go to the bank and get some of the bills paid and put in the mailbox before calling it a day.

Around four forty-five, Megan called my cell phone. "Hey, I'm sorry to have to do this to you, but I just got called into work. I can't come with you to interrogate Robert Larkin."

I held in a whine. "Ugh, of all nights to get called in."

"Cassidy is sick, and we haven't been able to get ahold of anyone else to come in. I might be able to leave early if someone calls us back, but that isn't really going to help us get up to Barton's at a reasonable time. It could take hours."

"I really don't want to wait," I said, and proceeded

to tell her about my visit with Joyce Han and what she'd said about Detective Bishop. "Would you be mad if I went without you?"

"I mean, I'm disappointed but I completely get it," she replied. "I thought you didn't want to go alone though? Who on earth are you going to get to go with you?"

I could only think of one person—aside from Megan—who was willing to go along with my hare-brained schemes. "I'll think of someone," I mumbled.

Megan was silent for a few seconds. "Oh my god, you're going to bring Kimmy, aren't you?"

"She might have crossed my mind," I said, non-committally.

"Lana, come on. Maybe you should wait for me."

"It's gonna be fine," I reassured her. "I've taken Kimmy places with me on a few occasions."

"Yeah, and she's a big mouth," Megan replied. "Ugh, fine. Call me when you're done. If I'm still at work, I want you to come by so I can hear everything that I missed out on."

We hung up and I let out a heavy sigh. Megan was not a fan of Kimmy and the feeling was mutual. Even though the two girls were my closest friends, they did not see eye to eye on basically everything in existence.

Vanessa Wen walked through the door at exactly five o'clock, out of breath and scanning the restaurant nervously, most likely for me. She bounced over to the hostess booth where I was waiting not so patiently with my purse. "Hey boss, sorry to keep you waiting. I hit a ton of traffic coming into the plaza. There was a four-car pileup down the road."

"Okay, well, you're here now," I said, slinging my purse over my shoulder. "Gotta go."

"Wait, wait, wait," my teenage helper said, holding up a hand. "Where's my lecture on coming in at the last minute and how there probably wasn't even an accident and I'm being dramatic and stuff?" She chomped on her gum. "Are you feeling okay?"

"I'm just in a hurry," I replied over my shoulder. "I have to catch Kimmy before she leaves."

Vanessa shrugged. "Cool. See ya, boss."

I flew out the door, giving Vanessa a casual wave without turning around and made my way over to the Asian entertainment shop. Kimmy was no doubt getting ready to leave for the day. She usually worked the day shift since both of her parents had part-time jobs at local factories to help make ends meet. Though business had picked up for them in recent months with the surge of interest in Asian film, they were still trying to get themselves back in the black.

Kimmy moonlighted as a waitress at a gentleman's club on Brookpark Road, and it was probably the best kept secret at the plaza since only Peter, myself, Megan, and Adam knew about it. If the Matrons ever got a hold of that information, it would be all over the plaza in no time, and the next thing you'd know, Kimmy would be shipped off to a Buddhist monastery in the most remote mountaintops that China's landscape could provide.

I found my friend behind the sales counter, chatting with her mother, Sue. Kimmy stopped mid-sentence as they both noticed me approaching.

"Hi, Mrs. Tran," I said, walking up to the counter. "Hey, Kimmy."

Sue gave me a big smile; her plump cheeks rising with the gesture. "It's so nice to see you, Lana. How is your mother? I haven't seen her in a while."

I shrugged. "She's okay. Busy with my grandmother and making sure she stays out of trouble."

Sue laughed. "When your parents get older, they can be a handful. My mother was the same way."

"What's up, Lee?" Kimmy said, breaking through the formalities. "Finally come to clear your conscience and fess up?"

Sue turned to her daughter. "What are you talking about, Kimmy? You are always giving people a hard time."

"Ugh, don't worry about it, Mom. I'm just teasing Lana. She can handle it. Can't you, Lee?"

I played the good-natured roll in front of her mother. "Of course. Just girls being silly with each other."

Sue seemed to approve, and nodded her consent. "I suppose it is good for young ladies to be playful. Just remember to be respectful."

Kimmy clucked her tongue. "Yeah, yeah. Come on, Lee, I'm outta here."

I said goodbye to Mrs. Tran, and we headed out into the plaza.

"So, what's up? You need me for something?" Kimmy asked once we were out of earshot.

I was just about to tell her the reason I'd come to see her when Peter approached. "Hey, ladies," he said, wrapping an arm around Kimmy's shoulders and planting a kiss on her cheek. "What are my two favorite troublemakers up to now?" He appeared more lively than earlier in the day and seemed to have caught a second wind.

Even though the two had been dating for several months now, it still weirded me out to see them together. Kimmy was brash and loud and loved a good crowd. Peter, on the other hand, kept to himself, preferred playing video games over leaving the house, and was one of the most introverted people I knew. But it must have been that whole "opposites attract" thing that made them work.

Kimmy softened her otherwise rough demeanor as she responded to Peter. "No clue, yet. She was just about to tell me before you came." She turned back to me. "So . . . what's up?"

"Um," I stammered. I couldn't talk about it in front of Peter. Not only would he berate me for getting involved in something I shouldn't be, he'd be even more upset that I was dragging his girlfriend into things. "Well, it's kinda . . ."

"Ohhhh, wait," Peter said, nodding his head as if he already knew. "That's right, you got some girl stuff going on, right?"

"Yeah," I replied quickly. "Yeah, you know me and my girl stuff. I was hoping to borrow your girlfriend for some advice."

He continued to nod and removed his arm from around her shoulders. "Right on, man. I'll leave you guys to your girl talk." Before walking off, he squeezed Kimmy's arm. "Call me later, I'll be at home."

I waved goodbye as he left and sighed relief that it was easy enough to get rid of him.

Kimmy whipped around to look at me. An agitated excitement lighting up her eyes. "Okay, dish. What's going on? The good detective isn't so good anymore is he? I'll punch him."

"Huh?"

"Your girl problems. Did Trudeau do something to upset you? I'll break his nose," Kimmy replied, balling her hands into fists.

I laughed. "What? No. Everything with Adam and me is fine."

"Oh," she said, sounding slightly deflated.

"I appreciate the fact that you're so protective, but that's not why I wanted to talk to you."

"Well then, out with it, Lana. Geez, a girl doesn't have all damn night."

I pulled her off to the side near the koi pond so we could talk without getting in the way of passing shoppers. When I finished my story with, "Well, what do you think? Are you free or do you have to work tonight?" I expected her to take a minute to think about it, but she didn't even pause.

Instead she grabbed my wrist and pulled me toward the plaza's main doors. "Come on, let's go. It's about time you came to your senses and asked me for help."

CHAPTER
22

We arrived at Barton's Adult Learning Center about a half hour later, only getting stuck in some mild traffic one time on the way over. Kimmy had been hyper the entire car ride, going on about conspiracies that had to do with staff betrayals and multi-layered affairs. "I can't wait to question the hell out of this guy," she said as we pulled into the school's parking lot.

I turned the engine off and twisted in my seat to face her. "Kimmy, this is serious, and I most likely have one shot to get this right. I didn't ask you to come so we could play good cop, bad cop. You're just backup in case he turns out to be a creep. I don't really want to be alone with the guy, and we definitely need to talk to him in private."

Kimmy crossed her arms over her chest and looked out the passenger side window. "Oh, I see. So, you only call on me when you need muscle then, huh?"

I groaned. I didn't have time for this. "Of course, you're not just my muscle, Kimmy, come on. It's just that I've been working on this for over a week now and I'm more familiar with the details than you are. That's all. Like I said, we have one shot at this and can't afford to waste time or mess up." I was hoping that she'd accept this explanation and we could get going. The longer we sat in the car, the more anxious I became. What if Robert Larkin wasn't even working tonight and I'd have to wait yet another day. I wouldn't be able to take it.

She lifted her chin. "So, what am I supposed to do? Just stand in the background and give him dirty looks? That sounds like muscle to me."

The idea of banging my head against the steering wheel crossed my mind for a split second. I felt like I was talking to a cranky five-year-old. "Okay, how about this? Let me ask the main questions, but you can ask follow-ups. How's that sound for compromise?"

Kimmy slowly turned her head to look at me. "Well, I guess that's acceptable. I suppose you're right about me not knowing as much as you. I just learned about it an hour ago."

I exhaled loudly. "Okay, good. Let's go." I took the keys out of the ignition and stepped out of the car.

The lobby and hallways were pretty empty when we walked in and I assumed that most of the classes were currently in session. It was a little past six o'clock.

"So how do we find this guy?" Kimmy asked, scanning the open space. "Is there like a janitor's closet or something?"

I shrugged. "I don't know, but I'm guessing so. Let's

just walk around and see if we can casually bump into him. Let's go this way." Leading Kimmy down the left side of the common area to avoid the administration office, I told her that I wanted to check out the room where the murder had occurred. I'm not sure why I felt the need to look at it again, but it had been hanging over my head since the last time I'd stopped by.

The crime-scene tape had been removed, and the classroom door was wide open. I poked my head inside, and glanced around. "It's so weird how everything just goes back to normal after a tragedy. You'd never know that something terrible happened in here."

Kimmy assessed the room. "So, you found her up here?" She asked, pointing at the instructor's cooking island.

"Yep, she was facedown there, right in the center." The memory flashed through my mind like a scene out of a horror movie. I squeezed my eyes shut trying to erase the image.

Kimmy tilted her head. "That's a pretty tight space." She walked into the room, and approached the cooking island. "Come over here."

"Why?" I hissed. "We shouldn't be in here."

She shrugged. "Why not? Who cares? Just come over here already."

I stomped my foot in defiance of her bossiness, but sulked into the room anyway. I knew she wasn't going to let this go, and I didn't want her to cause a scene that would attract unnecessary attention.

Kimmy grabbed my shoulders and maneuvered me to stand in front of her at the cooking station.

"What are you doing?" I asked, my pulse quickening.

"So, if I was standing behind you—" Kimmy paused.

I glanced over my shoulder and saw her raise her right arm as if she had a knife in her hand. "And I tried to stab you like this . . . ?"

"Excuse me, can I help you two?" A deep voice traveled from the doorway.

I flinched and turned in that direction, and then gasped when I realized it was the dimple-chinned man I'd seen talking to Margo that night, right as I was leaving. He was dressed in a casual, navy blue suit with no tie, and the button at his collar was undone. His sandy brown hair that I vaguely remembered being smoothed down was now mussed as if he'd just been running his fingers through it incessantly. He was attractive in that clean-cut, academic sort of way, but there was something about the dramatic curve of his lips that made him seem as if he were permanently smirking, and that bothered me.

The man appeared startled by my reaction. "Sorry to catch you by surprise, but you can't be in here unless you're students." He studied me a moment longer. "Do I know you? You seem familiar."

My voice caught and I found myself emphatically shaking my head in response.

Before he could object, Kimmy interrupted. "Oh, but we're going to be," she said. "We're going to take an arts and crafts . . . thing."

"This is a cooking room," he replied matter-of-factly. His attention drifted back in my direction.

"Well, right," Kimmy stammered. "We were just

scoping out the rest of the school in case we wanted to take other classes." She said in a manner that implied a "duh" could be added to the end of her explanation.

"I see," the man replied, his eyes returning to Kimmy momentary. He stuffed his hands in his pockets. Then he looked at me again, his brow furrowing. "Are you sure I don't know you from somewhere? I can't shake the feeling that we've met. Perhaps you've been in one of my classes before," he suggested.

"I'm sorry," I said, finally finding my voice. "I don't believe I have. What did you say your name was?"

"I didn't, but it's Anthony. Anthony Bianco. I teach Italian."

So, he was a teacher here. I adjusted the context that I remembered him in, originally thinking he was a student. When he came to visit Margo that night, it was a colleague coming to chat. I assessed his stature against my memory of the picture, and concluded that he could be the man in the photos.

He jutted his head forward. "Italian, have you taken it?"

I started to say no, but Kimmy cut me off. "Actually, she is a cousin of one your janitors, Robert Larkin. That's probably why she seems so familiar to you. She comes here to visit him from time to time. Does he happen to be here tonight?"

"Oh, Bob . . ." the man replied, his eyes never leaving mine. He nodded his head, briefly shifting his glance to Kimmy as he responded. "Yeah, he's around here somewhere." He gave me a once-over. "I wouldn't peg you for a cousin of Robert's."

I forced a chuckle. "Well, you never know who's in someone's family tree, do you?"

"I guess so. I can help you guys find him if you like—"

"Sure, that would be great!" Kimmy said enthusiastically. "We're kind of pressed for time anyways."

We followed Anthony out of the classroom, and I pinched Kimmy's arm when he had his back turned to us. She gawked at me and mouthed *"What?"*

He led us to a group of doors on the opposite side of the common area down a small hallway. The door on the right had a placard that read: JANITORIAL ROOM. He knocked assertively on the door before twisting the knob and poking his head inside.

"Bob, you in here?" he yelled.

A muffled "yeah" could be here coming from deep inside the room.

Anthony opened the door wider and stepped off to the side, allowing us to pass through. "Your cousin is here."

"My cousin?" the voice returned in confusion.

The narrow, cement brick room was painted a drab gray and outlined with metal shelving that covered both walls as you walked in. They were filled with cleaning supplies, replacement parts for plumbing needs, cans of paint, and every tool you could think of. Half of the stuff in here was beyond my knowledge of building maintenance.

Robert Larkin finally stepped into view from behind an area in the back of the room where there was a makeshift worktable. He stopped dead in his tracks when he saw that it was me. It took only a few seconds for recognition to set in.

"Hi, *cousin* Bob," I said through gritted teeth.

Kimmy whispered in my ear. "No one talks like that, weirdo."

I elbowed her in the stomach while maintaining the forced smile on my face. "We thought we'd stop by and see how you were doing."

"Yeah, you know while we signed up for our arts and crafts class . . ." Kimmy added.

"Oh . . . right," Robert replied. "Nice to see you again . . . cousin."

Anthony looked between the three of us, then took a step backward out of the room. "Well, I'll just leave you to your family reunion then. Have a good evening."

Robert's eyes drifted from mine to acknowledge Anthony. "Yeah, see ya later, Tony."

I waited until I heard the door shut behind us. I felt as if we had just escaped a close call.

Once we knew that Anthony was gone, Robert turned his attention back on me, running a hand through his shaggy hair. "What the hell are you doing here? And why did you pretend to be my cousin?"

Kimmy held up her hand. "That was my idea. Your pal, Tony, caught us snooping around in the cooking room so we had to be quick on our feet."

"And you dragged me into it?" he asked. "I don't need no trouble, and I don't know what you girls think you're up to, but leave me out of it."

"We came here to see *you*, smarty-pants," Kimmy replied.

I grabbed her arm and squeezed, urging her to step back a few feet. "Sorry, my friend is a little hyper tonight. I'm Lana, it seems you recognize me, so you know we met the night of Margo Han's murder."

"Yeah, I know who you are," he said. "And like I said before, I don't need any trouble."

"Well, that's just too bad, tough guy," Kimmy blurted out. "Because the cops already have their eye on you and my friend here. Only, we know she didn't do anything, so . . ."

Robert clenched his fists, and I remembered the charges he'd had on his record for assault. I whipped my head around at Kimmy and gave her my best glare. "Let me handle this."

"Ugh, whatever," she said, holding up her hands. "Fine, do whatever."

I took a calming breath and smiled apologetically at Robert. "Like *I* said, she's hyper tonight, but she does have a point. That's why I'm here actually. I think both of us are being investigated by the police."

He rolled his eyes. "Yeah, and what of it? I didn't do nothing wrong, so they can look into me all day long for all I care. I'm on probation, girly, so I'm not trying to get myself put back in jail for nothin'."

I took a step closer. "Aren't you worried they're going to try and make something up that isn't there? I don't know what your experience was with Detective Bishop, but I can't say that I enjoyed mine."

"It won't be the first time that something crooked like this happened. That's why you can't trust nobody nowadays. But I ain't gonna let it get the best of me. I'm just gonna keep my head down and let them do what they gotta do. You'd be smart to do the same."

I sighed. "I wish that I could. But, if I knew that something I did could make a difference, I'd feel pretty bad that I didn't at least try."

"That's nice and all that you still see the good in humanity, but that's how people end up like Margo Han. Always giving people chances."

"Did you know her well?" I asked.

He shook his head. "Nah, not really. She was a class act though. Probably one of the nicest people in this whole damn building. A lot of people don't tend to pay me much mind because of my position here. They think I'm lower than them or somethin' because I clean out the toilets. But, not Margo. She'd at least ask me how I was. One time she even made me a nice care package with leftover food from her class."

"Do you know if she was involved with anyone here at the school?"

He cocked his head at me. "Involved? Like how."

I blushed. "You know, like romantically."

"Oh, that kinda involved." He rubbed the side of his cheek, which was covered in five-o'clock shadow. "Eh, maybe she was seein' someone, but if she was, I didn't know who."

"Did you notice a change in her appearance?" I asked, thinking about the conversation I'd had with Sabrina.

He folded his arms across his chest and shifted, leaning to one side. "Yeah, now that you mention it, yeah. She did look kinda different to me after a while. Kinda sad-like."

"What about an affair?" Kimmy interrupted. "Do you know anything about any affairs around here?"

He snorted. "There's a lot of that around here. Sometimes I think it's something in the water." Robert laughed to himself. "Bunch of heathens, if you ask me."

I hated to ask, but I had to. "Do you know if Margo was somehow involved with something like that going on around here?"

He let out another snort. "Margo? Nah."

"What about enemies?" I suggested. "Do you know if she had any of those?"

"There's a lot of two-faced people around here. So, if you're wondering about that, your guess is as good as mine. But from upfront appearances, no, she didn't have any enemies."

"This sounds like a terrible place to work," Kimmy commented.

"It pays the bills." Robert checked his watch. "Speaking of which, I gotta make my rounds and get things going around here. You guys done asking me twenty questions?"

My shoulders sagged in defeat. "I guess so."

"Good, now try to stay out of things. You don't want to get mixed up with them cops if you can help it."

We started to leave, and as we exited the confined room, I stopped and turned back around. "Robert, can I ask you one more thing before I leave—then I swear I won't bother you anymore."

"Sure, what is it?"

"Why do *you* think Margo got murdered? I mean, you must think something. And if you don't think she had any enemies in the school, then what could have happened that night?"

"Look, kid, sometimes bad things just happen to good people. It's a cliché for a reason, you know? My best guess is she was at the wrong place at the wrong time. And that's about all I can say. Now if you'll excuse me, I have some floors that need mopping."

CHAPTER
23

"What a bunch of BS!" Kimmy shouted when we were back in the common area.

"Shhh!" I hissed at my friend. "Don't attract any more attention to us. We've already been caught staging a reenactment in the classroom."

She waved a hand at me. "Oh, like he knew what we were doing anyways. Don't be so timid, Lana. I can't believe I haven't rubbed off on you more by now."

I said a silent prayer of thanks for the fact that she hadn't. I couldn't even imagine myself being quite as abrasive as Kimmy often was. "Anyways, that was a total bust. We might as well go home."

"Nah, I don't think so," Kimmy replied. "I say we do more snooping. I didn't come out to Parma just to have a disappointing conversation in a broom closet. I want some action, Lee." She glanced around, hyper mode returning.

"I hate to break it to you," I replied, trying to usher her toward the exit. "There's not much we can do at this point. We came here to talk to Robert Larkin, and we did that."

"Didn't you tell me that Margo's sister said something about Margo having some teacher friends? Let's find them and see what they know."

"I only have their first names, and I didn't get to search the directory for who they could be."

"So, let's do it now." Kimmy said, clapping her hands and rubbing them together with enthusiasm. "This could be our lucky ticket to the missing clue."

I was beginning to regret bringing Kimmy with me, but maybe she was right. If I wanted to get the answers I was searching for, then I needed to try a lot harder.

We grabbed a program from one of the acrylic displays sprinkled around the learning center and found an empty couch that was out of the way.

Kimmy skimmed the left-hand pages, while I scanned the right side. Joyce had told me earlier that day that Margo had talked a few times about a woman named Melissa—which was an extremely common name—and then mentioned another woman by the name of Phyllis, which thankfully wasn't that popular of a name and would be easier to spot.

I found Phyllis listed under the arts and crafts section, which brought Kimmy a little bit of amusement.

Kimmy slapped the page with the back of her hand. "Well, looks like Phyllis teaches good ole watercoloring."

"We're not actually taking a class, Kimmy," I reminded her.

She snickered. "Speak for yourself. I can't let my boyfriend have all the talent in the artistic department. Maybe I'll sign up for this."

"Lana?" a feminine voice asked from behind us.

I shifted on the couch and saw Bridget smiling at me.

"How funny running into you here!" she said with a laugh. "Are you here to sign up for the new cooking class?"

"Uh, hi Bridget," I said, trying to gather my thoughts. What were the chances of me running into her today of all days?

"Well hey there, Bridget," Kimmy said with a hint of sarcasm, extending a hand. "I'm Lana's friend, Kimmy. Nice to meet you."

"Oh, nice to meet you too," Bridget replied, slightly taken aback by Kimmy's tone. "I hope I didn't disturb you two, but I just had to come over and say hi. I didn't think you'd be back here."

"I . . . didn't think so either," I said, unsure of how to explain myself. I definitely couldn't tell her the truth. "What's this about the cooking class being back on?"

Bridget gestured to the administration office. "Yeah, I just got done signing up for it. I assumed that's why you were here." Her eyes fell to the open course-listing program in our laps.

"Absolutely," Kimmy said, again beating me to the punch. "Me and Lana are going to take the class . . . together."

The excitement on Bridget's face dissipated. "Oh,

well I was hoping that we could have been partners. But it'll still be fun to have some friendly faces in the class with me. I wonder whether many people will be repeats from the last class. I hope I don't get stuck sitting next to that dull guy again."

As much as I was mad at Kimmy for volunteering us to take the class, what Bridget said did spark an interest in me. Could that mean the killer might be back too? I mean, if they wanted to look innocent, then they would be hiding in plain sight if they continued taking the class. Assuming that the killer had been in the class to begin with. I still wasn't sure what I felt about that. Right now, a majority of my suspicions were falling on Anthony. He *was* the last person I'd seen with Margo while she was alive. Which made me wonder . . . why wasn't that a concern of Detective Bishop's? I'd told him that I'd seen a man with Margo before I left. Had he even bothered to look into it? Perhaps now that I knew who Anthony actually was, I should relay that information to Detective Bishop. It was an adjustment to my original statement, after all.

"Lana?" Bridget asked, bending down. "Are you okay?"

"Huh?" I sprang back to the present. "Yeah, I'm fine. I was just thinking about the class."

"Yeah, the administration office is getting ready to close in thirty minutes; if you want to sign up and make it to tomorrow's class then you guys better get in there fast."

"Good idea, Bridget!" Kimmy said. "We're gonna head there now. So nice meeting you."

I cleared my throat, giving Kimmy a pointed look.

Kimmy pursed her lips. "Sorry, I'm a little hyper tonight."

Bridget smiled, though it didn't appear genuine. "No problem. I'll leave you guys to it, and I guess I'll see you tomorrow night."

We watched Bridget walk away and when she was out of range, I smacked Kimmy on the arm. "What the heck is wrong with you? Did you have to be so rude?"

Kimmy jerked a thumb over her shoulder. "That girl is weird, Lana . . . capital *W*. Something is totally off about your little friend there. It was like rolling off her in waves. Didn't you feel it?"

"She's a little overly friendly, but that's about it. Maybe she doesn't know a lot of people," I replied.

"No way, there's definitely something off about her." Kimmy stood up, knocking the program to the floor, and craned her neck to see if she could still spot Bridget, but she was long gone. She plopped back down, disappointed. "She's for sure weird. Capital *W* and then underline it."

"Adam thinks she's harmless. He called her a 'rubbernecker'."

Kimmy tilted her head. "A rubbernecker?"

"Yeah, you know, when people see an accident and they crane their necks to gawk at it."

"Oh! Okay, well whatever; he didn't meet her, right?"

"No, you're the first person to meet her. Although, Megan did have some suspicions about her, too."

Kimmy cringed, but didn't comment on her and Megan both having the same viewpoint. "Well, okay then.

Your boyfriend is hot stuff and everything, Lana, but it doesn't mean he's always right about everything. And trust me when I say that girl is strange."

"Fine, fine. I can see your point. It's very possible that her coming around is a little too convenient." I started to think back, remembering my encounters with Bridget, and how she seemed to always show up at opportune moments. I thought about the conversation we'd had the day she popped up at Asia Village and her insistence that I wanted to get involved and all the unknown variables that existed. At the time I had brushed it off as morbid curiosity, but maybe there was something to all of it that I hadn't acknowledged completely.

Kimmy tucked her hair behind her ears. "Great, I'm glad you agree with me on something." She leaned forward to grab the discarded program, and then stood up. "Now come on, we have a class to sign up for."

We left the school after both of us registered for the cooking class that would start back up the following day. Thankfully the evil woman who'd given me my refund wasn't working that evening, but neither was my intern friend Sabrina. Only one older lady was in the administration office, and I was relieved to find that she was quite the pleasant employee. Kimmy had worn herself out by then, but she did ask the woman behind the desk if Phyllis Ubert was teaching a class that night. When the woman told us no, Kimmy finally agreed it was time to call it a night.

I dropped her back off at Asia Village where she'd

left her car in the parking lot. It was already past eight o'clock, and I couldn't believe how much time that whole thing had taken. It was a good thing I hadn't waited on Megan after all.

Before pulling out of the plaza's parking lot, I took a moment to text Megan and see where she was and if she'd been able to leave work. A few minutes later she replied and told me that she was still at the Zodiac and I should stop by to fill her in on what happened at Barton's.

I was feeling hungry and didn't see myself cooking any dinner when I got home, so I decided to head straight over to the bar and get myself a big fat cheeseburger.

The bar was virtually dead when I got there, so I had my pick of seats. I chose my usual stool at the end of the bar anyway. Megan came out of the kitchen just as I sat down.

"You gonna eat?" she asked, plucking a liquor bottle from the shelf display that lined the bar.

"Yeah, I wanted a mushroom cheeseburger with extra pickles, and lots of curly fries with Cajun seasoning."

"Man, you really worked up an appetite, didn't you?" Megan returned the liquor bottle back on the shelf, and chose another to add to the drink. I had no idea what tonight's concoction would be.

I rested my head in the palm of my hand. "Dealing with Kimmy tonight was a lot. Normally she's not this amped up right out the gate."

Megan snickered. "That's what you get for taking her and not me."

"I didn't have much of a choice," I replied. "You're stuck here, and I really needed to get there tonight. It's a good thing I did too. Wait until you hear this."

She finished making my drink, which turned out to be something called a Lavish Libra. It could only be described as sipping on liquid cotton candy. Though it was quite delicious, it wasn't something I could continue to drink all night unless I wanted to be picked up off the floor.

Once I'd tested her new experiment and given it my stamp of approval, I went through the details of my day, giving her the extended version of what happened with Joyce and then my adventure with Kimmy at Barton's.

"I hate to admit that I agree with her," Megan began. "But from the beginning I have thought there's something odd about that girl."

"Like I've said before, she is a decent-sized woman," I said. "And could easily overpower someone of Margo's size. But as far as motives go, I still can't come up with one to save my life."

"Well, you're gonna have to get to know her better is all, Lana. It doesn't seem like she plans on going away anytime soon, so that's something in our favor. And then if things get too weird with her, you can always sic Kimmy on her."

I laughed. "It was a good move on Kimmy's part to have us join that class. I don't think I would have done it had she not been with me. Especially risking the fact that my mother or Peter will find out about it. Kimmy better not blab, that's all I'm saying."

"So, the girl was good for something tonight after

all," Megan smirked. "She's still not my favorite person, though I will say she's good at keeping a secret when it counts. I don't think you have to worry about her telling Peter anything. She'll probably get a kick out of keeping it from him."

"You know, one of these days you guys are gonna have to get over it and make nice with each other."

"One day . . ." Megan agreed. "But not today. Anyways, let me place your order. It shouldn't take long since no one has ordered food in over an hour. Dean is probably asleep back there."

I let my mind wander while Megan was away. There were two guys at the other end of the bar and neither one of them was talking. Both had their eyes fixed on the TV above them, and if I had to guess, they were probably watching the basketball game. One of the channels was set to the QVC channel and I doubted they had any interest in buying a floral-patterned silk scarf that the woman on the screen was currently modeling.

My food was ready in under twenty minutes, and I dug into my burger like I hadn't seen food in a decade. One of the guys who had been concentrating on the basketball game glanced in my direction for a minute, and I had a moment of self-consciousness, wondering what his inner dialogue might sound like. I imagined him thinking to himself, *"Wow, look at that little Asian girl go."*

Once I finished my food, cleaning my plate completely except for the decorative piece of parsley that came on every dish they served, I found myself sleepy and ready for bed. I only stayed for a few more minutes after I'd finished eating. I paid my bill and left my best friend a generous tip before heading out the door.

When I got home, I took Kikko out for her final tinkle of the evening, showered, and stuffed myself into my pajamas. I pulled out my notebook from under my mattress with the full intention of filling out the day's events, but I was so tired, I dozed off with the pen in my hand. I didn't realize it, of course, until I woke with a start around three o'clock from a nightmare. I'd dreamt that everything surrounding me was covered in black shadows, and when I called for help no one could see me, even though they were standing right next to me. As far as nightmares go, it was a pretty tame one for me, but it still left me sweaty and filled with a sense of dread.

I switched on the light to gather myself and tucked the notebook back under my mattress. The sooner I solved this case, the better. I enjoyed sleep too much to let it be ruined by my overactive imagination.

CHAPTER
24

When I woke up Tuesday morning, the remnants of my nightmare mid-sleep seemed like a distant memory. It's so interesting how fear seems more pressing in the early morning hours, and then with the light of day, safety and a sense of security return.

I dressed for work, made coffee, took Kikko on a short walk around the building, and then hopped into my car wondering what the day would bring.

The Matrons arrived on time, and reported that they had found nothing of use but were still on the case. At this point, considering how little everyone seemed to know about Margo, I wasn't holding out much hope. If someone wasn't friends with her directly, I didn't see anyone knowing anything much of use.

Our mailman, James, arrived as the Matrons were heading out. He said hello to all of them, and the group spent a few minutes chitchatting before the ladies continued on their way.

James greeted me at the hostess stand. "Good morning, Lana. I've got a special delivery for you today." He followed his announcement with a prideful smile as though he was just about to make my day.

"Morning, James," I replied. "Whatcha got for me?"

He handed me a square envelope that looked to be the size of a greeting card. "I thought it might be your birthday or something. They made sure to write your name in big bold letters."

I inspected the envelope. There was no return address or any marking to identify where it came from. It was postmarked as being sent the day before. "Thanks, James . . ." I mumbled, preoccupied by the envelope. "It's not my birthday though, it's already come and gone."

"Oh well, happy belated birthday, if that's the case," he said in a chipper tone. "You don't look a day over twenty-one to me."

I glanced up and smiled. I wasn't quite at the age yet where I wanted to look younger than my years, but from what my mother and her friends told me, that time would be coming around soon enough.

"Here's the rest of your mail," James said, handing over the remaining stack of envelopes. "Not a lot more excitement going on today, just looks like more bills."

We said goodbye, and I was left alone with an envelope that was beginning to make me anxious. I grabbed for the letter opener I kept stashed under the cash register and slid it through the slender gap to break the seal.

It was some type of greeting card. The card was face-down as I pulled it out of the envelope, and as I flipped it over, whatever had been stuck in the middle fluttered out onto the ground. The front of the card showed three giraffes with party hats, and a speech bubble that read SURPRISE!

I hopped off the stool and reached for what had fallen. It was a photo, and as I stared at the picture, trying to make sense of what I was looking at, a chill ran down my spine. It was Sabrina and me sitting at the bar on Sunday hovered over the pictures and the note she'd received in her work locker.

Forgetting my surroundings, I was completely caught off guard when the bells above the door jingled and I jumped backward, dropping the card and photo onto the ground while also knocking over my stool.

It was Ian Sung, the property manager, who was staring back at me. "Lana, are you all right? I didn't mean to startle you." His eyes traveled down to the card and photo, which was facing backside up. "Here, let me—"

"No!" I yelled, maybe a tad too aggressively. "I'll get it. It's fine."

He furrowed his perfectly arched eyebrows at me. "Okay . . ."

Bending down as gracefully as I could in the knee-length skirt I'd chosen to wear that day, I picked up the card and photo, making sure not to expose the picture in the process.

Ian watched me with intrigue. "Is everything okay with you? You look a bit rattled."

In truth, I felt like a mess. I wanted to run and hide

in my office, call Adam, and not come out until he came here fully armed. This meant that someone was watching me . . . and Sabrina. I needed to talk to her. But I couldn't exactly tell any of this to Ian.

"I'm fine," I replied, falling short of sounding truthful.

"If you're sure." He looked so composed compared to how I felt. Though Ian was always put together well in his fancy French suits and polished Italian shoes. His raven black hair was usually slicked down and combed to the side with a distinguished part off to the left. He kept the sides short and faded, and apart from his thin sideburns, he never entertained anything besides a clean-shaven face. Everything about him reminded me of a classic 1930s gangster sans fedora—which he did own and often sported during the colder months.

I stuffed the card and photo back into the envelope and shoved it underneath the counter. I'd noticed some writing on the inside of the card, but I'd have to wait until Ian left before I could look at it. "Really, I'm okay. What can I help you with?"

He held out a hand and moved around me, picking up the stool and setting it back down properly. "I just wanted to swing by and see how you were. I haven't seen you in a few days and got a little concerned. You missed a board meeting the other night."

I smacked my forehead. "Ugh. I'm sorry, things have been crazy lately, and it slipped my mind."

"Is there something you need to talk about it?" he asked, looking me over. "You're not sick, are you?"

"No. Really, I've just been busy and forgot all about it. I'll be at the next one," I said.

"Okay, Lana, just remember if you need anything . . . I'm always here for you." He diverted his eyes as he said the last bit, and if I didn't know any better, I'd say he was on the verge of blushing.

For the most part, Ian was respectful of my relationship with Adam, but I knew there was still a level of personal interest for him that I did not share. Even if Adam hadn't come along when he did, I can't say it would have made any difference in my feelings toward the handsome property manager. Yeah, I admit that he's handsome . . . in my head. Those words would never actually leave my mouth, however.

"Um, thanks," I said, feeling awkward. "Did you need anything else? I really have to get this mail sorted."

"Oh, of course, I'll leave you to your day." He bowed his head before turning to leave.

Once he'd left the restaurant, I pulled out the envelope and removed the contents again. My hands shook as I opened the card back up to read the message inside.

There was only one sentence written in small script, but all capital letters just as the envelope had been addressed. It read NEXT TIME, SMILE FOR THE CAMERA.

I felt sweat start to collect on my palms, and I wiped my free hand on my skirt. I didn't like that whomever sent this mentioned a "next time." My eyes immediately darted toward the door to the restaurant. I scurried over and peeked out into the plaza, scanning the scattered patrons for anyone who looked out of place. A couple sat at one of the benches near the koi pond outside the restaurant. From what I could tell, they appeared unsuspecting and not at all as if they were keeping an eye on me.

Aside from the couple, there wasn't anyone milling around, and that brought me the slightest bit of relief.

I needed to call Sabrina.

I grabbed the stack of envelopes and tucked it under my arm to bring back with me to the office. When Peter saw me come through the kitchen door, he removed his ear buds to greet me. "What's up, dude?"

"Can you watch the front for a few minutes? I have to drop this off in my office and make a quick phone call."

"Sure thing," he said, giving me a thumbs-up.

I continued on to the back, opened the door to my office and dumped the mail tub on my guest chair, then rushed to my purse to grab my cell phone. Finding Sabrina's number in my call log history, I selected it and listened while her phone rang. It went to voice mail, and I let out a frustrated groan.

At the prompt, I left my message: "Hi Sabrina, this is Lana Lee from . . . um . . . Ho-Lee Noodle House. I need to talk to you as soon as possible, so please call me back as soon as you get this. It's urgent. Thanks."

When I disconnected the call, I went through my favorites and dialed Megan's number. She didn't answer either and I figured she was probably still sound asleep. I didn't bother leaving her a message because I knew that half the time she didn't listen to them. Instead, I left her a text telling her to call me as soon as she woke up.

Next, I planned on calling Adam, but before I hit CALL I paused. If I told him about this right now, he most likely would get involved and not allow me to go to the cooking class with Kimmy. To make matters even worse, he currently wasn't aware that I was going back to Barton's at all. We'd kept missing each other the night before, and hadn't had a chance to talk on the phone. I felt like my news of returning to the cooking class was not something for a text message.

I put away my phone and decided to hold off in order to give myself some time to think. I mean, he was probably busy anyways, and there was no sense in disturbing him until after lunch. Right? Right, I confirmed with myself.

I sat down in my office chair for a minute and tried to calm down. The last thing I needed was for Peter to give me the third degree. I resolved that I would be fine as long as I was in the restaurant and Peter was here with me. Whoever this person was probably wouldn't approach me unless I was alone. For now, I was safe in the confines of Asia Village.

My hands had stopped sweating, so I decided to head back out to the dining room, bringing my cell with me in case Sabrina or Megan called me back. When I exited the kitchen, I found Peter up front at the hostess station chatting with Kimmy.

They both turned as I approached them.

"Hey there, Lana," Kimmy said, giving me a wink while Peter's back was still facing her. "I just came by to see how things were going with that *girl situation.*"

Peter jokingly covered his ears. "La la la, let me get

back in the kitchen before you guys start your girl gab-bin'."

Kimmy batted his arm jokingly before he shuffled away.

I watched him disappear into the kitchen. "What do you suppose he thinks we talk about all the time?"

Kimmy shrugged and with a laugh said, "Probably our periods or something stupid. But hey, whatever gets him out of our hair works for me." Her attention drifted from the kitchen door back to me, and she leaned forward, studying my face. "What the hell is wrong with you?"

I took another peek at the kitchen door to make sure that Peter was definitely gone, and then whispered, "I got a weird thing in the mail today."

"What do you mean by a *weird thing*?"

I told her about the card and photo inside.

Kimmy gasped. "You're lyin'. Really? I wanna see it."

"I left it in my purse back in the office," I said. "I don't want to leave the dining area again; Peter is going to get annoyed with me."

"No sweat," she replied and started to head back toward the kitchen. "I'll just go take a quick look."

"Kimmy . . ."

She waved a hand over her head without turning around. "Be right back, Lee."

I sat on my stool, and tapped my shoe impatiently on the footrest waiting for her to come back. It was good she'd come by because I did want to talk to her about this, but I didn't know if the restaurant was the best place for it.

Kimmy returned a few minutes later, an expression of shock on her face. "Holy crap, Lana! That picture is legit. Are you freakin' out or what?"

"Uh, yeah," I spat. "How else would I feel right now?"

"Okay, chill out, don't worry about it. It's broad daylight and we're in the plaza. It's totally safe. Some weirdo stalker isn't going to come in and just murder you for all to see."

I cringed. "Don't say it like that. I don't even want to think about it."

"Well then don't. Try to think about something else until it's time to go to class."

"Easy for you to say," I mumbled.

"Trust me, Lee, it's going to be fine. You know what this means, don't you?"

"That Sabrina and I have targets on our backs?" I asked sarcastically.

"No, smarty, it means that you're gettin' close to something, and when we go to that school tonight, we're goin' to find out what."

CHAPTER
25

Kimmy's reassurances did very little to make me feel better. She was right though. If someone wanted me to know they were watching me, that meant I was on to something. Only I didn't know what. And I felt this person might have more faith in me figuring it out than I had in myself at the moment.

The hands on the clock ticked slowly as I waited for the afternoon to pass. Nancy must have asked me at least five times what was wrong with me, and I tried my best to convince her that I had a headache and nothing more.

As it neared two o'clock, I methodically counted the cash deposit and filled out the bank slip, shoving everything into the security bag. For once, I was dreading my trip to the bank because it was the only time during the day when I would be completely alone. At least after work I could be comforted by Kimmy's presence until I got home later that night.

I still hadn't called Adam and avoided telling him too much in my response text when he asked about my day.

On my way to drop off the daily deposit, I kept checking my rearview mirror every five seconds to make sure that I didn't have a tail. In the parking lot of the bank, I sat in my car for a few extra minutes to make sure that no one was lurking around. I felt ridiculous, and overly cautious, but I reminded myself that I hadn't been aware someone was watching me on Sunday while I was at Hooley House, and yet there was clear evidence that someone had been. And as I thought about it more carefully, it struck me as odd that Adam hadn't noticed someone had been there either. Who the heck was this person and how did they get around being noticed by one of the best detectives I'd ever met?

My return trip to Asia Village mimicked my drive to the bank, meaning I kept a close eye on my rearview the entire time. I felt a little safer once I'd reached the plaza's parking lot. It wasn't by any means packed, but there were enough people around to make me feel like I wasn't alone.

Carefully exiting the car, I glanced over my shoulder a few times on my way to the main entrance, and once I was inside, I quickened my pace back into the restaurant where the sight of Nancy's kind face brought me a little solace.

"You were very fast today," she said as I walked through the door.

"No traffic," I replied.

"Your mother and grandmother are here."

Inner groan. "Oh yeah?" I glanced toward the back booth near the kitchen that my mother often frequented. "Where are they?"

"In the kitchen, talking to Peter."

I nodded and headed toward the back to greet them. They couldn't have picked a worse day to stop by.

When I pushed open the door to the kitchen, my mother swung around to see who it was. "La-naaa!" my mother blasted in a singsong voice. "There you are. I was looking for you."

My grandmother grinned at me, shuffled over to where I was standing, and raised her hand to pinch my cheek. She was the only person on the face of this earth that I would let get away with something like that.

"Hi, Mom," I said when my grandmother let go of my cheek. "What are you guys doing here? Isn't it half-off buffet day at the casino?"

"Oh yah." My mother nodded. "But I wanted to come see you first. Have you been thinking about this restaurant? We need to make it more beautiful and you are taking too long."

I huffed. "Yes, Mother, I'm working on it, but you're being so picky. I need a little more time to find something we both like."

"How about you, me, and A-ma go shopping today when you leave work, yes? We can go downtown and then eat dinner at Siam Café."

"Uh, I can't tonight, Mom. How about tomorrow night instead?"

"Why not tonight?" my mother asked, placing her

hands on her hips. "What is it so important that you cannot go with Mommy and A-ma?"

"I have to do something later . . . with Kimmy." My eyes shifted to see if Peter was paying attention to our conversation. So far, it seemed he was in his own world.

"What do you have to do?"

"It's . . . private."

"Why?"

"Mom . . ." I slid a look at Peter and then winked at my mother. "It's personal."

My mother scrunched up her face in confusion, glanced at Peter, then back at me. It took her a moment to put together an assumption. "Ohhh, okay, okay, I see," she said, nodding.

I have no idea what she'd come up with in her head, but it didn't really matter. As long as she thought I wasn't telling her because it involved Peter somehow.

"Okay, tomorrow," she said. She translated the conversation we'd just had to my grandmother, and my grandmother stole a glance at Peter and then grinned at me, giving me a thumbs up.

They said their goodbyes and my mother promised that I would see her tomorrow. I let them leave first before heading back to the dining room.

"Lana," Peter said, catching me on my way out.

"Yeah?

"What are you and Kimmy up to?" he asked, pointing his spatula at me.

"Nothing, we're not up to anything, I swear."

"So what was all that with you and your mom just now? What don't you want me to know?"

"Oh that," I said with a snort. "I just made that up so I didn't have to go with them tonight. I've got a headache and don't feel like dealing with it. You know how my mom won't take no for an answer."

"Yeah right. Kimmy told me she couldn't hang out tonight. I know you guys are up to something, and I'm just going to find out anyways."

"Peter . . ."

He turned his back to me and faced the grill. "You guys think you're slick, but I always end up figuring it out."

After work, I met Kimmy at China Cinema and Song where we agreed to take separate cars so we could go straight home after class. We followed each other out to Parma, and I made sure to stick close to her car in case anyone was following us. The last thing we needed was to get separated.

Arriving thirty minutes later, we found two parking spots next to each other and had a quick meeting in the lot before going in.

Kimmy was holding a rolled-up program and waved it at me as she got out of her car. "I forgot to tell you about this before we left Asia Village, but I was going over the course schedules in this program, and as luck would have it Phyllis is teaching her painting class tonight. It runs the same schedule as the cooking class."

"Well, how does that help us? I asked.

"The minute we leave class, we'll go over to the art studio and asked her a few questions. She's probably got a lot of cleaning up to do with all the paint and whatever, so she'll be around, don't you think?"

I shrugged. "It's worth a shot."

She slapped the rolled-up program against her thigh. "Hot damn, we're on the case! Now, let's go to school."

Shaking my head, I followed behind Kimmy as she strode into the learning center like she owned the place. I, however, did not feel so self-assured. I was still worried about the photo, and I was a little annoyed that Sabrina had never gotten back to me.

We had some time to spare, so I asked Kimmy if she wouldn't mind swinging by the administration office with me. It would be closed by the time we got out of class later that evening.

Since the outer walls of the administration office were windows, we were able to see inside without having to actually go in. I tried to be inconspicuous about it, and from what I could tell, it was just Grumpy Pants and the alternate intern who had helped Kimmy and I register for the class. Sabrina was nowhere in sight.

"Maybe she's in the back room?" Kimmy suggested. She was standing on her tiptoes to see farther into the office.

"Kimmy, don't be so obvious. If that old witch sees us, she'd probably call security."

Kimmy smirked. "She doesn't know who I am. I'm going in."

Before I could object, Kimmy sauntered into the office. I took a few steps back to shield myself from view.

A few moments later, Kimmy walked out shaking her

head. "Sabrina didn't come in or call off today. Total no call, no show."

"That's odd."

"Also, that one lady is total b—"

"Hey, guys!" a chipper voice screeched from behind us.

It was Bridget.

"Hi," I replied, putting on an exaggerated smile.

Kimmy appeared less enthused. "'Sup."

Bridget ignored her and held her attention on me. "Are you ready for our class? The new instructor is supposed to be a well-known chef in the area. They got him last minute."

"Oh, really? I hadn't heard anything about it," I said. My stomach was churning uncontrollably, and my eyes darted to the restroom. If I didn't calm down, I was going to make myself sick.

"Yeah, maybe you know him, he runs that cool place downtown, Wok and Roll."

Kimmy and I gawked at each other and our jaws dropped in unison.

Bridget raised an eyebrow. "What? Is that bad or something?"

I laughed. "Oh no, no. Everything's fine. Just surprised is all."

Kimmy tilted her head from left to right, cracking her neck. "Well, let's get these shenanigans under way."

The three of us headed toward the cooking room, and with each step I took, it felt like my feet were made of lead. Stanley Gao, the owner of Wok and Roll, was someone I knew personally. I didn't know him well or anything, but you could consider us seasoned acquaintances at the very least. Our last encounter had been during Cleveland's Best Noodle Contest some months back.

Stanley had been one of the contestants and was someone I was generally wary of. Though he was nice enough, he tended to talk to me like I was a naïve little girl he would gladly take under his much more experienced wing. On top of that, he was kind of a womanizer, and that never sat well with me.

Bridget had walked ahead of us, while Kimmy and I lagged behind. She elbowed me in the ribs and said out the corner of her mouth, "This town is getting too small."

I didn't say anything back, but I agreed. Things were starting to get a bit claustrophobic.

I'd have to say something to Stanley at some point this evening because I didn't want him running his mouth to anyone in the community that he'd seen Lana Lee and Kimmy Tran in an Asian cooking class. My only hope was that he didn't find our request odd.

Kimmy and I stepped cautiously in the room, expecting to see Stanley Gao front and center, but he hadn't yet arrived. I released a breath and nudged Kimmy to follow me to a table in the back. Bridget had taken a seat toward the front, but when she saw us taking our seats in the back row, she got up and moved to the table directly in front of us.

Kimmy scowled. I knew what she was thinking. If Bridget was sitting in front of us, we'd have to be very careful about what we said because she'd without a doubt hear everything we were talking about.

I checked the time on my cell phone, and we had about five minutes before class started. I was subconsciously tapping my shoe on the footrest, which must have been driving Kimmy crazy because she put a strong hand down on my thigh and glared at me.

"Sorry," I mouthed.

While we waited, I skimmed over the other people in the class. A few looked familiar, and I noted that the angry woman who I'd seen in the first class was back. Only now, she seemed less angry.

It was two minutes after seven, and I was beginning to think that Stanley wasn't going to show. Wouldn't that be a stroke of luck?

But no such fortune came our way because just as I was starting to feel like we were in the clear, the bald, lanky chef, Mr. Stanley Gao, walked in with a flirtatious smirk that he flashed toward the women in the room.

"Gag me," Kimmy whispered.

"Hey everyone, I'm Stan." He saluted the room with his free hand. "And tonight, we're gonna get into some Asian goodness. Who's ready?"

His enthusiasm was a little overboard for the participants in the room, and only a few people replied with a cheerless "yeah."

He set his things down on the counter and pulled out a manila folder from a black backpack that he'd removed from his shoulder. "Okay, let's get started with roll call."

He began calling names in alphabetical order. When he got to Bridget's name, I made a mental note that it was Hastings.

When Stanley got to the *L*s, he paused and let out a chuckle. "Lana Lee?"

I cringed. "Here," I said, waving my hand.

He followed the sound of my voice to the back of the room. "Whoa . . . Lana. You continue to surprise me with your random pop-ups." He squinted. "Hold up, is that Kimmy Tran back there with you?"

Kimmy waved. "Hi, Stan."

"Whoa." He laughed. "Okay, ladies, see me after class."

CHAPTER
26

Stanley was a showman of sorts. He liked to flash his impressive cooking techniques by flipping spatulas and igniting high flames on open grills any chance he got. Also important to him was plate presentation. He considered food to be art and always took great care in strategically designing his dishes as if they were going to be displayed at the Cleveland Metropolitan Museum of Art at any given moment. In truth, Stanley was the perfect choice for a replacement instructor, but I was disappointed for my own selfish reasons.

He came from around the back of the cooking island and leaned casually against the station, folding his arms across his chest as if he were getting comfortable for a nice long chat with a group of his closest friends. "So, from what I've reviewed from your previous instructor's itinerary, the next class was supposed to be hands-on learning with some fried rice. But I know due to the circumstances, none of you really knew what would go down next. I decided we're going to keep her schedule intact."

A woman sitting in the front row raised her hand. "We didn't bring any supplies with us though. How will we cook anything?"

He held up his index finger. "Ah, but never fear! If you guys weren't already aware, I'm the owner of Wok and Roll, which by the way, if you haven't come by before, you really need to check it out." Stanley winked at the woman. "I've very graciously agreed to donate the needed supplies for this class since I figured there would be no time for you guys to get them beforehand."

The woman who'd raised her hand began clapping, which sent the rest of the class to follow suit. Kimmy and I clapped half-heartedly.

Stanley bowed dramatically, without a doubt soaking up all the attention he was getting. *What an ego boost*, I thought.

When he was finished with his theatrics, he clapped his hands together. "Since I'm supposed to demonstrate how to make orange chicken afterward, let's get started so you have plenty of time to watch a master in action." His eyes fell on Kimmy and me, and he smiled wide. "Ladies, would you mind being my assistants and help pass out the ingredients and utensils to get started?"

Kimmy muttered something under her breath as we both got up to make our way to the front of the class. I really didn't like being the center of attention, but I thought this might be a good chance to look everyone in the face without having to obviously stare.

Stanley pulled out a large plastic tote container that he'd had stored behind the counter. He removed the lid and instructed us to pass out a box to each student. I had to say that I was impressed with his organizational skills. In separate boxes, he had provided everything each person would need almost as if it were a meal kit. It would have taken someone an entire day to put all of these together. Though I had a sinking suspicion that he had his employees handle it for him.

While I walked around the room, I noted the thin blonde woman from the first class who had thought I might be the instructor. I headed over to her and she smiled at me as I handed her a box. Again, she was seated next to the lady who'd had an attitude. I paused as I stood in front of her, trying to search her face for something that could explain what her deal was. But there was nothing. She was an attractive woman with messy curls of strawberry blonde hair that hung well past her shoulders. I couldn't guess at her age because it was clear by the rigid skin around her mouth and eyes that she'd had some work done. Her outfit, which consisted of tight stonewashed jeans and a low-cut top that accented her cleavage, spoke not only of her generational peak but also of the attention she craved. A rose tattoo poked out from behind her scandalous neckline. My eyes traveled down to her black stiletto ankle boots that were a little much for an evening cooking class.

She noticed me checking out her footwear, and flared her nostrils while extending her hand. "Hello?"

I blanched, my gaze traveling up to meet hers. "Sorry, I was just admiring your shoes," I said. "I love them."

She glanced down at her boots, and shifted her foot as if to model them for me. "They are pretty badass, aren't they?" The outer side of the boots had chains that connected to a zipper and made a tinkling sound as she wiggled her foot.

"Totally," I replied, attempting to sound as if I were gushing.

The woman found this acceptable and gave me an approving smile. I returned it with a polite nod and kept on moving until I'd distributed all the boxes I was holding.

Kimmy and I made it back to our seats and exchanged a look before sitting down. Here we were . . . the moment of truth. I glanced down at my box as if it were my worst enemy.

Kimmy did the same. "How hard can this be? I mean . . . tons of people make fried rice, right?"

"Uh-huh. Piece of cake."

We opened our boxes simultaneously and began pulling out the contents, setting them up in front of us.

Frying pans had been provided and sat on the solitary burners at our stations. I twisted the knob to ignite the flame, and began heating my pan.

Kimmy unwrapped her stick of butter, which had been divided into the appropriate amount, and flung it into her pan. "You know," she said, watching the butter begin to sizzle and melt, "this is kind of dummy proof, if you think about it. He has everything separated and divided into the correct proportions."

I added my own butter to the heated pan. "Hey, I'm not complaining."

She smirked as she dumped in her container of mixed vegetables. "I'm going to get an *A*. This might be a first."

"We don't get graded," I told her.

She elbowed me in the side. "Don't ruin my happy moment."

We went about our cooking lesson, adding the ingredients as Margo had showed us the first time around. Stanley walked around the room, observing and giving people helpful tips about making sure to keep the rice moving so it didn't burn or cook unevenly.

When I looked up to see who he was talking to, I noticed that Anthony, the last person I'd seen with Margo before her murder, was standing outside of the classroom, looking in. I couldn't tell exactly whom he was making eye contact with, so I scanned the room.

Bridget had stopped stirring her rice and was staring at him, but her face was a blank. I realized that he was looking at the woman with the rose tattoo. The only reason it became obvious to me was because of her body language, which appeared flirtatious, at least from this angle. You didn't see many women gyrate their hips in a cooking class.

Anthony's line of sight transitioned and it took me a minute to realize he was now looking at me. I could tell that recognition was trying to form in his mind. Then his eyes darted to Bridget and he disappeared from sight.

I watched Bridget furiously begin to stir her rice around the pan.

Without realizing it, I had let my rice sit, and I heard

a cracking sound coming from my workstation. When I looked down, I realized that the flame had been too high and the butter had dried out, leaving my rice stuck to the pan.

Kimmy looked over at the burner and giggled. "Even fried rice you mess up. Are you sure you're Asian?"

I scowled at her and removed my pan from the burner. "Shut up, Kimmy, just shut up."

Once everyone was finished with the cooking portion of the class, it was time for us to sample our own work, and I would be going hungry that night. My distraction had led to a predominantly overcooked experiment. I sampled a few bites, but all I could taste was burnt butter and salt.

Kimmy handed me a small serving of fried rice from her pan. "Taste this *A*-plus dish," she said with a sense of pride.

I ate her offering with a scowl.

Stanley called for a break while he set up his cooking island to show us how to make orange chicken. I, of course, had to run to the bathroom, so I scurried away leaving Kimmy to her own devices.

On my way out of the restroom, I noticed the woman with the rose tattoo standing behind one of the brick columns, talking with someone who was out of my line of sight. She was leaning against the brick with her hip jutted outward, and as I neared her position, I thought I heard her giggle.

Before I could get any closer, Bridget stepped in front of me. "Hey there. Sorry about your rice. Maybe the next dish will work out better for you."

My body sagged at the mention of my failed cooking attempt. "Yeah, I was a little distracted. Hey, do you know that lady over there?" I pointed to the woman with the rose tattoo. "She looks familiar."

"Oh her?" Bridget scoffed. "Just another desperate housewife, I'm sure. I mean, could your neckline be any lower?"

"She was in the first class, right?" I knew that she was, but I wanted to see what Bridget would say.

She tilted her head. "Um, yeah. I think. Anyhow, wanna get back in there? I'm excited to get started. Orange chicken is my favorite Chinese dish."

"Yeah, okay," I agreed, sensing I wasn't going to get rid of her. I wanted to see who the woman was talking to, but I couldn't think of an excuse to ditch Bridget.

We walked back into the room together, and I spotted Stanley and Kimmy talking to each other near our cooking station. When Kimmy and I made eye contact, I saw her shush Stanley, and he turned around to acknowledge Bridget and me.

"Hey there, Lana," Stanley said with a wave. "Kimmy and I were just catching up."

Bridget smiled politely and shimmied her way between the cooking stations to sit back down. She didn't seem to be too interested in our conversation.

"Good to see you, Stanley," I said. "It's been a while."

"Right? Since that craziness with the noodle contest."

His eyes rolled toward the ceiling. "Absolute madness. Glad things have settled down for everyone."

"Uh-huh," I replied. Things hadn't really settled down for me, but I wasn't going to point that out at this particular point in time.

We exchanged a few more pleasantries about the restaurant business and then he asked how my family was doing. I confirmed that everyone was doing just fine, and then he excused himself to continue the class.

The entire group huddled around the main cooking island just as we had during Margo's class. I wasn't paying the slightest bit of attention because I was too preoccupied watching the woman with the rose tattoo and how she was acting. Didn't seem as if she cared much either because her attention kept traveling to the door. When I turned around to see what Bridget was doing, I noticed she was staring at the woman just as I had been.

The hour of demonstration ended, and I was relieved because I was becoming very restless and my legs were starting to hurt from standing in the same place. Kimmy and I planned to rush out of the class and head straight to the art studio where we'd attempt to interrogate Phyllis Ubert.

We hurriedly packed our things after Stanley dismissed us and beelined for the door. Stanley called out before we could get away.

Kimmy let out a loud groan. "Oh my god," she exclaimed. "Just go on without me. I'll take care of Stanley."

"Are you sure?"

"Yeah, I'll meet you there. Just go before she can leave."

I nodded in agreement, gave Stanley an apologetic wave as Kimmy distracted him, and rushed out of the room before Bridget could stop me.

CHAPTER
27

- - - - - - - - - - - - - - - -

The art studio was on the second floor, and I rushed up the stairs noting how quickly I lost my breath. I really needed to start working out.

Because I was so distracted by trying to find the classroom, according to its placement on the map, I wasn't paying attention to where I was walking and ran right into the lady with the rose tattoo, stepping on her foot.

She yelped, and a curse word flew from her now cherry-painted lips. "Ow! Watch it!"

"Sorry," I said, taking a step back. "I'm so sorry."

She glared at me, but softened when she realized who I was. "Oh, it's you. What's your rush, honey? There's no fire."

"I, um, needed to catch someone before they left for the night. Sorry, again. I hope I didn't hurt your foot."

"Don't sweat it, honey. But look, don't apologize so much. It's unattractive on a woman, you know? Just say sorry once and move on. Especially with a man."

I tried to appear appreciative of her advice. "Thanks, I'll keep that in mind."

"Also, you may want to practice your cooking skills, darlin'. You know what they say, the way to a man's heart is through his stomach." She gave me a wink, patted me on the shoulder, and moved past me to descend the stairs.

Someone else in recent history had said those same words to me. I mean, I knew it was a common expression, but how many people actually say it?

I shook the thought away because I didn't have time to worry about it, and continued to look for the art studio. The room was listed as 205 on the program, which was to the left of the staircase. The door was open, and I could see a woman with wild curly black hair gathering open paint containers and straightening up her work area.

When I stepped farther into the room, I noticed a straggler student packing up their things. The curly haired woman lifted her head when she realized I'd entered the room. "Hello, can I help you?"

She had on thick glasses with large black frames that reminded me of the 1950s musician Buddy Holly. A floral-print scarf was tied in her hair, though it didn't seem to serve the purpose of keeping her hair out of her face.

"Are you Phyllis Ubert?"

She nodded, straightening up and abandoning her

paint supplies. "Yes, that's me. My class for this semester is full if that's what you're wondering."

"Actually, I was here about—" I stopped, glancing to the student who was loitering nearby. "Margo Han," I continued in a lower voice.

Phyllis looked over at the student, then toward the door, and signaled me with her eyes to step out of the room. I followed her to a remote corner in the corridor right outside her class.

"Now, what's this about?" she asked, scrutinizing me. "Are you a family member?"

Taking a moment, I considered lying about who I really was. But it wasn't a risk I was currently willing to take. Should she find out that I wasn't who I said I was, she could end up reporting me to the police and I'd look more suspicious than ever. I opted for the truth, and as calmly as possible, introduced myself and told her the story from start to finish about my involvement in finding Margo's body.

She cradled her chin in the palm of her hand, and stared at the floor as I spoke. She didn't comment in between my pauses, and when I was finished, she took a few minutes to reply. "Well, Miss Lee, as luck would have it, I'm not a fan of the police . . . actually any law enforcement really, but that's a story for another day. Which is a good thing for you because had I been someone else, I might have taken this wackadoo story right to the cops."

I swallowed back some anxiety and tried to appear humble. "I know it sounds pretty crazy."

"Oh, it's beyond crazy, my friend," she said, brushing

some curly strands from her cheek. "But I'm more apt to believe what you're saying instead of that crackpot detective who's been running around here interrogating everyone about that poor janitor."

"You mean Robert Larkin?" I asked.

"Yeah, that poor SOB," she said with a shake of her head. "He's just trying to get his life together. Margo really felt sorry for him, and she'd go out of her way to be nice to the man any chance she got. If anyone could even dream of killing someone who was that nice to them, they'd be crazy."

"So, you don't think he's capable of doing anything to harm her?"

Phyllis laughed. "Not at all. But do you want to know who I think is capable of being a total slimeball and murderer?"

She said it kind of on the loud side and I flinched, reflexes causing me to glance over my shoulder. "Please tell me."

"That scumbag, Anthony Bianco . . . that jerk."

My mouth dropped. "The Italian instructor?"

"Oh, so you're familiar with that sleazeball? I'd bet my money on his guilt any day."

"You clearly have no love for the man. Can I ask why?"

"He's a Casanova for sure. I hope you understand that reference."

"I've heard it once or twice," I replied.

"I'm pretty sure he cheats on his wife with half the students that sign up for his course. He gives tutoring lessons off the clock, if you catch my drift."

My stomach sank. Anthony was the last person—to my knowledge—to see Margo alive, and everything started to fall into place. The photos, the note, him stopping by the class the night she was murdered. He had to be the man in the photos. But who was the woman he'd been having a "study jam" with?

"Do you know who his current mistress is?" I asked.

"Ha, try that sentence again in plural," she said with disgust. "Like what kind of man does that sort of thing? What kind of example is he setting for his family?"

"Does he have kids? I've seen him around and he doesn't look like any kind of dad to me."

"He's not. He has a stepdaughter. His wife, Caroline, is a real pleasant woman. Any time we have a work function, she comes and is all smiles, even though she's gotta know her husband is a total rat. Anyhow, she brought her daughter a few times—she's grown, of course. I think her name is Brittany, or Brandy, something like that."

My throat dried. "Bridget . . . would that be her name?"

She smacked her head. "Bridget, yeah that's it. I'll tell ya, your memory starts to go faster than you'd think. But yeah . . . beautiful girl, looks just like her mom."

I thanked her tremendously for the info and asked her to keep our conversation between the two of us. She agreed wholeheartedly and wished me luck with an added warning to be careful of Detective Bishop.

Flying down the stairs to meet up with Kimmy, I checked the cooking room first, wondering what had been holding her up this whole time. She was going to be disappointed that she'd missed my conversation with Phyllis.

I found her and Stanley in a heated debate. Kimmy currently had her index finger in his face and a string of swear words were flying from her mouth just as I entered the room.

"Whoa, whoa, whoa," I said, stepping in between them. "What the heck is going on in here?"

Kimmy huffed. "This jerk won't keep his mouth shut. I tried to tell him we're here on official business, and he can't tell Peter that he saw us, but he won't budge."

Closing my eyes, I pinched the bridge of my nose, and took a deep breath. *Patience, Lana.* "Stanley, it's really important that you not breathe a word of this to our families, or to Peter. It could cause a lot of problems."

"No way," Stanley said with a laugh. "And miss out on telling everyone that I schooled Lana Lee on cooking fried rice and she *still* messed it up."

My heartbeat started to quicken. "Fine, what will it take for you to keep your mouth shut?" I asked.

He stopped laughing. "Wait, what?"

"What do you want?" I asked, gesturing with my hand for him to hurry up with a response. "Everybody wants something. What is it that *you* want?"

Kimmy gawked at me. "Don't give this guy anything, Lana. He doesn't deserve it. We have other ways of keeping him quiet."

I rolled my eyes. "No, we really don't."

"Shhh!" Kimmy hissed. "He doesn't know that unless you give it away."

"All right," Stanley said, interrupting us. "How about this. You and Kimmy have to come to my restaurant at least three times a week, one time on the weekends for two whole months. Bring your beaus, the more the merrier." He smiled, clearly taking pride in his offer.

I wasn't going to accept this deal at face value, however. No matter what corner we were backed into. My mother, of course, had taught me how to haggle with the best of them. "Two nights a week, we bring a group of friends, for one month."

Stanley tapped his chin. "One month, two times a week, but you have to bring your hot roommate with you."

Kimmy made gagging noises next to me.

"Megan?" I asked. "She's a manager at the Zodiac and a fill-in bartender. I'm lucky if I get to hang out with her two times a week."

"Okay fine . . . she's gotta come at least one night a week with you . . . as long as she comes you only have to show up for a month."

I extended my hand. "Fine."

"Deal," he said, taking my hand and giving it a firm shake. "See you this weekend."

I grabbed Kimmy's arm and pulled her out of the room before she lay into him again.

She jerked her arm out of my grasp. "I can't believe you just agreed to that, Lana. You didn't even ask me if I'm willing to go along with it."

"Well, you have to, unless you want Peter giving you a hard time about what we're up to. And if my mom finds out I came back to this class, then I'm dead. It's only a month."

"Fine, but you're paying for my drinks."

"Ugh, whatever, let's go. I have a lot to tell you." We exited the building and headed toward our cars. "Can you come to my place? I think it's time for all of us to have a powwow."

Kimmy shrugged. "Sure, I don't have anywhere I need to be."

We got into our respective cars and headed to North Olmsted. I called Megan on the way there to make sure she would be home and warn her that Kimmy would be with me. Thankfully she was off that night, and I told her I'd be there in about twenty minutes, barring traffic.

Right before we hung up, she whispered into the phone, "Be prepared. Adam stopped by unannounced."

CHAPTER
28

Before we went inside, I alerted Kimmy to the fact that Adam had unexpectedly stopped by and how much I had failed to tell him. It was all going to come out now, but I wanted it to come from me, not Kimmy.

She agreed without any convincing, promising to keep quiet until I had relayed the whole story of recent developments. As I unlocked the door, she patted my shoulder and said, "Don't worry, girlfriend, I got your back."

Kikko's head was the first to pop up as I stepped into the apartment. When she realized I had brought a stranger home, she released a series of yips and howls as she flew off the couch to inspect our new visitor. Kimmy opened her hand and turned it palm up for Kikko to sniff. After a few snorts, Kikko must have established that Kimmy was acceptable and gave her thumb a lick.

In the meantime, Adam had risen from his seat on the couch and I couldn't tell by the expression on his face whether he was going to strangle me or kiss me. Megan had been seated at the kitchen table with her laptop open and hadn't bothered to get up.

Adam stood towering over my small frame, looking at me with disappointment. He kissed my forehead without saying anything, though I knew that if we were alone, he probably would have started in on a lecture.

Kimmy stepped forward, squeezing Adam's bicep. "Hey there, Detective Hottie Pants, glad you could join us."

Adam's face reddened and he stammered his response. "N-Nice to see you again, Kimmy."

Despite the amount of stress I was feeling at the moment, I couldn't help but laugh. Kimmy was great at making awkward situations even more uncomfortable, but adding some humor to it at the same time.

Adam had been coined "Detective Hottie Pants" when we first met, and all of my friends knew that if they wanted to give him a rattle, that was the way to do it.

I removed my purse from my shoulder, and hung up my keys. "Well, I don't know about you guys, but I could sure use a drink."

Adam followed behind me to the kitchen. In a low voice meant just for me to hear, he said, "I could use an explanation, Miss Lee."

"Don't worry," I replied. "I'm going to tell you everything tonight."

"It's about time," he said.

Adam and Megan already had beers open, so I worked on fixing some mixed drinks for Kimmy and me. She wasn't a huge fan of whiskey and Cokes, but she'd drink just about anything if it was free.

We all sat at the table, the first time in a long time utilizing all four chairs. Kikko sat at my heels, pawing at my leg, no doubt feeling left out that she wasn't seated at the grown-ups' table. I picked her up and put her in my lap.

There were still parts of the story that Kimmy didn't know, which was everything that I had discussed with Phyllis Ubert. But I needed to start at the beginning of what Adam was missing—which was basically everything that happened since the previous morning.

Trying not to rush, I went over the details of what had transpired. Megan was only partially listening at the beginning since she was basically all caught up. In mid-explanation I'd gone to retrieve my purse and pulled out the card I'd received in the mail for Adam to inspect.

He did so with a sour expression on his face, but allowed me to continue the story without interrupting.

It felt like I had been talking forever by the time I got to the part where I spoke to Phyllis. My throat was feeling scratchy, and I paused to sip my drink.

When I'd finished the complete story, and Kimmy had voiced her opinions of disbelief at the new information, we all took a moment to gather our thoughts in preparation of debate. I'd left out the part about Stanley Gao and our deal for the moment because I felt it wasn't a relevant part of what we needed to accomplish. Megan and Adam would learn about it soon enough.

Adam was the first to speak. "I can't believe you didn't bring any of this up when I texted you." He waved the card and photo at me. "This is pretty important stuff, Lana."

"I know, but I couldn't have you stop me from going back to the school. I knew that I'd learn something useful if I could just get back there, and look . . . we did."

Adam tossed the card and photo onto the table and leaned back, scrubbing his face with both his hands. "You're really turning me gray here, babe."

Kimmy whistled. "Gray hair on men is hot!"

Megan clucked her tongue. "All right, enough comic relief, Tran. Let's be serious. This new information lines things up for us." Megan rested a hand on the greeting card, and pulled it close to inspect it further.

Kimmy held her hands up in defense. "Okay, sorry, Miss Killjoy."

Megan opened her mouth to say something, but must have thought better of it and let Kimmy's comment go. I silently thanked her for that.

"We just have one problem," I said to the group. "I still haven't heard back from Sabrina Hartford."

"Who cares?" Kimmy said, dismissing my concern with a wave of her hand. "That girl isn't going to help us with anything."

Megan leaned forward. "She's in danger though. Clearly the person who took the pictures is aware that she knows something she isn't supposed to."

Adam snorted. "If you ask me, she's the one who took the damn pictures to begin with."

"What?" Megan asked with gasp. "You think she's the photographer?"

Adam nodded with confidence. "For the original photo . . . absolutely." He jabbed the giraffe card on the table. "And she's the one who sent this to Lana too. Getting her there was a setup to keep her quiet."

Megan shook her head, unconvinced. "I think she's just an innocent bystander. She's too young and inexperienced to pull this off."

"Lana, what do you think?" Kimmy asked, ignoring the other two's bantering.

I petted Kikko's tiny head and tried to organize the thoughts I'd come up with on my way home. "Three people are in that original photo . . . and two of them are guilty of an affair. The man has got to be Anthony Bianco. If he's having a slew of affairs, then chances are it's him that was caught on camera. And clearly we know that Margo Han is the one who saw Anthony with our unknown mistress."

"Okay . . ." Kimmy said, as she followed along. "But then what? They killed her to keep her quiet?"

"Maybe," I replied. "Anthony would be my best guess, considering I saw him with her last. But it bothers me that she seems disappointed or maybe even sad in the photo of her sitting in the car. Let's say she was involved with him, and he's the secret boyfriend: she would be devastated that he was sleeping with someone else."

Kimmy shook her head. "Man, I wish we had that photo to look at."

"I know, it would be really helpful right about now." I glanced down at my phone, which still had no correspondence from Sabrina. It was nearing ten o'clock and felt a little late to call someone I didn't know. I decided to send her a text message instead. Maybe she was still up. I typed a quick *Call me ASAP. It's urgent.* and set my phone back down with the screen facing up so I could see her response right away.

"You don't think it's weird she hasn't answered you all day?" Adam asked. "After she was seemingly so helpful?"

Megan rolled her eyes. "How can you think this poor girl is so guilty? She's probably scared out of her mind."

"Or . . ." Kimmy interjected, "the killer already got to her."

My stomach sank at the notion. "Let's hope that's not the case. Maybe she's just busy with schoolwork or something."

"So, what now?" Megan asked. "What do we do with a half-baked theory and what about Bridget? Are we going to talk about *that* hot mess?"

Kimmy lifted a hand up to her ear and used her index finger to make a circular motion. "Girl is cuckoo."

Megan scoffed. "Finally, something we agree on."

"I have to admit," I said, "she is beginning to seem a bit off to me, but more than likely, I think that she's aware of her stepfather cheating and trying to catch him in the act or something. From what Phyllis said to me earlier, she thinks that Anthony's wife is aware of his romping around. . . . Maybe Bridget caught on a while ago too?"

Kimmy nodded. "She was staring down that rose-tattooed hussy something pretty fierce."

Adam sighed. "Okay, well, I agree that Bridget may have an idea about her stepfather messin' around, especially if she's going to classes at the learning center. She could have witnessed something."

I gasped. "Do you think *she's* the one taking the photos?"

He folded his arms. "Doubtful, babe. I think if she was the one taking the photos, she could have gotten him in trouble already. I don't think she'd play all these games and just let him continue cheating on her mother."

"Yeah, but what if she was trying to be sneaky about it?" I suggested.

"What would be her purpose in getting Margo Han involved? Seems like a waste. Besides . . . sounds like he's involved with this supposed hussy woman—she'd be the one to go after," Adam said.

Kimmy threw up her hands. "You guys, it's getting late, can we wrap this up? I have to open the shop in the morning. Lana, you need your beauty rest too, no sense in sporting eye bags all day."

I checked the time and it seemed the minutes were flying by. We were already coming up on eleven o'clock.

For about fifteen minutes, we all exchanged some banter on our final conclusions. My ending argument was that Anthony Bianco was the most likely of our suspects to have killed Margo. It made the most sense considering the note that had been included with the photos challenging Margo to whistleblow on his cheating ways. It was obvious that Margo knew about the affair since she was in the photograph, and if the picture had been given to Anthony in a similar matter as a sort of blackmail, then I would gather one of his loose ends was keeping the Asian cooking instructor quiet.

Adam seemed to be coming around to my way of thinking after I'd explained myself further, but he still thought that Sabrina was somehow involved and told me to trust his detective instinct when it came to the helpful intern.

Megan threw a curveball by bringing up Robert Larkin, who I'd let fall to the wayside after Phyllis talked about how kind Margo had been to him, and that he was just a nice man who was misunderstood. However, my best friend didn't seem to think so. "He probably mistook her kindness for romantic interest. Then when she turned him down, he got mad and killed her so no one could have her."

I cocked my head at her. "But what about the photo stuff? Then that wouldn't make any sense."

Megan pursed her lips. "This whole thing could be a coincidence and have nothing to do with the photos. Or!" she said, holding up a finger. "On second thought, maybe Mr. Janitor is the one who took the photos. If she was sad in the photos as you say, maybe he took the photos because she was also sleeping with Anthony Bianco, and Janitor Man knew it and thought if he got the other man out of the picture, Margo would come crawling to him for comfort."

She did have a point, but did I agree that Robert Larkin would kill her so no one could have her? That I wasn't sure on quite yet.

Kimmy surprised me by suggesting that the rose-tattooed woman was the culprit and that it would explain her crappy attitude in Margo's initial class. "Didn't you say she was giving her the death stare throughout the whole two hours? Maybe she's in a better mood now that she knocked out her competition."

I tried to envision the middle-aged rocker-esque woman stabbing Margo Han in the back. I wasn't sure I could fully buy into it, but at this point, anything was possible. It would have really helped if we could see the woman in the photo now and compare it to the memory of our strawberry blonde friend.

We said goodnight to Kimmy and watched her get into her car. Megan shut off her laptop and announced that she would be calling it a night as well. She claimed the ping-pong of all our speculations had given her a headache.

I said goodnight to my best friend before retiring to my bedroom with Adam lagging behind and Kikko racing me to get there first.

Sleep came quickly and I was relieved that I made it through the night without any bad dreams to wake me up. I checked my phone as soon as I was coherent and to my disappointment, I had no return messages or calls from our missing intern.

It was only eight in the morning, and I was just about

to see Adam off when I decided to call Sabrina one more time. She was a college student, so I assumed she would be awake, getting ready for class, or she was already at school. I planned on leaving her a very curt voice mail about how rude it was to not return calls when someone says there's an emergency.

The phone didn't ring and immediately went to a recording. I held the phone away from my head so Adam could hear as well. *"I'm sorry, but the number you are trying to reach is disconnected. If you have received this message in error, please hang up and try your call again."*

I hung up the phone, and stood staring openmouthed at Adam.

Knowing him well enough by now, I could tell that he was trying his best to remain mature, and not throw an "I told you so" in my face. Instead, he went for a milder version, and said, "Now what was it you were saying about Sabrina being an innocent bystander?"

CHAPTER
29

I drove to work in a daze, which isn't the best way to function during rush-hour traffic, but my saving grace was that I didn't need to take the freeway to get to work.

I couldn't stop thinking about Sabrina's disconnected cell phone and wondering if Adam had been right all along. Had the seemingly helpful intern been playing me this whole time? Adam, of course, thought so and assumed that no one had been following us and secretly taking pictures. He had a hunch that perhaps it was staged, and Sabrina knew that the picture was being taken. She had shown up before me and picked the table. Was it strategic?

When I got to the plaza and was safely tucked away in Ho-Lee Noodle House, I contemplated reaching out to Detective Bishop to inform him of what had developed since I last saw him. My only worry was that somehow this whole thing was going to make me look even guiltier. And then would he try and get me on ob-struction of justice since I was technically holding onto information?

Well, at the very least, I could inform him that I now knew who the mystery man was that I saw with Margo right before she was killed. I concluded that I should take the chance. Once I had gotten everything situated at the restaurant, I could slip into my office and give him a call.

I wouldn't tell him about the note or photos just yet. I had another class the following evening, and maybe sometime before then I would come up with a solid plan of action. If I could confirm my suspicions somehow and actually assist in solving the case, maybe Detective Bishop would be a little more lenient with me.

Before Sabrina went missing, it was my hope that she'd be the one to uncover all the pertinent details to the grouchy detective.

As I straightened up the restaurant, using my most critical eye to search for imperfections, I began to won-der why Sabrina would show me the photos to begin with. What would she have to gain by doing this? Was she trying to implicate me? If I knew about the pho-tos along with her, then I couldn't turn anyone over to the cops . . . especially with the damning photo of us meeting at the Irish pub.

Peter arrived ten minutes later, tapping the drum line to a Metallica song on the window. I opened the door, still lost in thought, trying to make sense of the infor-mation I had.

He noticed immediately, and when I turned back

around from shutting the door behind him, he was staring me down. "Fess up, Lana," he said. "I know you and Kimmy were up to something you weren't supposed to be doing last night. I wanna know what it was—and tell the truth, because I know when you're lying."

I didn't have the mental capacity to come up with anything clever this morning and I really just wanted to be left alone with my scattered thoughts. "Peter, it's better if you just drop it for now." I sulked away, feeling discouraged that I couldn't get my brain to function better than it was. Something had to click for me at some point.

"It's something to do with that teacher lady who got murdered, isn't it? You're involved with it somehow, aren't you?"

"No," I said plainly.

"Yes, you are. I know you, Lana. Just come out with it."

I whipped around, agitated with his persistent prodding. "Okay fine. I am, all right? That detective who was here last week has his eye on me and some janitor I don't even know. And if I don't do something about it, then who knows what will happen?"

Peter was stunned by my response and took a moment to collect himself. "See? Why couldn't you just tell me that?"

I let out a frustrated sigh. "Whatever, Peter. Because you get all holier than thou when I tell you what I'm up to. I can't confide in you when it comes to this stuff."

"Oh gee, sorry. Sorry that I care about your general safety and whatever." He threw his hands in the air.

"You and Kimmy, man, always making me out to be the bad guy. I just care. So, *whatever.*" And he stormed off into the kitchen without giving me a chance to respond.

Originally, I had planned on going into my office until I unlocked the doors for the day, but I didn't want to run into him and give him the chance to snap at me when I passed through the kitchen. I stayed at the hostess station and waited for nine o'clock.

The Matrons arrived promptly, and Helen seemed more excited than usual to see me. "Lana, do we have good news for you!" she boasted as they headed to their table. "We have found out some information that will help with Margo Han."

I followed behind them, my heart doing a little pitter-patter with the promise of a missing puzzle piece finally presenting itself. "And?" I asked, practically on the balls of feet, ready to hop up and down. "What did you ladies find out?"

The four women sat down, taking a few moments to get situated. You could tell that all four of them knew what I wanted to know, but it was Helen's privilege to start the story.

"Margo Han was having an affair with a married man!" Helen practically screeched with excitement. Thankful for all of us that the restaurant was otherwise empty, or we might sound like a bunch of lunatics excited about someone's damaged marriage.

"Aha!" I yelled. "I knew she looked sad in the photo."

The four women exchanged confused expressions.

"What does this mean, Lana?" Wendy asked for the group. "What photo?"

I explained about the photo and how Margo had seemed sad after seeing the couple's rendezvous. "The photo must have caught her finding out for the first time that he was cheating on her as well."

Opal continued the story. "You are correct. We also learned that she was no longer seeing him because she found out that she was not the only one. In recent months, she had become very sad and kept her distance from many people."

I shook my head in disbelief. "How did you manage to find this out?"

Helen beamed. "We ran into Julie Peterson at Asian Accents."

"Who's that?" I asked, unfamiliar with the name.

"Julie is the wife of John Peterson who is also a teacher at the learning center you went to. He is friends with Anthony B-B . . . how do you say?"

"Bianco?" I offered.

"Yes, this is the man. He is good friends with John and told him a story about Margo. He is so stupid," Helen said, clearly disgusted.

"Yah," Wendy agreed. "He tells John, and John's wife is Chinese. He doesn't think maybe they could know each other? *Only* two Chinese teachers in the whole school, and he does not think this?"

The four ladies shook their head making tsking sounds.

I felt rejuvenated by this confirmation, and headed into the kitchen with some extra pep to grab their tea and place their order. Peter was still agitated with me, and barely grumbled an acknowledgment when I told him the Matrons had arrived. But I didn't let it get to me. I felt justification that I had been right about the secret boyfriend being Anthony Bianco.

But the question that had been mystifying all of us involved popped back up yet again: *So now what?*

In my spare time after the Matrons left, still feeling mighty proud of themselves as they walked out the door, I texted Megan to update her on what I knew. This only cemented her belief that Robert Larkin had taken the photo to upset Margo and win her over. And though it was possible, I was now convinced that Anthony had to be our likeliest suspect. He obviously had been there right before Margo died. I'd seen him with my own two eyes.

But playing devil's advocate with myself, I couldn't ignore the fact that Robert Larkin had come to my rescue pretty fast. Was it possible that he'd just doubled back? How close had I been to actually witnessing the murder? I'd never stepped foot into the room, so it's not like I knew if her body was warm or if she'd been like that since I'd left the first time.

The Matrons information definitely helped solidify the story, but there were still missing pieces. Had it been Anthony who had taken matters into his own hands? Or was it the unknown female in the photo? It would seem those two people had the most to lose, and everything to gain, from Margo's death.

I pondered these questions while I served the few people who had come in for a light breakfast. When

Nancy arrived, I burrowed away in my office just so I could think. I twirled around in my chair, trying to let my mind relax and wander on its own.

The original picture would be really helpful right now, and I couldn't let it go. But it was useless to keep obsessing over it, considering that the person who had it was now missing.

I thought about that for a moment too, still wondering what role Sabrina played in this whole thing. If she was the photographer, what purpose would it be for her to bring the photos to me in the first place? Sure, as Adam said, she could very likely have done it to implicate me, but why, when she could just burn the photos? Was she worried that Anthony and the unknown woman would share their copies with someone? But why would they? They would then be implicated themselves. It would be better off to eliminate evidence of the photos completely. After all, one of the witnesses to the affair was already dead.

That thought sounded an alarm in my brain. One witness to the affair *was* already dead. And the person who had the photos meant for Margo in their possession was now missing. If you eliminated the person who took the photos, there would be no one left to blab.

Trying to get into the mind of the unknown photographer, I thought about what their original purpose might have been. Surely, the photo had gone to Anthony—who had to be the man caught on camera—then possibly a copy went to the mystery woman, and then, of course, intended delivery to Margo.

Assuming that Anthony would come to the same

conclusion—that Margo knew about the photographs—he may have approached her that evening to find out what she planned to do about it. Then when she tells him she doesn't know what he's talking about, he becomes enraged and ends up killing her to keep her quiet.

The only loose end I couldn't figure out is how would he know that Sabrina had the photos? Of course, I was assuming that she had been taken against her will. And that didn't really fly with the fact that her phone had been disconnected. Without knowing her role in this whole thing for sure, I was at a loss.

I slapped my desk. "This doesn't make any sense!"

Supposing that Adam was right, and Sabrina had intentionally brought me into the middle of this, what would her endgame be?

Massaging my temples, I went through my meeting with her one more time, walking myself through the motions of getting out of the car and then entering the pub. I could see Sabrina trying to hand me the photos, me rejecting to pick them up, and her spreading them out on the table for me to review.

I tried to remember our conversation to the best of my ability, but nothing struck me as odd or damning against her. I recalled thinking she was innocent and could almost hear her complaining about getting the photos to begin with.

That's when it struck me. I'd forgotten about the end of our conversation. She'd mentioned to me that she'd checked some kind of logbook at work to compare the handwriting from the note with samples of the faculty's handwriting. She hadn't found anything similar. But all of that had slipped my mind, and now I wondered if I'd been sitting on the perfect clue this entire time.

Quickly, I dug in my purse and found the torn piece of receipt that I'd received not too long ago. I assessed the handwriting, which was all in caps, just like the greeting card I had stashed away with my detective notebook.

But I had to be sure that I wasn't creating this theory out of thin air. I had to get home and compare the two side by side. If I was right about this, it meant I knew exactly who the photographer was—and if I could figure that out, then Anthony probably could too.

I grabbed the deposit bag off my desk, shoved it in my purse, and sprinted up front. There was hardly anyone in the restaurant, and as I checked the clock I noted that it was only a little after twelve.

"Hey, I have to run out, it's kind of important. I'm going to swing by the Tran's shop and see if Kimmy can help you if there's a lunch rush."

Nancy scanned me over, her lips curved in a frown. "What's wrong? Should I call your mother?"

"No, no, nothing like that. I just have to get something I left at home. I'll be really quick, I promise."

She nodded in agreement and I exited the restaurant heading straight for the Tran's shop. I gave Kimmy a quick rundown of what I was doing, and asked if she could help Nancy should a lunch rush bombard the restaurant out of nowhere. Kimmy accepted. "Sure, my dad's in the back room taking inventory. You go. I'll head over to the restaurant after I tell him where I'm going."

"Thanks!" I yelled over my shoulder. "Be back soon!"

"Let me know what happens," she hollered back.

I raced to my car, took a deep breath, and reminded myself not to speed home. I couldn't afford to get a ticket just as I was about to add an important puzzle piece to this case.

CHAPTER

30

It took everything I had in me not to slam my foot on the gas pedal and speed my way down the length of Center Ridge Road. I tried calling Megan on my way home to see if she was still around, but there was no answer. Normally she was up by now, so I couldn't imagine she was so dead asleep that she wouldn't hear her cell phone ringing.

Minding the speed limit, I still managed to make it home in record time, and I flung myself out of the car feeling the anxiety pump through my body.

I unlocked the door, catching my dog off guard with my arrival. She jerked her head up from a curled position on the couch. Just as she opened her mouth to bark, she realized that it was only me barging in. Unimpressed with my surprise return, she lowered her head again, most likely annoyed that I had interrupted her daily nap.

I scurried into my room and stuck my hand under the mattress, digging out my notebook and removing the envelope I had stuck in the middle. My hands were shaking uncontrollably, and I scolded myself to pull it together.

Finally getting the card out of the envelope, I opened it and placed the photo of Sabrina and me off to the side so I could study the writing. I set the envelope down with my name and address on it, put it next to the card, and then retrieved the torn receipt out of my purse.

I studied the handwriting, and reread the message to myself: NEXT TIME, SMILE FOR THE CAMERA.

I compared the *E*s first, since that was used most frequently and was also on the receipt. The *I*s were the same as well, and included a curved flourish at the bottom of each letter.

There was no mistake. The person who had written the card was the same person who had jotted down their name and phone number on the receipt.

And that person was Bridget Hastings.

I practically jumped up and down at my newfound discovery. Bridget Hastings had been the photographer, catching her stepfather in the act of his illicit affairs. And then, she must have thought involving Margo would work in her favor. But what exactly did she assume would come from that? Did Bridget want Margo to be the one to tell her mother, so she didn't have to? On the other hand, why not just send the photos to the learning center and get the guy fired? Wouldn't that have been more effective at hurting him and ruining his reputation? It definitely would have made his cheating more public.

Clearly there was something I still didn't understand.

Now that I knew Bridget was the photographer of the affair photos and the photo of Sabrina and me, I had to wonder what her angle was in sending me the card.

She'd been at the pub that day, taking photos of Sabrina and me. How would she know that we were even there? Now Adam's theory of Sabrina being involved was starting to ring true.

It perhaps started involuntarily. Bridget must have realized that she unknowingly implicated Sabrina by putting the photos in the wrong locker. I envisioned a discussion taking place where they figured out I was involved, and Bridget requested Sabrina's help in setting me up.

Bridget, after all, had tried to spark my interest in Margo's murder from the very beginning. She probably also had come to the conclusion that her stepfather had killed Margo, and knowing that it was basically her fault, wanted my help in bringing Anthony to justice. Turning in those photos to the police could have gotten her into trouble for blackmail once her stepfather was questioned. Then not only would the police know about Bridget's involvement, but so would her stepfather. If she had never taken those affair photos to begin with, then Margo might still be alive today. Now Bridget was most likely in danger as well and didn't even realize it. If *I* could figure out that it was her handwriting, wouldn't Anthony be able to figure it out at some point, considering he was her stepfather?

I flopped backward on my bed, and groaned. I closed my eyes and tried counting to ten. I had to let Bridget know that I knew what was going on and warn her that she may be next. And maybe she'd know where Sabrina was.

I picked up the receipt and dialed the number Bridget had given me. There was no answer and a generic voice mail greeting. I left her a message attempting to sound casual so she wouldn't be worried about my confronting her. Obviously, she didn't want me to know that she'd taken the photos or had been watching me at Hooley House.

I got up and went back into the living room, coaxing Kikko to stir from her nap. I might as well take her for a walk while I was home. And maybe the act of walking and being outside would clear my mind and help me think about what to do next concerning Anthony Bianco.

After I put her collar on, the two of us exited the apartment and Kikko, now having livened up, scuttled over to her favorite tree trunk to give it a good sniff. There was a toy fox terrier that had just moved in three apartments down and I suspected that Kikko was excited to mark her territory.

I needed to talk this over with Kimmy, and Megan . . . and probably Adam. Adam could help me figure out what to do in regards to Detective Bishop. Without the original affair photos, it would be difficult to prove that Anthony Bianco would have a motive for killing Margo.

Trying to imagine my conversation with Adam, I ran potential scenarios of what he might say. And I knew without a doubt, the first thing he'd say was, *"There's nothing connecting Anthony to the crime scene besides your word. You were the only one who remembers seeing him talk to Margo that night."*

Then I could see him reminding me that both Sabrina and I had withheld evidence from the police, and that was maybe the only evidence that would convince Bishop of foul play enough to make him look into someone other than Robert Larkin and me.

I cursed the situation, which startled Kikko, and she stared at me as if to say, *"What did I do?"*

Giving her a reassuring coo, I encouraged her to keep sniffing, and we went on our way around the cluster of buildings to the next group of apartments. We spent about twenty minutes ambling around when Kikko decided she was ready to return home for more nap time.

As I removed her leash and pulled out her bag of treats, I convinced myself that what I needed was a confession from Anthony Bianco. But just exactly how was I going to pull that off?

Getting into the car, I sat for a minute before turning the engine on. My mind was moving a thousand miles a minute. Though I had more information than I'd had this morning, it still wasn't enough to come completely clean with Detective Bishop. In the excitement of everything going on earlier that morning, I'd never gotten the chance to call him like I'd planned to.

I turned the car on, checking the time. I decided to make a pit stop before heading back to Asia Village.

* * *

As I trudged along down Ridge Road, I realized the error of my ways. Thinking there wasn't going to be much traffic on the way to Parma was a mistake I'd never make again. But I was almost there and had to keep going at this point. To calm my nerves, I practiced the apology I would recite to Nancy upon my return to the noodle house.

I finally pulled into the parking lot of the Parma police station and let out a heavy sigh. *Here we go, Lana.*

Stepping into the vestibule, I reminded myself to breathe normally and to remember that I was, in fact, an innocent person trying to be a good citizen. There was no reason to appear as if I'd been caught with my hand in the proverbial cookie jar.

A woman, slightly older than myself, with her hair in a French braid that looked as if it was tugging at her scalp, stared up at me as I approached the plexiglass partition that separated us.

Her muted voice came through the slot at the bottom of the plastic wall. "Can I help you?"

"Yes, I was wondering if I could speak with Detective Bishop? My name is Lana Lee, and I wanted to update something on a statement I recently gave for a murder investigation."

She sized me up, appearing unimpressed with my professional adult voice. With little emotion, she gestured to a grouping of chairs across from her counter. "Have a seat. I'll see if the detective is available."

I smiled a thanks, and turned to see the cluster of

chairs that had undoubtedly seated several a nervous visitor.

Feeling the tension in my throat, I cleared it—perhaps a little too loudly—and the dispatcher flicked her eyes up at me with what I couldn't deny as annoyance.

I folded my hands in my lap and circled my thumbs anxiously one around the other, trying to make as little noise as possible so as not to gain her attention. Though she hadn't gotten up from her seat, I didn't imagine her to be much bigger than myself. However, I still wouldn't want be caught alone with her in a dark alley.

A few minutes later, I heard a door open, and footsteps coming in my direction. I turned around to see the detective approaching me with papers in one hand and a pen in the other.

I stood when he'd reached my seat. "Hello, Detective Bishop."

"Miss Lee," he replied with a nod.

"Sorry to bother you midday, but I didn't think I should wait any longer."

"My dispatcher told me that you had an addition to make to your statement."

"Yes," I replied. "You see, I—"

He thrust the paper and pen at me. "No need to recite it to me verbatim, Miss Lee. Writing it down on this form will be satisfactory. I have some things to attend to. Why don't you go ahead and turn this into the dispatcher when you're finished. I'll call you if I have any questions."

I pursed my lips at his dismissal, but let's face it, I wasn't going to talk back to an officer of the law. I forced a smile. "Sure thing, Detective." I took the pen and paper from him and sat back down.

He left without saying anything further.

Detective Bishop hadn't bothered with a clipboard, so I awkwardly knelt at the coffee table that was centered between the chairs. It was too far away from the seat to be of use, and I didn't want to drag it across the linoleum and annoy the dispatcher further.

I quickly scribbled down the information about finding the identity of Anthony Bianco, and emphasized that he was the last known person to be seen with Margo Han while she was still alive.

I capped the pen and rose from my crouched position, taking the paper over to the counter where the dispatcher had been eyeballing me. "All finished then?"

I nodded and slid the paper and pen through the slot.

She took them from me and wished me a nice day.

I'd made it halfway through the parking lot when I heard a man's voice yell, "Hey!"

Turning around, I saw that it was Detective Bishop, and he was jogging toward me with a frown on his face and what I assumed to be my new report clutched in his hand.

I met his frown with one of my own, but let him speak first.

"Are you kidding me with this?" he said, shaking the paper in his fist. "I distinctly remember telling you to stay out of it. But you can't seem to follow instructions."

"Well, I didn't do it on purpose," I lied. "I was signing up for a new class, and I ran into him while I was there. I learned his name and figured you should know who he was. It could help the investigation."

He scowled. "First of all, Miss Lee, I don't need your help in solving a murder investigation. *I'm* the trained professional in this scenario. Not *you*."

"I never said I was," I replied. It came out timidly, but I hadn't meant it to.

"Second of all, I hope you understand how serious it is for you to try and falsely incriminate someone else. I don't have time to play games with you, and this smells of you trying to throw me off."

"I would never do such a thing," I said, feeling my face warm. "I really just want to help, Detective."

"More like help take the attention off you and that janitor, Larkin." He jabbed the papers in my direction. "Mark my words, Miss Lee, if I find out at all that this is fabricated in any way, I will make sure that you see the inside of a jail cell for obstruction."

I stood staring at him as he challenged me with his eyes to say something else. I didn't. With satisfaction, he spun on the heel of his cheap dress shoes and stormed back into the building.

This time, I knew it was a threat, and I didn't think anyone else would mistake it for anything less.

CHAPTER

31

Rushing back to Asia Village feeling frazzled, I worried less about the speed limit when I realized just how long I'd been gone. I still needed to stop at the bank, and fortunately it was on my way back to the plaza, so I didn't have to go out of the way.

I was no longer concerned with being followed because I knew the only person it would be was Bridget, and I needed to talk with her anyway. Where was a stalker when you needed one?

When I returned to Ho-Lee Noodle House, I found Kimmy and Nancy lounging at the hostess station having what appeared to be an amusing chat. I watched the two women and wondered if one day, Nancy would be Kimmy's mother-in-law.

I glanced around the dining area and noted that only two tables were filled, and they were both in mid-meal. I approached the women, trying to appear as if I weren't out of breath, and laughed. "Well, looks like my worries about a lunch rush weren't necessary after all."

Kimmy gestured to the two tables of customers. "These are the first people to come in since you left. It's been pretty slow in the plaza all week, really. I'm not that surprised."

Nancy nodded in agreement. "It's this nice weather we're having. Everyone likes to be outside. Pretty soon, it will be too late to get some sunshine."

The three of us acknowledged the truth in that statement, and then Nancy excused herself while she went to check on our customers. When she was out of earshot, Kimmy grabbed my arm and steered me toward the lobby area so we couldn't be overheard. "Where have you been? You took forever."

I filled her in on my impromptu visit with Detective Bishop.

"Damn," she replied. "You might have just made it worse for yourself, Lee. I wish you would have told me you were going, I would have talked you out of it."

"It's too late now," I said with a sigh.

"Well, forget about that for now. We have other things to think about it. What happened with the handwriting? Did they match?"

"They did," I told her. "And I think Bridget could be in danger."

"Okay, so what are we waiting for? Let's go take down Anthony Bianco ourselves. Forget that stupid Detective Bishop. We've got this handled."

I huffed. "We can't do that. Technically we don't have concrete proof."

"Yeah, but he was there that night and he's probably the one we want anyways," Kimmy said. "We can try and get him to confess somehow and record it on our phones. Then you can take that evidence to Bishop."

"And how do you suppose we'd get someone to confess to committing murder? Maybe if we had the photos, we could use that angle, but with no evidence to go on, we just sound like crazy people. Then he'd probably call the cops on us, and Bishop's hopes of getting me into a jail cell would become a reality."

Kimmy threw her hands up. "Well damn. I don't know what else we can do, Lana. We're so close to getting this damn guy. You're right there, if only we had that picture to prove he was into some shady stuff, then we'd be set. We could really use that Sabrina chick right about now. Hell, if she had just gone to the cops with the photo, there'd be no need to implicate ourselves in the snooping around we've done."

"That's what Adam said too. That's why he thinks she's guilty of something. But now all I think is that she's guilty of helping Bridget suck me into this mess."

"Okay, we have to come up with something. Let's do this. Obviously, we're both stuck working for the time being. Let's finish our shifts, think of a plan before the end of the day, and then we can get together after work to figure out what our next step should be."

With a sigh, I concurred, and she left the restaurant wishing me a speedy afternoon.

* * *

One of the conclusions I came up with that I couldn't work around was that we needed evidence of the three photos that started this mess. If Bridget called me back, I could set up a time to meet, confront her, and ask her for the originals. She had to have kept a copy for herself. Maybe she could shed some light on where the heck Sabrina had been hiding too.

I also considered that Kimmy and I may need to get back up to the school and find some information on Sabrina. I doubted that anyone in the administration office would give me personal details about an intern, but maybe I could play the part of cousin again.

My mind drifted back to Robert Larkin and I wondered if there was any way he could be of help. Being a staff member, he may be able to get what I needed to track down Sabrina.

Around quarter past five, my mother and grandmother strolled into the restaurant, and I held back the urge to scream. I'd forgotten all about our intended shopping trip for that evening.

I had to figure out a way to get rid of them as quickly as possible. I had about fifteen minutes before I was supposed to meet Kimmy.

"Oh hey, Mom," I said casually. "What are you doing here?"

My mother's eyes widened. "What do you mean what am I doing here?" She sauntered up to the hostess podium giving me her best mom glare. "We are going shopping tonight. Did you forget about Mommy already?"

"I thought you said tomorrow," I said, smacking my forehead. "I already have plans tonight."

She clucked her tongue at me. "No, no, tonight. We are going tonight. We are already here," she said, waving a hand of dismissal at me and storming toward the kitchen.

My grandmother shrugged at me, smiled, and followed after my mother.

"Crap," I mumbled. "Now what do I do?"

Hopping off my stool, I went into the back to somehow convince my mother that tonight was not going to work. I found her and my grandmother in the kitchen, chatting with Peter.

"Mom," I said, interrupting their conversation. "Really, I can't do tonight. You told me Thursday so that's what I had planned."

My mother wagged a finger at me. "I am getting old, but not that old, Lana. I know we said we would go today. Now go get your purse, it is almost time to go."

"It's my fault," Peter blurted out.

We both turned to him, equally surprised.

"What is your fault, Peter?"

He let out a theatrical huff and bobbed his head back and forth. "I didn't want to tell you, but Kimmy and I are having problems and Lana is trying to help us. I need to pick out a really good present to win back Kimmy before it's too late."

If I could have started clapping, I would have. Peter knew this was exactly the sort of thing my mother would cave for—the man admitting that he had erred.

My mother assessed him. "If this is true, maybe I should help too."

"No, Mom," I said, taking a step forward and putting a hand on her shoulder. "That would probably embarrass Peter. It's better if it's just the two of us."

My mother looked to Peter for confirmation.

He nodded. "Yeah, Mama Lee, it would be too weird. Can I just borrow Lana tonight, and then I promise even I will make her go shopping with you tomorrow." His eyes slid toward me.

"Okay, okay," my mother said, throwing her hands in the air. "You young people go do young people things." She relayed the story to my grandmother who nodded and declared, "Buffet!"

My mother accepted the suggestion and they said their goodbyes.

Peter and I stood in the kitchen, silent and maybe waiting for the other to speak.

"Thank you," I whispered.

"Yeah, yeah, you owe me."

CHAPTER
32

I met up with Kimmy after work and told her about what had happened with my mom showing up and Peter saving the day.

"Wow," Kimmy replied. "I'm totally surprised by that."

"Me too. He told me that I owed him, so I'm sure I'll have to deal with that later, but I can worry about that another day. Right now, we have more pressing issues to be concerned with."

"So, what's the game plan?"

"Well, Bridget hasn't called me back yet. I sent her a text message to let her know that it's me calling her in case she didn't recognize the number or listen to the message. I don't know what she does for work, so maybe she's busy right now. In the meantime, we need to head to Barton's and see if we can find out about Sabrina."

We decided to drive together, so we could hash things

out on the way over. I filled her in on the rest of the plan, which was to get some contact information on Sabrina by pretending to be a family member.

Kimmy agreed it was a good course of action. "Maybe I should be the cousin this time though. You didn't do very good with your last acting performance."

The parking lot at Barton's was practically full, so it was good we'd driven together. There was a spot toward the back of the lot, and I hurriedly parked the car before anyone else could come by and take it.

Classes must have just been starting because there were a ton of students in the common area. We made our way through the maze of people ambling around, and stopped in front of the administration office. Both of us shocked by what we saw through the windows.

It was Sabrina Hartford.

She was unfortunately sitting next to Grumpy Pants, and I dreaded having to acknowledge the woman's presence. Kimmy agreed to go into the administration office without me and ask Sabrina to come out and talk with us.

My blood was boiling. Here I was worried about the slim possibility that she had been kidnapped and there she was acting as if today were just another day. Now I was convinced without a shadow of a doubt that she was working with Bridget Hastings. The sneaky little rats.

A few minutes later, Kimmy came out of the administration office with Sabrina in tow. I reminded myself to keep cool because we were in public and I couldn't afford an outburst with Grumpy Pants in the immediate vicinity. Knowing my luck, she'd have me escorted out of the building.

As Sabrina approached me, appearing rather confused, I folded my arms across my chest, and gave her the best look of disapproval I could muster. "Well, what do you have to say for yourself, young lady?"

"Huh?" she asked, her upper lip curling. "What do I have to say for myself? Nothing?"

"Where the heck have you been?" I asked. "My friend Kimmy and I were looking for you the other day and they said you were a no call, no show."

"Oh, I had food poisoning the other day," she explained. "I sent them an e-mail letting them know I wasn't coming in because I forgot to pay my cell-phone bill and it got shut off. They just never checked the e-mail box."

Kimmy blew a raspberry. "Likely story."

Sabrina's mouth dropped. "I'm telling the truth. I swear. My phone is turned back on, and if you really want, I can show you the e-mail I sent to the supervisor."

I pulled out my phone. "So, you're telling me that if I call you right now, that your cell phone would ring."

She reached into her back pocket and pulled out her phone, showing it to me. "Yeah, go ahead."

I found her number in my recent history and tapped the CALL icon. Sure enough, the phone in her hand began to ring.

"*Now* do you believe me?" She tucked her phone back into her pocket. "Now what the heck is all of this about? Why are you acting so crazy?"

"I've been trying to get ahold of you to let you know that I got a photo of us at Hooley House that day. It was sent to my work."

She covered her face with her hands. "Ugh, I know, I got one too."

"You could have told me—" I paused. "Wait, did you just say you got one too?"

Sabrina uncovered her face. "Yeah, it was sent here to the administration office. Scared the crap out of me."

"Hang on," Kimmy said, holding up her hand. "Aren't you working with Bridget Hastings?"

"Bridget Hastings?" Sabrina exclaimed. "Who the heck is Bridget Hastings?"

A voice behind us interrupted our conversation. "Okay, I know I heard my name. Lana, is that you?"

I whipped around to see that Bridget was only about three feet away from where we were standing. "Bridget, oh my god, I tried getting a hold of you earlier today. I really need to talk to you."

She nodded apologetically. "Sorry I didn't get back to you, it's been a busy day. I planned to call you later tonight."

Sabrina gawked at all of us. "Hey, are we done here? I need to get back to work before you-know-who lays into me."

My eyes drifted over to the administration office where we were being watched by Grumpy Pants herself. We made eye contact and she gave me a scowl before turning back to the paperwork she held in her hands.

"Sure, sorry," I said. "We can finish talking about this later. Keep your phone handy."

Sabrina nodded and said goodbye, rushing back into the office.

"Lana," Bridget said, grabbing my arm, "you look upset." She glanced over at Kimmy and then turned her attention back to me. "What is it that you wanted to talk about?"

"I think you might be in danger," I whispered, checking over my shoulder.

"From who?" she asked, her eyes traveling around the room.

Right as I was about to tell her I knew about the photos, I spotted Anthony Bianco in the distance. He'd most likely spotted his stepdaughter and was heading this way.

I reached for her hand, and signaled to Kimmy. "Come on, we gotta get out of here. Now."

I didn't say anything else until we were outside of the school. Bridget's face was a mixture of confusion and impatience. "What is this about, Lana?"

"Do you still have the photos?" I asked, holding off on the explanation.

"Photos?" Bridget asked. "What photos are you talking about?"

"Quit the innocent act, Bridget," Kimmy said. "We know you took the photos of your stepfather gettin' freaky with some lady."

Bridget gasped, her eyes flicking up to the door. "We probably shouldn't talk about that here."

"Agreed. Where should we go?" I asked.

"Anywhere," she replied, her voice quickening. "Just away from here. My stepfather is coming this way. I think he might know what I've been up to. He knows you saw him that night."

I felt a jolt of panic move through my body like lightning. "Come on, we can take my car. It's this way." I pointed to the back of the lot.

Bridget shook her head. "My car's parked right here. Let's take mine instead. It'll be quicker."

With limited time to think, the three of us got into the blue Chevy Cobalt, and Bridget cranked the engine, backing out of her spot so quickly that her tires squealed in protest.

As I put my seat belt on, I glanced toward the entrance to see if I could spot Anthony Bianco coming after us, but there was no one there.

We were well down the road before I realized that I'd never told Bridget I'd seen Anthony the night of Margo's murder.

A second later, it occurred to me that Kimmy and I should have never gotten into the car.

CHAPTER
33

At the present moment in time, I was the only one who knew that Bridget had slipped up. I didn't have a way to tell Kimmy, who was lounging comfortably in the back seat completely unaware of what might happen next.

Bridget appeared to be calm, and I wanted her to stay that way until we could get out of this car. I didn't know how to get her in a position to tell the truth without harming one of us in the process.

She continued on down York Road heading north, and hadn't said a word since we'd left the learning center's parking lot. I didn't know what to say and had to be careful with my choice of words.

Kimmy was the first to break the silence. "We need to get those photos, and then you have to come clean to the police about your creep stepfather having an affair. We know what went down, Bridget."

"I knew you'd figure it out," Bridget replied.

"You really threw us off for a little while there. I thought you were some kind of loon, the way you were following Lana around like a lost puppy dog." Kimmy laughed.

Bridget chuckled in return. "Imagine that."

To me, her laugh sounded fake and borderline evil. Goose bumps ran down my back as the sound filled the otherwise quiet car. Couldn't she at least turn the radio on?

A few minutes later, we were turning right onto Big Creek Parkway, a branch of the Cleveland Metroparks that looped through the city.

Kimmy sat up straight in the back seat. "Hey, where are we going? Is this where you live or something?"

Bridget did not respond.

I had to say something, but I felt like I'd lost the ability to form words. "Bridget . . ." I started. "I know it was probably difficult to find your stepfather cheating on your mother like that. But just think, now we can get justice for her and get him out of both of your lives. We'll just take the photos to the police and explain—"

"Oh drop it, Lana," Bridget said, watching me from the corner of her eye. "We both know I messed up. You can stop pretending like you didn't catch it. I could see it in your face when we left the school."

Kimmy leaned forward, putting her hand on the headrest of my seat. "Lana, what the heck is she talking about?"

We came up to Big Creek Reservation and she made another right, pulling into the picnic area that was well known for having a piece of land the locals had dubbed "Monkey Island." She proceeded around the winding bend, and parked the car near a small pavilion tucked all the way in the back of the property. There was no one else around despite the particularly sunny weather, and my only hope was that I could scream for help at a jogger who might be passing by.

"Lana," Kimmy repeated with agitation. "What is going on? And why are we at the Metroparks? Shouldn't we be taking these photos to the police?"

Even though Bridget had parked the car, she hadn't shut it off. She shifted in her seat, and pulled a butterfly knife out of her back pocket. "Good thing I carry this around for protection." Opening the knife, I saw the blade was double-edged and serrated. She glanced over her shoulder at Kimmy and then at me. "Do you want to tell her? I mean you're the great detective, aren't you?"

I adjusted in my seat so I didn't have my back to Kimmy, but also kept an eye on the knife. I didn't know how much damage a butterfly knife like that could do, but I wasn't about to find out the hard way. "When we left the school, Bridget said that her stepfather knew I recognized him from the night Margo was killed."

Kimmy scrunched up her face. "Yeah, so?"

I rolled my eyes. "I never told Bridget that I saw her stepfather that night."

My confused friend took a moment to comprehend what I was telling her. I saw it register on her face and then moved to grab for the door handle. But it didn't budge.

Bridget smiled, shaking the knife at Kimmy, "Child-proof locks. Plus, if you did get out, I'd just run you down with my car anyways. I hate to break it to you, but I can't just let you guys leave now. I'm not throwing my life away for this."

I turned to her, trying to find some sensibility buried in her eyes, but I couldn't see any. All I could see was fear and anger. "Do you understand that you gave yourself away? I was prepared to go to the police to testify against your stepfather."

She glared at me. "Do you have any idea what I've been through this past week? Do you think I meant to kill Margo Han? It just happened, okay? I've been a nervous wreck this entire time. Lying to everyone . . . you, my mother, that wretched man she calls a husband. It's exhausting."

"What *did* happen?" I asked. "It doesn't make any sense. I was so sure that your stepfather killed Margo to keep her quiet. I mean, he was there that night, in what would have been minutes before everything happened."

"I lost it. That's what happened," Bridget replied, sounding disgusted with herself. "After I sent the photos to my stepdad, I thought for sure he'd tone things down. Maybe he'd think twice knowing that someone out there knew exactly what he was doing behind my mother's back. I followed him the next day, and he still met up with that stupid home-wrecker. That slutty woman in our class," she said, pointing to her chest. "The one with the trashy tattoo."

"Aha!" Kimmy said from the back seat. "I knew she was a hussy."

Bridget paused to gawk at Kimmy, then continued with her story. "*Anyways*, he was still going at it. I didn't know what else to do. But I knew that Margo Han had seen what I had. I just didn't know that she was involved with him too."

"She had stopped seeing him," I said. "Months ago."

She rolled her eyes. "As if that matters."

"So why did you leave her the pictures?"

"At the time, I thought maybe she would help me if she knew that she'd been caught on camera. So, I got into the administration faculty room with some story that I needed to leave a note from my mom for my stepdad. I didn't know I'd put the photos in the wrong locker. Good thing I'd had the mind to follow you from the beginning. It wasn't until you met up with that intern that I fully understood what was going on. When Margo told me she didn't know what I was talking about, I assumed she was lying to me."

"And that's why you stabbed her?" I asked. Half of my brain was searching the car for a way to get out without her stopping us or stabbing me in the process. I didn't know what she had in mind, but I knew she wasn't going to just let us go.

"No, I stabbed her"—Bridget's breathing started to quicken, and tears began to form in her eyes—"I stabbed her because she wouldn't listen to me. She actually felt bad for my stepdad, he couldn't help himself, she'd said. Yeah, well what about my mom? What about her feelings?"

"I'm guessing she wouldn't turn him in?" My eyes traveled past her to the driver's console on the armrest of her door. If I could knock the knife out of her hand and push her back, I could unlock the childproof option from the back doors, and Kimmy would at least be able to get out and use her cell phone to call for help. Since I was in closer proximity, it might be more difficult for me to get out without her catching me.

"No," Bridget whined. "No, she wouldn't turn him in because she still loved him. She didn't want him to lose his job. Can you imagine? Then she asked me to leave. That cheatin' bitch didn't even have the courtesy to look me in the eye." Tears started to stream down her face. "I panicked. I totally lost it. I saw the knife on the counter, and I reached for it, just to threaten her. Something had to get through to this woman. But before I knew what happened, I'd stabbed her in the back. And I just ran. I went in the bathroom and threw up. Then I heard your scream."

"You were in the bathroom that whole time?"

"I had to sit in there all night," she admitted. "Once I heard the police leave, I was afraid to come out. I didn't know if I would set off some kind of alarm, so I stayed in the stall all night, not knowing what to do. I killed someone, Lana. You don't know what that does to a person."

A part of me felt bad for her. It was apparent that she hadn't meant to do Margo any harm, but got lost in the heat of the moment. "Let me help you," I offered. "We can go to the police together."

She snorted. "You're such a champion of justice, aren't you? Do you really think anyone would believe my story? Besides, either way, I'm going to prison, and I just can't. Who will my mother have then?"

Kimmy interjected. "You should have thought about that before you totally lost your brain. You can't blame anyone for what you did. So what, your dad is a skeevy guy. Doesn't give you the right to act the way you did."

Bridget lunged toward the back seat, holding the knife near Kimmy's face. "*Step*father, you mouthy bitch, *step*father."

Kimmy leaned back against the sheet, holding up her hands. "Okay, okay, I'm sorry."

My heart was racing, and I didn't know how to handle this with Kimmy being in the car, especially if she was going to run her mouth and aggravate Bridget further. "Okay, well if you won't let me help you, then what are you going to do? Kidnapping us isn't going to help anything. My boyfriend is a detective and he'll have the entire city looking for me in a matter of hours. You're better off letting us go."

She sniffed back some tears and wiped her nose, readjusting herself in the driver's seat. "No, that won't work. I have to turn you guys in. I have the photo of you and that Sabrina girl. And I got a few photos of that Robert Larkin guy talking with her too. It might be a little farfetched at first, but I can convince them that you guys caught me following you and *you* kidnapped me."

"No offense," Kimmy said, "but that's the stupidest idea I've ever heard."

Bridget narrowed her eyes and twisted in her seat to threaten Kimmy again. Her arm was at a strange angle and I thought it might be a good weak point. I decided to make my move, and with all the force I could muster, I grabbed her wrist and bent it backward.

"Ow!" she yelled. "Let go of me."

I used my grip on her wrist to hoist myself forward and reach for the console, which proved to be a struggle because my arm wasn't long enough. I tried to push off with my right foot to lean even farther forward, but my shoe kept slipping.

"Owww!! Let go of my hair, you crazy b—"

"Call me that one more time, and you're going to have a bald spot, you psycho," Kimmy returned.

It bought me enough time to move myself forward, and I hit UNLOCK on the console and yelled, "Kimmy, get out now! Get help!"

I heard the door open and slam shut while I still struggled to keep Bridget from moving out of the awkward angle I'd managed her into. Her head was almost flush with the floor partition in the back seat. I saw her hand waving around to the right, trying to blindly find her knife, which I couldn't let her do. I pulled her back up and was going to attempt punching her in the face, but she shoved me, and I smacked the back of my head onto the passenger side window.

I shielded my face with the fear she was going to hit me, but when I opened my eyes, she'd turned the car on and threw it into reverse. "Where'd Kimmy go? She moves pretty quick for a heavier girl." Bridget put the car in drive as I searched the small road for signs of Kimmy.

I spotted her running around the bend, checking over

her shoulder. Down a little ways farther there would surely be people that Kimmy could ask for help. I could see her holding the cell phone up to her head. Hopefully she was talking to a dispatcher and they were already sending someone out. But what would happen in the meantime? I started to panic wondering if I'd just inadvertently put myself in a high-speed chase.

"Stop the car, Bridget!" I yelled. "This isn't going to work."

"Shut up. If you would have just minded your own damn business like you said you would, we wouldn't be here."

When she turned to look at me, I saw in her eyes that she had come completely undone, and any hope of rationalizing with her was gone.

I took a deep breath, holding back tears. I couldn't let her get away or try to take me with her should she attempt some type of escape. Without allowing time to talk myself out of it, I grabbed firm hold of the steering wheel, and jerked it to the left, forcing the car off the tiny road right into large oak tree.

I remember seeing the look of shock on her face, hearing the airbags deploy, and feeling the extreme pain in my head. As I closed my eyes, I watched Bridget do the same.

CHAPTER

34

I woke up in University Hospital of Parma, feeling like my head was separate from my body. It hurt to open my eyes, and when I tried to move my neck, I cried out in pain. Adam came into view and put a gentle hand on my arm. "Don't try to move yet, babe. You're pretty banged up."

"Is Kimmy okay?" I struggled to say.

He squeezed my hand. "Yeah, Kimmy's fine. Don't you worry."

I closed my eyes again and drifted back to sleep.

The next morning, I woke up with the sun streaming into my room and both of my parents standing over me.

"It's about time you woke up, sleepy head," my dad said playfully. "I was going to rename you Rip Van Winkle."

I gave him a little smirk, but winced with the gesture. My mouth felt swollen and stiff.

My mother brushed a strand of hair away from my forehead. "No more trouble, young lady. Next time, Mommy asks you to go shopping, you go. Okay?"

I forced a smile and attempted to nod my head.

A half hour later, a doctor came in to check on my status and told me that I was cleared to go home as long as I wasn't alone. Megan was in the waiting room, and told my parents she would take me home.

The nurse who helped me gather myself put me in a wheelchair and pushed me out to the waiting area where Megan sprang out of her seat to greet me. "Don't do this to me, Lana. I'm a mess." She bent down and hugged me, her body shaking as she wrapped her arms around me.

"Don't squeeze so hard," I whispered.

"Oh, right," she stood up, wiping a stray tear from her cheek.

When we got home, we were surprised to see Kimmy and Peter waiting outside our apartment with a bouquet of flowers.

As we approached, Kimmy thrust them forward at me. "You know I don't do the mushy thing that good, but I wanted to say thank you for putting yourself in danger to save me. Someone else might have saved themself first."

"Hey, what are friends for?" I took the bouquet, smelling the fragrant mixture of stargazers sprinkled with roses, and waited for Megan to open the door.

Kimmy and Peter followed behind us, and when we were all inside, Peter gave me a once-over. "Man, you're pretty beat up, Lana."

"Thanks for pointing that out, Peter," I replied sarcastically. "A woman always loves to hear she looks like crap."

He ran a hand through his hair. "Well, I guess what I'm trying to say is . . . thanks for what you did. It let Kimmy get away, otherwise she might have been in the hospital too. So yeah . . . you don't owe me anymore." He ended the sentence with a crooked grin.

I laughed. "I guess you're not that bad of a guy after all."

EPILOGUE

It took me a few days to recover and gather my bearings. Adam stayed by my side as much as he possibly could while I healed from the injuries I'd sustained from the accident. The doctor had told me I was lucky I hadn't broken my collarbone in the process.

Bridget had sustained injuries as well, and once she was deemed fit to leave the hospital, the cops took her in to a policed medical ward to await the next steps in her arrest. Officer Weismann, the young police officer who had taken my statement the night of Margo's murder, had come to see me in place of Detective Bishop. Weismann didn't come out and say it, but he did hint—with a smirk—that it was because Bishop didn't want to face me knowing that he'd clearly been wrong about my and Larkin's guilt. The young officer updated me on what happened after Bridget and I had separated that day. He assured me that she was considered a flight risk and would mostly like not be released on bail.

Aside from not visiting me himself, Detective Bishop avoided me to the best of his ability on any matters in regard to the case, and all further communication was handled by Henry, who was still acting as my lawyer. He'd managed to also get me out of trouble somehow, but told me if Bridget didn't plead guilty, I'd have to go to trial and testify. Kimmy too.

For now, I was safe, and no one was going to come after me for withholding evidence. Sabrina, for all it was worth, took on the brunt of the blame. She did agree to fully cooperate with the police, and since she was an otherwise upstanding citizen, they were going to go easy on her.

A few days after Bridget's arrest had been made public, Joyce Han reached out to thank me for my part in finding the person who really killed her sister. She told me that her family, though still working through the emotions they felt, could now find some peace knowing the truth.

Out of everything that happened, that knowledge is what made me feel like the whole ordeal had been worth it.

The following Friday, Megan had gotten herself excused from working the entire weekend, so we could have some fun. After showing her boss the story that had graced the *Plain Dealer*, listing my name more times than I would have liked, he readily agreed to let her have the time off.

Megan and I primped in the bathroom, and I hogged

the mirror while I tried to expertly apply concealer on some of the bruises that were starting to yellow on my face.

"So where are we going?" Megan asked, running the makeup brush over her cheekbones.

"Wok and Roll," I said.

She met my eyes in the mirror. "Why the heck are we going there again?"

"I told you, I owe Stanley Gao a favor. I can't go back on my word."

"Ugh, fine. But tomorrow night, let's do something else. I feel like dancing."

"You can dance tonight. Put them heels on, girl-friend," I said, bumping Megan's hip with my own.

She giggled. "Why are you making me get so dolled up just to go to Wok and Roll?"

"No reason. I just wanna get dressed up."

"Uh-huh. Come on, Lana, who do you think you're lying to?" she asked, pointing the makeup brush accusingly in my direction.

I held up my hands. "Okay, fine. Truth is . . . Stanley thinks you're hot stuff. And getting you to come with me was part of our deal."

Mean gasped. "I can't believe you, Lana Lee. Are you putting me on display?"

Placing my hand over my heart, I did my best to look taken aback. "I am both shocked and appalled that you would even suggest such a thing."

"Right. My little angel." She rolled her eyes and exited the bathroom.

I followed behind her and we both searched for our

shoes. "Don't worry, I'd never let him near you with a ten-foot pole—he's kind of a playboy. It's just for show. I can't have him telling Asia Village I was in his cooking class. It hasn't come up yet and I'd rather he didn't remind anyone."

"But you're not going back, right? You're done with this whole cooking class scheme?"

I found the shoes I wanted to wear in the hallway closet. "Yup, I give up on trying to learn how to cook Chinese food . . . for now. If I really want to learn, I'll save us all a bunch of trouble and just ask Peter."

Megan was digging under the couch, and pulled out a red stiletto. "Good. Well, I hope you know that you're going to owe me for this little shenanigan."

I spread my arms out. "Thus is the cycle of life."

We heard a car horn sound in the parking lot right outside of our apartment. Adam was picking us up and we planned to meet Kimmy and Peter at the Asian fusion restaurant to check out some 80s cover band making their debut performance.

Megan dug out the other shoe and slipped it on, adjusting her skirt. "I'm glad to hear you say that."

"Oh?"

"Yeah, I already have something in mind." She sashayed over to the dining room table, grabbed her handbag, and tucked it under her arm. "You ready?"

I nodded, grabbing my own purse off the couch, giving Kikko a pat before following Megan out the door. "Well are you going to tell me?"

"I'd like to use Ho-Lee Noodle House for an entire evening . . . privately."

"What? Why?" I asked.

She twisted the knob, and glanced over her shoulder, giving me a sly smile. "I have two words for you, my friend: Speed. Dating."